LAS
HERMANAS

Raedene Jeannette Melin

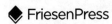 FriesenPress

Suite 300 - 990 Fort St
Victoria, BC, V8V 3K2
Canada

www.friesenpress.com

Copyright © 2018 by Raedene Jeannette Melin
First Edition — 2018

Author photo by Jason Hutton Photography

ISBN
978-1-5255-1957-4 (Hardcover)
978-1-5255-1958-1 (Paperback)
978-1-5255-1959-8 (eBook)

1. FICTION, ACTION & ADVENTURE

Distributed to the trade by The Ingram Book Company

Of the 40 million people living in modern slavery, 71% are female. Of the 4.8 million humans trafficked for sexual exploitation, 99% are women and girls[1].

1 in every 3 women will be physically or sexually assaulted. Over 120 million girls have been raped or sexually defiled[2].

Every year, 66,000 females are violently murdered. Out of the top 10 countries with the highest rates of femicide, 7 are in Latin America[3].

This is for them.

1 International Labour Organization, Walk Free Foundation and International Organization for Migration. (2017). *Global Estimates of Modern Slavery: Forced Labour and Forced Marriage.* Geneva.

2 United Nations Department of Economic and Social Affairs. (2015). *The World's Women 2015: Trends and Statistics.* New York: United Nations.

3 Nowak, M. (2012). *Femicide: A Global Problem.* Geneva: Small Arms Survey Graduate Institute of International and Development Studies.

Chapter One

With a racing heart and pounding feet, she ran as fast and hard as she could through the trees. Her eleven-year-old body shook with fright as the sound of sporadic bursts of gunfire ripped the air, silencing the cries of those dying in the village behind her. Consumed by the chaos and fear, she didn't notice her brother whimpering softly in her arms.

She continued to run farther into the jungle, the screams slowly fading as the distance increased between them. As she fled, her mother's voice rang loudly through her mind. *"Adi, run!"*

Adi shook her head, trying to clear the vision of her mother shoving Benito into her arms, but it was no use. The image took hold of her, forcing her to watch as her mother jerked violently, the bullets tearing through her body.

She ran for about a minute before stopping, unable to take another step as the grief and despair weighed her down, cementing her in place. Releasing Benito from her grasp, she dropped to her knees, struggling to breathe as her body shook uncontrollably. The immense pain of her heartbreak trapped her there until the sound of Benito's terrified cries broke her from her anguish.

"Adi!" he said, gripping her shoulders, the tears streaming down his face. "Adi, get up. They're coming!"

Fear seized her once more, forcing the agony out of her mind as she heaved herself onto her feet. As soon as she stood, the sound of people coming rapidly towards them reached her ears and she picked up her four-year-old brother.

She ran as quickly as she could but less than a minute later, her muscles started to ache, unable to stop the exhaustion. The group behind her was gaining and the sound of their thudding footsteps told her she wouldn't be able to outrun them, not like this.

Thrusting all her remaining energy into one last sprint, she stopped at the base of a large cinchona tree and lifted Benito above her head. Needing no instruction, he grabbed onto the overhanging branch and swung himself up.

"Hide," she said quietly. "Don't come out for anything."

She watched as he submerged himself under a dense clump of leaves before darting deeper into the trees. She knew the terrain well, advancing through the thick, convoluted clusters of vines and brush effortlessly. After her family moved here from the city four years ago, she had spent every spare moment in the jungle with the village healer, learning about the plants and animals. Señora Reyes taught her everything, including how to hunt and how to heal, and Adi had never been so happy. But that was before everything went wrong. That was before the jungle had turned on her, killing the people she loved one by one. Now she hated this place.

She felt her cheeks flush, her fear morphing into anger as she loudly zig-zagged through the jungle floor. Using the damp ground and moist ferns, she created obvious tracks for her pursuers to follow, leading them into the thickening forest. Once she had them lost and going in the wrong direction, she would double back for Benito.

After a few minutes, she stopped and listened. It took a moment to quiet the thumping of her heart, but eventually she heard them. Their footsteps were louder, quicker, and much closer than she wanted. Running faster, she used fallen trees, rocks, and roots to camouflage her footprints. She was looking behind her, trying to see her pursuers, when she tripped over a vine and fell head-first down the suddenly sloping terrain.

Her body bounced hard against the ground, forcing the air out of her lungs as she tumbled down the hill in a loud, noticeable clump. Slamming into the exposed roots of a large kapok tree, Adi finally stopped rolling and lay there motionless at the bottom of the ravine.

Sharp, painful convulsions shot through her body as she gasped for air. Every part of her hurt, from her head to her toes, and it took a minute before she was able to stand back up. There was no way she could run now.

Limping into the dense foliage, she found a thick vine and began to climb, slowly hoisting herself up. Once she was a few feet off the ground, she pushed against the tree next to her and swung towards another one a couple feet away. It took several swings to get close enough, but eventually she made it, landing uncomfortably onto a branch as a red howler monkey screeched in protest above. Not pausing for a moment, she climbed to the other side, found another vine, and jumped, making her way across the jungle through the air. As she squeezed into the split trunk of the third tree, the forest quieted around her, an eerie silence settling down into the woods.

Adi steadied her breathing and waited, the pain from her fall radiating through her body as she leaned against the branch, hidden by the dense leafy canopy. She was examining the ripped skin on her hand when her mother's screams echoed through the air, causing her to jerk her head up just in time to see four camouflaged, masked men slowly emerged from the trees below.

She watched them as they tracked her footprints to the vine and stopped, cautiously surveying the area around them. One of the men crouched, tracing her footprint with his finger, when he suddenly looked up and called, "Adelita. Adelita Alvarez. Where are you?"

A chill ran down Adi's spine and her heart beat faster. How did he know her name?

"Your papa sent us to find you," the man continued. "Don't be afraid, you're safe now."

Adi gripped the tree to steady herself as a thousand thoughts ran through her head. Could it be true? Her father had been missing for over three months. Was he alive after all this time? Unsure of what to believe, she stayed hidden behind the leaves, not moving a muscle.

"Enough," she heard one of the others say. "I'm not wasting any more time looking for a fucking child. Everyone else is dead. She won't survive out here on her own."

The first man ripped off his mask. "Shut up, you idiot," he hissed angrily. "She's close. I can feel it."

As he turned his head, Adi saw his pale, gringo face. There would've been nothing special about it had there not been a long scar that curved from the left corner of his mouth to his eyebrow. It hadn't healed well and left an ugly, jagged line.

She studied him for a moment before shifting her gaze to his friends. While they were all dressed alike, it didn't take her long to figure out that three of the four men were white. Besides the fact that they noisily clumped their way through the jungle, they obviously weren't used to the stifling humidity, as their shirts clung tightly to their bodies, drenched with sweat. But the fourth man did not experience the same discomfort and appeared quite relaxed. He moved through the jungle with ease, as if he were familiar.

He must be a traitor, Adi thought, scowling. People like him were evil. They betrayed their own, doing anything for money. Because of men like him, her family was landless and had to fight just to survive.

Adi sat in silence and watched the men continue their search, passing her on the ground below. She was happy to rest and wait them out but as she leaned her head on a clump of leaves, the distinct sound of hissing slithered loudly into her ear.

Jerking her head forward, Adi found herself staring into the grey-blue eyes of an emerald tree boa. While she had encountered these green predators before, she had never been stuck in a tree with one. Forcing herself to stay calm, she slowly inched away from it.

Her movements seemed to agitate the snake more and it struck at her, forcing her out of the tree and back into the open. Latching onto the twisty vines that cloaked the trunk, she silently climbed down.

When she landed softly on the ground, Adi stood still against the tree and waited, listening for any sound or movement. Distracted by the snake, she had lost sight of the men and had no idea if they were close. Hearing nothing after a minute, she was about to step out and head back to Benito when she saw him crouched low, his white, scarred face visible as he searched through the trees. In an instant, their eyes connected and a small smile crept across his lips.

Adi immediately turned and fled, running as fast as she could away from the man. A loud whistle cut through the air and the footsteps pounded behind her once more. She dashed through the trees, jumping over logs and sidestepping large rocks as she urgently looked for something that would help her. The sound of rushing water broke her from her panic and she ran towards it.

While the river wasn't particularly large, it roared with power as the rainy season had just ended, drowning the jungle in storms that lasted for days. The downpour had caused the river to swell and it now flooded over the bank and into the trees, trapping large pools of water as it receded. Going along the marshy shore, Adi hopped through the mud, looking into the pools until she saw grey, snake-like shapes slowly swimming back and forth within them, their beady white eyes staring up at her from their flat heads. Moving to the other side of the pools, she stomped through the sludge, making obvious tracks for the men to follow, before slipping farther back into the trees.

The first man awkwardly made his way through the mud, not seeing her hiding a few feet away. The rest of the group wasn't far behind and she watched as they walked across the murky and wet terrain, looking around them as they tried to follow her tracks. Spotting the more noticeable footprints she had left up ahead, one of the men moved forward with confidence, not seeing the deep pool beneath him, and sunk down into it, water swallowing his legs.

He struggled for a moment, trying to wrench his feet out of the clay, when he suddenly screamed in agony, his torso shaking. The other men rushed forward to help, but as soon as they touched him, their bodies lit up with the electric currents being transmitted from the angry eels in the pool below.

Adi couldn't help but smile as she watched the men being shocked over and over again, their groans drowned out by the sound of the river. They would be unable to move, the electricity paralyzing their muscles, so she left them crying behind and went back through the jungle.

No longer being chased, the adrenaline began to leave her body, revealing the many injuries she had collected during her flight. While she could easily treat them, she wasn't stopping until she had Benito with her again. She was almost to the top of the ravine when she heard a shot.

The sharp bite of a bullet ripped along the outside of her thigh, causing her to stumble to her knee. Fear and panic returned, clawing up her throat as she tried to stop her leg from shaking. She was still attempting to stand when the butt of a gun slammed forcefully into her back, sending her sprawling face-first into the dirt.

Adi wheezed in pain as she rolled off her stomach and looked at the tall man standing over her, his silhouette casting a dark shadow. It took all her willpower to blink away the tears and focus in on his face. The man with the scar stared back with curiosity and satisfaction.

Adi pushed her torso off the ground but was stopped by the heel of his boot smashing into her head, knocking her back down as ringing filled her ears. She could do nothing but watch as he dropped his gun and climbed on top of her, sitting down hard on her stomach.

"You are an interesting individual," he said calmly, his strong fingers wrapping around her throat.

Adi frantically grabbed at his hands as he squeezed, the pressure constant and unrelenting.

"I've never had someone evade me for so long," he continued, ignoring her flailing arms and heaving chest.

The sound of his voice faded in and out as the lack of air caused her body to scream in anguish. She tried with all her might to remove his hands from her throat, but she soon gave up and started scratching at his face.

"It is a shame you didn't last longer," he was saying, completely composed as he shifted his head out of reach. "I was beginning to enjoy it."

As Adi's consciousness began to flicker, the man suddenly jerked in pain and gasped. Swatting at something on his foot, he unexpectedly released his grip from her throat and she rasped in relief as air entered her lungs.

She simply lay there, breathing desperately and coughing, her vision blurry and her ears still ringing. After several minutes, she pushed her body up and looked at the man twisting in pain on the ground. She didn't have to wonder what was making him suffer: she could see the large, black bullet ant scampering underneath his clothes, stinging him repeatedly as his body jerked. In his eagerness to kill her, he had unwittingly jammed his boot into the ant's colony at the base of a tree, and she knew that the amount of pain he would feel for the next twenty-four hours would be unforgettable. Taking one last look at him writhing in front of her, she turned and left, going as fast as her wobbly legs could carry her.

She stumbled, tripped, and fell her way forward, no longer caring about how loud she was. The jungle was a death trap and she needed to get out. When she finally arrived at the tree, she hoped she wasn't too late.

"Benito," she rasped.

The seconds felt like hours as she waited for some sign that he was still there. When his head finally poked out through the leaves, a relieved sigh escaped her throat.

"Come," she whispered. "We need to go."

As soon as he was on the ground, Adi grabbed his hand and they ran farther into the jungle, away from the village and the men. She had no idea where they were going or what they were going to do. The only thing she knew was that they needed to get as far away as possible from the place they called home.

Chapter Two

Using her legs to grip the tree, Adi reached towards the papaya hanging just out of her grasp. She could feel how ripe it was as her fingers grazed its skin and she stretched her arm, her thighs shaking with fatigue. They had been running for days, only stopping when it was dark, but even when night came, she thought of nothing but the man, her mind refusing to let her body rest. She was more than just tired; she was empty. As her fingers finally latched onto the stem of the papaya, her muscles gave out, sending her freefalling into the dirt.

"Adi," she heard Benito cry, his voice filled with worry. His blurry face appeared above her.

"I'm okay," she said. She blinked fast, trying to clear her vision.

She couldn't feel anything, a numbing sensation blanketing her body, but the moment she took a deep breath, she immediately regretted it, the gesture racking her torso with pain. She struggled to stand, the agony radiating from her ankle. Unwilling to show how much she was hurting, she gave Benito a smile and limped towards the river.

A small sob burst from her lips the instant she submerged her feet in the water, gingerly lowering herself down onto a rock. She winced as the pounding in her head intensified, her once-dull headache now spiking in full force as she looped a thick strand of brown hair behind her ear. Even though she could feel the heat radiating from her thigh, the bullet wound fully inflamed, she ignored it and dipped her hands in the river.

It shocked her how cold the water felt as she splashed it on her face, a firm shiver running down her spine. She knew her head was hot, unable to explain why else she was constantly sweating, but as she looked back up feeling suddenly cold, a pair of eyes met hers from across the river.

Adi froze in place, refusing to look away as a jaguar slowly walked towards the water, steadily holding her gaze. She knew she should run, the river no barrier to the predator, but as she watched it stop at the edge and take a drink, sharp shoulders emerging from its muscular back, she couldn't look away. She had never seen anything so terrifyingly beautiful, and as she watched the sunlight glint off its body, a shimmering movement of yellow and black, she remembered what her mother had told her.

"Bright colours mean danger," her mama said as they knelt close to a frog, black and blue splotches covering its body. It had been so small, Adi almost missed it. "You must never touch those."

A hand on her shoulder broke her from the memory and Adi looked up, seeing her brother standing above her. She knew she should say something to alleviate the concern etched across his face, but she had no idea what. She had never been good at talking; that was her sister's talent. Leti was five years older than her and could talk her way out of anything. But Leti was gone and Adi was left to figure it out by herself.

They kept moving, Adi refusing to think about how slow they were, now that she could only limp her way through the trees. Her headache had gotten progressively worse, making her brain feel fuzzy and numb, and while her skin was burning, she couldn't stop shivering. Sometimes as they were walking, she would reach out to support herself against a tree, but every now and again, the tree trunk would vanish before she touched it, sending her stumbling forward as she awkwardly tried to catch herself. She figured she was just tired, but when she felt her legs buckle underneath her and the darkness close in, she knew something was horribly wrong.

The moment she felt her heels drop into the dirt, a single thought rang like an alarm through her head: He had them.

Opening her eyes, she struggled against her constraints, unable to break the vines that held her tightly to the roughly-made stretcher. But as soon as she turned her head and looked at the brown-haired boy crouched beside her, she stopped.

"Pablo," she said eventually, not believing it.

He smiled, a mixed look of confusion and concern flickering across his face. He opened his mouth to say something, but then closed it for a minute. "You alright?"

Adi took a breath, trying to calm her racing heart, and nodded. "Where's Benito? Is he here?"

"He's just up there, with the others." Pablo looked past her towards the voices that she heard somewhere ahead of them.

Unable to hide her relief, she closed her eyes and exhaled loudly. When she looked at him again, his face was different.

"You're a long way from the village," he said. "What are you doing out here?"

Adi thought about what to say, watching a red-headed manakin fly above them. Pablo had been born in that village and his entire family lived there. How was she supposed to tell him they were all dead?

"I asked Benito," he continued, "but he wouldn't tell me."

Adi felt his gaze even though she was looking straight ahead. Just as she was about to answer, another boy walked up.

"She's awake," he said, warily looking at her. He casually leaned his arms against the gun slung over his body. "Can you walk?" As soon as she nodded, he said, "Good. Untie her. We need to go."

They moved in silence through the trees, three boys in the front and Pablo in the back. While they weren't going fast, the steady pace and rough terrain were almost too much for Adi's stiff muscles and aching leg. She was about to ask for a break when they reached their destination.

She could smell the camp before she could see it, the scent of roasting meat making her mouth water and her stomach clench hungrily. Walking into the clearing, she searched for it, ignoring everything else. Spotting the fire a few feet in front of her, she bee-lined towards it.

Adi had never wanted something so badly as she stared longingly at the frogs sizzling over the fire. The boy roasting them looked up at her oddly from his seated position, but she didn't care.

"Give me one of those," she said, not taking her eyes off the frogs.

"Me too," Benito said, suddenly beside her.

"They're not done yet," the boy replied, irritated. "And you can't just demand food."

Adi was about to reach out and take one when Pablo walked up, stabbed one with his knife, and handed it to her. Not waiting a second, Adi grabbed the frog and was about to bite into it when she stopped. She could feel Benito's eyes intently watching and she knew he was just as hungry as she was. It took all her willpower to hand him the frog and watch him eat it, hot juicy grease dripping down his chin.

"You can't do that," the boy was saying. "It's against the rules."

"Here." Pablo ignored him, offering Adi another frog. "Eat."

Almost crying in relief, she eagerly shoved it into her mouth, not stopping even when the meat burnt her tongue.

The frogs were devoured in less than a minute and she was about to ask for another when Pablo said, "Come."

Adi and Benito reluctantly followed him away from the food and through the camp, allowing her to notice it for the first time. It was well organized, the fire in the centre with a few structures around it. While she hadn't known what to expect, she was surprised by how many kids she saw and she watched as they hung wet clothes, smoked pirarucu, and weaved a wall of vines together. She spotted a girl a little older than her climbing up a sapodilla tree before they entered a small hut that sat on the edge of the clearing.

It wasn't very big, having only enough room for a small makeshift table and a few stumps, but it was dry and cozy as the sides were packed with leaves. Once inside, Pablo told them to wait before he turned and left the hut.

Adi was content to sit and do nothing, completely exhausted and happy for the chance to rest. Looking at Benito already sleeping on the floor, she knew he was too. Sleeping in trees was never comfortable and she couldn't remember what it felt like to lie flat. She was about to join him on the ground when Pablo returned with two other boys in tow.

She watched as they made their way around the table, looking at her intently as they sat down. She recognized one of the older boys, but couldn't place him.

"Adi," Pablo said, directing her attention to the smaller boy beside him, "this is Salvador. He's the leader of our camp."

Salvador wasn't very tall, but she could tell he was strong. His eyes were a sharp green and he sat confidently.

"And Rodrigo you already know," Pablo said. He motioned to the boy she had recognized.

Rodrigo, she thought. *Rodrigo Padilla.*

As soon as she remembered his name, the vision of her sister's bullet-ridden body flashed before her eyes. It felt like she had been punched in the stomach and she doubled over, the heartache threatening to collapse her right on that stump.

"...clean your wounds," Pablo was saying. He placed a bucket of water beside her.

Adi sat back up, trying to regain her composure as the boys stared at her from around the table.

"Pablo and Rodrigo tell me you're from their village," Salvador said, bringing her attention to him.

She nodded.

"What are you doing so far away from home?"

She studied him. While he wasn't an adult, he talked and acted like one, folding his hands neatly on top of the table. The other boys slouched and moved around on their stools, but he sat up straight and was perfectly still.

"Where are we? What is this place?" She asked in return, avoiding his question. While she knew they would make her tell them, she didn't want to and hoped to delay it as long as possible.

Salvador smiled patiently at her. "This is a place, a community of sorts, that I started about a year ago."

"Why?" She didn't understand why they would build a community in the middle of the jungle. There were other villages they could live in, and cities too.

"To protect people."

"What kind of people?"

"People like me, like Pablo and Rodrigo. Like you."

"Kids, you mean."

He smiled. "Yes, kids."

Adi paused. "What are you protecting them from?"

"From danger," Salvador replied. His voice softened as the smile faded from his face. "The kind that I suspect brought you and little Benito here today."

She looked away, her eyes landing on her brother's sleeping body.

"Adi," Rodrigo said. His voice betrayed the worry he felt as he leaned towards the table. "You remember me, right?"

She reluctantly looked at him and his dark hair. She nodded.

"You remember that day, a few months ago, when the rebels came and told us we were joining their movement?"

"Yes," Adi whispered. How could she forget? That was the day everything changed. She had never seen so much violence, and it wasn't long before kids just a bit older than her were taken away to fight. Leti had been one of them and the night before she had to leave, Adi laid next to her, lost for words. She simply took Leti's hands in her own and never looked away. When she woke the next morning, they were in the same position, hands tightly intertwined, Leti's eyes red and swollen.

"I love you," Adi had whispered.

"I love you," Leti whispered back.

Rodrigo's voice broke her from the memory. "That night my parents told me to leave. They said if I stayed, I would die, so I left, along with Pablo and a couple others. We were supposed to go to my abuela's village, but when we came across Salvador's camp, we decided to stay." He paused, as if he was trying to figure out what to say. "Whatever's happened, Adi, you can tell us."

Unable to contain the despair she felt, tears ran freely down her cheeks. "It's gone. Everyone's gone."

"Who's gone?" Pablo asked intently.

She looked up and saw his anxious face. "Everyone. The whole village."

"What happened?" Salvador asked after a moment, his voice quiet.

She shrugged. "They came and just started shooting."

"Who came?" Rodrigo asked. He was clearly struggling to understand. "The ranchers?"

"I don't know."

Silence filled the room as the boys tried to comprehend what she was telling them.

"How did you escape?" Salvador asked eventually.

She wiped away the tears with the back of her hand. "I was picking fruit when I heard the trucks, but by the time I got to the village, the shooting had already started. My mama gave me Benito and told me to run."

Salvador nodded as he thought it over. "And what happened when you ran? How did you get all those bruises on your throat?"

Adi self-consciously touched her neck. While it was sore, she didn't realize that there were visible marks. "We were followed," she replied, remembering the man with the scar. He had been on her mind from the moment she left him, but the memory of her family had made her forget his sinister face.

"By who?" Rodrigo asked.

"I don't know." She was tired of giving them the same answer. They expected her to know everything, but she had no idea why this happened. "They tracked us from the village."

"Why would they do that?" Salvador asked out loud to no one in particular.

"Maybe they saw her get away," Pablo suggested.

Adi ignored their conversation and replayed her escape through the trees. There was something important she was forgetting, but she couldn't remember what. Her brain hurt and it was hard to remember everything that had happened.

"Could be," Salvador was saying, unconvinced.

"Even if they did see her, why would they care?" Rodrigo asked. "Why would they hunt down two kids?"

Suddenly, she remembered and she stood up, knocking over the pail of water. "They could be out there, following us here," she said, her heart in her throat.

Salvador looked at her, puzzled. "Why would they do that? Why would they track you all this way?"

"Three of them were white," she said, remembering another detail.

Salvador was quiet and shook his head. "A lot of white men work around here. That doesn't mean anything."

Adi sighed. He wasn't getting it. "You don't understand," she said. She was convinced that he was still out there. "They didn't see me leave the village. They knew I was missing."

"Maybe they were looking for people hiding in the jungle and found you by accident," Rodrigo offered.

"No," she said. "It wasn't an accident."

"How do you know?" Salvador asked.

"He knew my name. He called me by my name."

☙

Adi sat silently as the boys discussed how the men knew who she was. While one day she might figure it out, right now she didn't care. It didn't matter who they were or why they did it; all that mattered was that they—he—could still be out there and she needed to get Benito as far away from him as she could.

"Benito," she called. "Get up, we have to go."

"Wait," Salvador said. "Where are you going?"

"Doesn't matter," she said as Benito slowly stood. "We can't stay here."

Salvador scoffed. "You can't leave. Look at you. With those injuries you won't last a day."

Adi shrugged. "Maybe not, but I'd rather die out there than let him catch us."

"Him who?"

She had wasted too much time already and didn't feel like explaining it. "The man who chased us. The man with the scar. It's not safe to stay."

"You'll be safe here," Salvador said. "We can protect you."

Adi looked at him sceptically. "How?"

"We're well hidden, we have lookouts, we're armed. No one knows we're here."

"He'll still find us," she said. "He'll track us down."

Salvador hesitated. "We'll cover your tracks. Pablo can get rid of them."

She was quiet as she considered it. While her body ached for a chance to recover, she didn't know if it would be enough to prevent him from finding them.

"I'll tell you what," Salvador said. "Stay here, just for the night, and then if you're still convinced it's not safe, you can go. I won't stop you."

She hesitated so Salvador continued.

"I don't think that man is following you," he said, "but if he is, eliminating your tracks will buy you a few days at least."

She was still uncertain, but as she looked at Benito's exhausted face, she knew she couldn't say no. "Alright. One night."

The rest of the day passed quickly as Adi and Benito ate what they could and then fell asleep on the hut floor. She woke up several hours later and was examining her bruised side when Rodrigo walked in.

"Here," he said, handing her a plate of food and a cup of water.

Adi said nothing as she reached up and set it on the floor beside her. They had given her more food than she could eat and for the first time in a while, she was full. Hoping Rodrigo would leave, she returned her attention to her torso.

"I can fix that for you, if you want," he said, still standing there. Seeing the confused look on her face, he elaborated. "Your shirt. I can patch it up."

"No thanks," she said quietly. She avoided his gaze as she pulled her shirt back down. She didn't feel like talking and he was the last person she wanted to have a conversation with, but when he sat down on one of the stumps, she knew she didn't have a choice.

The silence in the room was deafening. He obviously wanted to say something but was struggling to start. "Are you and Benito alright?"

Adi simply looked at him. While she could tell that his concern was genuine, she didn't care.

"You've been through a lot," he continued, his voice fading a bit. He cleared his throat and carried on. "I can't imagine what it was like to be there when it happened, all by yourself."

It took all her willpower to keep her mouth shut and not tell him how much he disgusted her. Here he was, sitting in front of her, blabbering on about things that didn't matter, when all she wanted was for him to admit what he'd done.

"I'm sorry about your family," he was saying. "Your parents were always nice to me. And Leti, Leti was..."

It was too much for Adi to take. "Don't talk about my sister," she said. She fought to keep herself from yelling. "Don't ever talk about her."

A look of confusion settled on Rodrigo's face. "She was my friend," he started to say, but she interrupted him again.

"No, she wasn't. If she was, you wouldn't have killed her."

Rodrigo sat there baffled. "I did *not* kill her."

"Yes, you did."

"I wasn't even there!" he exclaimed. He stood, the anger in his voice filling the shelter.

"Exactly!" Adi yelled. She jumped to her feet. "You weren't there!"

He still didn't get it.

"You weren't there when all the men died, you weren't there when they sent kids to fight, and you weren't there when they noticed you were gone."

He shook his head. "I don't understand what you're saying."

"You abandoned your family and ran away!" Adi shouted at him, not caring that Salvador and Pablo had entered the hut, looking concerned. "They put a gun to your mama's head and forced her to tell them where you went. And you weren't there!" She swallowed hard, forcing the lump in her throat to go away. She would not cry. She had cried every day since it happened and she was tired of it. "You weren't there to protect your own mama," she said, "but my sister was. And they killed her for it. *You* killed her."

The hut was completely silent. Rodrigo met her gaze. "Hate me all you want, Adi, but you're just as guilty as me."

She was about to protest when he continued, his eyes full of tears. "If I'm responsible for Leti's death, how many people did you leave behind to die when you ran?"

Stunned, Adi took a step back as if she had been hit and looked at him, seeing nothing but anger.

"How many deaths are you responsible for?"

"Enough," Salvador said with authority. He moved forward, preventing Rodrigo from saying anything else.

Unable to stop the tears, she looked down as Rodrigo stormed out of the hut. While Salvador tried to reassure her that there was nothing she could've done to change what happened, she couldn't help but wonder if what Rodrigo said was true, if she had left her mother behind to die.

Chapter Three

Adi woke the next morning drenched in sweat.

It's not real, she told herself, trying to get the nightmare and the man's face out of her head. She had been running from him in her sleep as he taunted her, but the feeling of his hands had been too real. "It's just a dream," she said out loud. "He's not here."

Although she had been sleeping for hours, her muscles ached with exhaustion and as she stood, she was stopped by the pain shooting up her leg. She didn't have to touch the wound to know it was infected. Her thigh was hot and the gash swelled with pus.

Gingerly pushing herself off the floor, she left the hut and made her way down to the river. Not bothering to take off her clothes, she simply walked into the current, feeling every cut on her body as the water soothed her aches and pains. After a few minutes, she sat down, scrubbing her skin with sand as her feet floated underneath the surface. Finally clean, she dragged her water-logged body out of the river and walked through the trees towards the camp.

The jungle had come alive with the morning and Adi listened as birds called back and forth to one another, their whistles and squawks filling the air. Spotting the tree she was looking for, she grabbed a small rock off the ground and sliced into the bark repeatedly until red sap oozed out. Holding a leaf underneath, the liquid dripped slowly, creating a small pile of sticky goo.

Relief flooded through her as she smeared the sap over her thigh, covering the gaping hole. It was soothing, the sap killing the pain and infection as it sealed the wound shut. She rubbed it into every cut, scrape, and bruise, and when she was finished, more than half her body was red. Collecting a bit more, she wrapped it in the leaf and made her way back.

By the time she got there, the camp was in complete chaos. Kids were scattered everywhere, crawling on the ground as they puked, their distressed cries filling the air. Unsure of what was happening, Adi sprinted towards the hut.

"Benito," she called as she entered.

The silence that answered frightened her to the bone and she ran back out, panic filling her chest. Seeing someone jogging past, Adi asked, "Have you seen my brother?" She got no reply. Unsure of what to do, she ran around the camp, searching the shelters as the crying increased. She was about to give in to the hysteria when a small hand lightly touched her elbow.

She grabbed him, pulling him close as his head smooshed against her stomach. Her heart was pounding so hard she could feel it pulsating through her thigh. Desperate to stop the throbbing, she took a few deep breaths, trying to slow it down.

Benito took a step back. "You need to come."

Taking her by the hand, he led her across the camp and into a small, partially-closed lean-to. Upon entering, Adi saw Rodrigo and Pablo huddled around a boy lying on the ground.

"Adi," Pablo said, looking up hopefully when she entered. "Benito says you can help."

She ignored the angry glare from Rodrigo and approached, kneeling next to Salvador. He was deathly pale and his body was covered in sweat. He shook uncontrollably.

"Do you know what's wrong with him?" Pablo asked. "He was fine last night, but when I found him this morning, he was like this."

She didn't reply as she continued to look him over. While his head was radiating with heat, his body was cold. When she gently squeezed his leg, he let out a small groan. She had just opened her mouth to speak when a girl burst into the lean-to.

"They're getting worse," she announced as she walked in. She was older, about Salvador's age, and had long brown hair that was hastily tied up into a ponytail.

"How many?" Rodrigo asked, standing up.

The girl shook her head. "I don't know. I've lost count. About twenty."

"We need to find what's causing it." Rodrigo paused. "Could it be the water? Maybe there's something in it."

The girl shrugged.

"What about the food?" Pablo asked. "Maybe some of it was bad."

Rodrigo let out an exasperated sigh and was about to say something when Adi interjected. "It's not the water or the food," she said as she stood, wiping Salvador's sweat off on her pants. "It's malaria. They all have malaria."

"How do you know?" Pablo asked.

"If the water or the food was bad, they'd be puking, but they wouldn't be shaking and sweating this much."

"So, because they're shaking its malaria?"

Adi nodded. "It's in their muscles. That's what makes them tired and sore. Bad water or food don't do that."

"But we've had malaria before," the girl said, baffled. "It's never been close to this bad."

"There are different types," Adi replied with a shrug. "Some you barely notice, others hurt a lot."

"How can this many people have malaria at the same time?" Rodrigo asked angrily. "Even at our village, no one was this sick."

Adi didn't want to talk to him. She had planned on never speaking to him again, but as the others waited for her answer, she relented. "That's cuz we had Señora Reyes. She helped them before they got this bad."

"How?" Pablo asked. "Do you know?"

She nodded.

"Can you do it?" he asked, his eyes lighting up.

Adi hesitated. While she knew how to treat them, she wasn't sure she wanted to. It would take hours, if not days, and that was time she didn't have. She needed to get away from this place. Her dilemma was interrupted by the feeling of a hand sliding into hers.

"Adi," Benito said quietly. "Help them."

As she looked down into the steadiness of her father's eyes staring back at her, she sighed. "Put all the sick together," she said. "I need a knife, a bowl, and a small fire."

Pablo nodded eagerly. "Ivanna, go." The girl immediately left the lean-to. "What else?"

"We have to cool their heads and warm their bodies."

"Okay, I can do that," Pablo replied. "Rodrigo, give her a knife."

Adi turned around. Rodrigo was standing with arms crossed, a scowl on his face, not moving a muscle.

"Rodrigo," Pablo said louder with annoyance.

Huffing noisily, he reached behind him, pulled out a knife and slapped the blade into her hand.

Adi ran through the trees, searching for the right ingredients. She didn't want to be out there any longer than she had to. Being alone in the forest made her anxious. It felt like the man with the scar was going to jump out at any moment. When she spotted the cinchona tree, its long trunk and bushy top extending upwards, she pushed her fear aside and got to work. She cut the bark off in short, thin pieces, and within an hour, she had enough. The next tree she needed was a bit more difficult to find, but after a few minutes of running around, she finally spotted one. The kamalame tree was quite large and had shaggy, red-copper skin that glistened in the sun. Peeling away the bark, Adi dropped the paper-thin strips into the bucket and ran back to camp.

Over the next few hours, Adi didn't stop, working as fast as she could to prepare the medication. The cinchona bark had to be dried and then smashed into powder while the kamalame peels had to be boiled and made into tea. As she sat grinding down the dried strips, she watched Pablo and Ivanna work under the lean-to, wiping the sweat from the kids' bodies and trying to warm them. Adi remembered what it felt like to have malaria. Her muscles would clench and shake for hours while her head felt as if it would explode at any moment. It was like the earth was constantly wobbling and she could never get warm, no matter how long she sat in the sun.

"Benito," she said, calling him away from stirring the tea. "Bring this to Pablo." She handed him a leaf full of freshly ground cinchona powder. "Make sure everyone gets some."

He nodded and carefully carried the powder towards the lean-to while Adi placed some more bark in the bowl and started grinding again. While the symptoms would soon die down, they would be back in twenty-four hours and Adi needed to strengthen their bodies before the next attack came. She was helping one of them drink some tea when Ivanna walked up and crouched beside her.

"What does that do?" she asked after a moment.

"Brings down the fever and helps with the pain." Adi lowered the cup from the kid's lips.

"And the powder?"

"Kills the bugs and relaxes the muscles."

Ivanna nodded thoughtfully. "Salvador's feeling better. He wants to talk to you."

Adi followed her through the camp and into the small lean-to as the sun began to set. Pablo and Rodrigo were already there and they stood around Salvador, who was sitting on the floor, a blanket covering his legs.

"Adi," he said with a smile as she entered.

She walked up and handed him a tin mug. "It'll help the aching."

"Thank you," he replied, wrapping his hands around it. "Pablo tells me you're the reason I'm feeling better."

Adi shook her head. "No, it doesn't work that fast. It's the bugs. They've stopped."

He gave her a weary smile. "And will they be back?"

"Yes."

"When?"

"About a day."

Salvador sighed and nodded. "How long will this continue?"

"At least a week, maybe two."

He was quiet before he turned to Rodrigo. "How many are sick?"

"Sixteen, including you."

"That leaves twelve of you to do everything. The patrols, the hunting, the cooking."

"We should stop the patrols," Pablo said, grabbing Adi's attention. "We don't have the people. It'll be hard enough finding food."

"No, we need the patrols," Rodrigo replied, much to Adi's relief. She was already uncomfortable with how long she and Benito had stayed. If the patrols stopped, there would be no one to warn her if the man was coming. "We can't sit here unprotected," Rodrigo continued. "We wouldn't survive a surprise attack, not like this."

"Who's gonna attack us?" Pablo asked. "There's not a single person out there."

"Benito found us. There could be others. They could follow them here."

Pablo shook his head. "No, they can't. I covered their tracks. There's nothing to follow."

"Being unguarded is stupid. It defeats our entire purpose," Rodrigo argued. "These kids came here because we told them we would protect them. I'm not gonna stop doing that just because some of us are sick."

"Some of us are sick?" Pablo asked. "More than half the camp has been puking their guts out. They have to be treated, and that takes time. We can't waste it on pointless patrols."

"Okay," Salvador said sternly, bringing the argument to an end.

As Adi waited for him to make a decision, she tried to ignore the anxiety twisting her stomach into a hard knot.

"We keep the patrols," he said after a moment, relief washing over her, "but in four teams of two. Two for the day and two for the night. That will have to work until we get past this."

Satisfied with the plan, Adi left the shelter, found something to eat, and laid down next to Benito, eager to get some sleep. But when she woke the next morning, she realized that things were going to get much worse.

The sound of sickness filled her ears as she walked out of the hut. She looked over at the group of kids under the lean-to, expecting the distressed cries to be caused by them, but as the noise increased, she realised it was coming from the opposite direction. Following the groans across camp, she found Pablo, Ivanna, and a few others lying on the ground covered in vomit.

"They're all sick," Rodrigo said as he walked up carrying a small girl.

Adi reached out and touched the child's forehead, but jerked her hand back. "She's burning."

"I found her outside camp against a tree. She shouldn't have been there."

Adi was about to reply when calls for help interrupted them. Turning around, she saw two kids walking into the camp carrying a young boy.

"Take her." Rodrigo placed the girl in her arms and ran towards them.

Although the girl was only four or five, Adi struggled to lift her and she quickly carried her over to the lean-to.

"We need to cool her off," she said as Benito came out of the hut. She laid the girl down. "Cover her with wet rags and as soon as they get hot, dunk them back in the water. Okay?"

Seeing him nod, Adi walked over to Rodrigo and the others. They were standing around the boy on the ground and he wasn't moving.

"What do we do with him?" one of them asked.

Adi knelt down and examined him closely. She didn't have to touch him to see that his skin was clammy and his clothes were covered in puke and sweat. He had been dead for a while.

"We need to bury him," the other replied.

Adi looked at the dirt around them. While they buried the dead in her village, the ground here was different, full of roots, and the soft soil on top soon turned to clay. Digging a grave would take hours and they didn't have energy to waste.

"It'll take too long," Rodrigo said, echoing her thoughts.

"What else are we supposed to do?" the first one asked. "We can't just leave him to rot."

"We'll float him." They turned and watched as she stood. "If we make a raft, the river will take him away. That'll be fastest."

Rodrigo was quiet before he nodded. "Go help the others," he said to the boys as he picked up the body. "Come on."

Adi followed Rodrigo down to the river, collecting long, thin vines along the way. They worked quickly, gathering narrow logs and branches that were strewn across the jungle floor. Once they had enough, they placed the logs in the river and began stacking them on top of each other in rows, twisting the vines around the criss-crossed pieces.

"We should save his clothes," Rodrigo said. "We don't have very many."

Adi was standing in the water, tightly wrapping the edge of the raft together. She looked over at the boy lying on the riverbank, but didn't move. She had handled dead bodies before, forced to strip them of clothes, supplies, and anything else they could reuse at the village, but she had always done that with her sister, and as she stared at his pale face, she only saw Leti's, her sunken eyes perfectly still in her grave.

"Adi," Rodrigo said, urging her to do it.

She walked out of the water and knelt down beside the boy, unable to deny the feeling of dread as she began to remove his clothes. His body was already stiffening and every time she touched his cold skin, a wave of nausea slammed into her. She had managed to move his shirt up, but when she tried to lift it past his head, her eyes fell into his lifeless stare and suddenly, she was surrounded.

She could barely breathe as the bodies piled up around her, the smell of their rotting flesh overwhelming her senses and making her gag. No matter where she looked, she couldn't escape them, their cold eyes burrowing into her skin. She tried to push herself up, but her muscles refused to move and just as she was beginning to panic, she felt two hands grab her shoulders and shake.

It took a moment for her vision to clear as the bodies melted away, but when it finally did, she found herself staring into Rodrigo's worried face. She inhaled deeply but her stomach clenched and she turned and puked, just barely missing Rodrigo and the body.

He said nothing as she wiped her mouth with the back of her hand, but when she reached out towards the boy, his firm grasp held her in place.

"I'm fine," she said, her voice barely above a whisper.

He hesitated, but eventually let her go and returned to the raft.

The air was still as they placed the boy on top and watched the current take him down and away. As he drifted out of sight, Adi felt Rodrigo looking at her, but she ignored him, unwilling to talk about what happened. It had seemed real—the bodies, the smell, the way their eyes latched onto her—and even though she knew it wasn't, she couldn't shake the frightening feeling that she was losing control.

The day passed quickly as Adi and the others worked hard to treat everyone and gather supplies. When they finally finished, it was dark and she walked over to join them, sitting down heavily in front of the fire.

"Is this all we have?" She looked dejectedly at the small collection of fruit beside her. While she was hungry enough to eat anything, her body craved something more.

Rodrigo nodded. "We gave the last of the meat to the others. We'll get more tomorrow."

Adi wasn't so sure but didn't bother saying so. She picked up a mango and bit into it.

"We built sides on the lean-to," Rodrigo said after a few minutes, "but we'll still have to keep watch. The smell will attract animals." They had tried to remove all the vomit, but they couldn't keep up and the camp reeked of sickness.

"I'll take first watch," Adi said, surprising him. While she was exhausted, she wouldn't be able to sleep.

"You sure?" The other boys left the fire and went into the lean-to. She nodded and Rodrigo stood.

"Here."

Adi looked at him standing above her and saw the gun in his hand.

"Take it," he said when she didn't move, the handle pointed in her direction.

Adi reached up, but the moment she felt the cold steel against her skin, the image of her mother's bullet-ridden body reappeared and she jerked back, dropping the gun.

"I don't need it," she said quietly, trying to hide the pain on her face.

Rodrigo bent down and picked it up. She could tell he wanted to say something, but she was grateful when he didn't and simply walked away.

The night crawled by and Adi kept busy by checking on the sick and mashing bark and roots into powder. She was so tired her hand could barely hold onto the bowl, but she continued to work, afraid of where her mind would take her if she stopped. She was sitting against a stump, grinding bark into smaller pieces when the fatigue overwhelmed her and she nodded off to sleep.

The sound of someone choking jolted her awake. The bowl still in her lap, it fell to the ground as she scrambled towards the lean-to. The older boy was near the back of the shelter, trying to roll himself over as vomit filled his mouth, but he didn't have the strength. Dropping to her knees, Adi grabbed his shoulder, struggling to pull him towards her, but when she finally got him sideways, she saw that it was too late. The boy's chest no longer moved as he laid perfectly still, his lifeless eyes staring forward as saliva and puke dripped from his mouth.

"No," Adi whispered, not wanting to believe it. "No," she said, this time louder as she roughly shook his shoulder. So wrapped in her despair, she jumped when she heard a voice behind her.

"He's gone."

Adi turned and looked at Ivanna, shivering on the ground a few feet away. She was grossly pale; the only colour in her face was the redness of her eyes.

"Nothing you can do."

Adi stayed there for a while, battling the guilt she felt. She had only fallen asleep for a second. If she had just gotten there sooner, she would have been able to save him.

The light of the morning interrupted her reverie and she picked herself up off her knees, knowing what she had to do. Grabbing the boy by the ankles, she walked backwards, struggling to drag his dead body out of the lean-to and towards the river. She was almost out of the camp when Rodrigo jogged up.

He silently looked from her to the body, and then back again, the confusion on his face fading. But when he bent down to pick up the boy, Adi stopped him.

"Don't."

"Let me help you."

Irritation flowed through her as she shook her head. She didn't want his help or his sympathy. "I'll do it myself." Grabbing a hold of the boy's legs once again, she continued pulling him towards the river.

For the next hour, she worked at building a raft, stripping the body, and heaving it up onto the wooden float. As soon as she got the boy on top of the raft, she saw that a few vines had come loose on one side, causing a couple logs to separate, but she didn't bother fixing it. Once it was in the fast-moving water, the current would hold the raft together as it carried the body downstream.

Pushing it out into the river, Adi watched the dead boy bob along and as he drifted away, the only thing she felt was anger. She was doing everything she could but it wasn't enough, they were still dying. She was trying to stop the hot tears welling in her eyes when the sound of frogs croaking on the riverbank distracted her. Forcing her emotions down, she turned her attention to her next meal.

ψ

The next several days melted into each other as they did nothing but tend to the sick and search for food and supplies. By the time the malaria relented nine days later, they had eight more bodies to float. It took them an entire day to build the rafts and once it was done, Adi ached from head to toe.

With Salvador and the others finally better, Adi collapsed into a heap under the lean-to and slept solidly for hours, the weariness in her body taking over and trapping her there. She woke the following night still tired, drank some root tea, and went back to sleep, but this time it was not so serene. She woke up in a fright, sweat running down her face, as flashes of dead bodies and children screaming filled her head. Unwilling to face her nightmares, Adi grabbed a suma root and ate it, washing it down with more tea.

It didn't take long for the remedy to kick in and she was soon fast asleep, the pain melting away with the night. It was unusually peaceful in her dream-like state as her mind was still and finally quiet. Her body felt weightless, as if it was floating through the air, a slight breeze gently pushing a stray strand of hair across her forehead. She could hear the tranquil sounds of the early morning as insects chirped to one another and tree rats made their final calls as darkness lifted. She could imagine the cool feeling of mud squishing between her toes and the revitalizing sensation of water slowly climbing up her legs, as if she was lowering herself into a bath. She felt relief as she slept, free of nightmares, pain, and guilt, and she relaxed every muscle, inhaling deeply with contentment.

Water rushing into her lungs jarred her awake and she thrashed around violently, confused and terrified as the current took her down river. She kicked with all her might, propelling herself upwards and out of the water, choking and spitting when she was finally able to breathe. She swam towards the shore as hard as she could, but the weight of her clothes and the increasing speed of the water held her back, making it almost impossible for her to get any closer to the bank. The river was becoming louder and the thought of what was coming drove a new spike of fear into her as she swam for the edge with a renewed sense of panic. She had made it halfway to the shore when she saw it: a large cluster of rapids roaring less than ten feet in front of her.

Pulling her legs up, she braced for impact and was forcefully carried with the water into the terrain of large boulders that bulged out of the river. The first few rapids she got through unscathed but by the third batch, her strength was waning and the moment her legs dropped, she slammed into a rock that hid just below the surface, stopping her dead in the water.

Adi forced herself to ignore the pain reverberating through her legs and climbed up the stone, a few inches of water rushing over her feet as she stood on top. Looking for a way out, she searched the foaming water and as soon as she saw the path, she brushed the wet hair from her eyes and jumped onto the slab beside her. She carefully moved towards the riverbank, her muscles shaking as she climbed, jumped, and shuffled across partially-submerged rocks. When she finally stepped onto the shore, the comforting feeling of earth beneath her, she collapsed in the dirt.

She didn't know how long she laid there, but eventually her chest stopped heaving and she pushed herself up, beginning the long walk back to camp. She had been trudging along for almost an hour when she heard something moving through the trees in front of her. Too tired to be afraid, she stood and waited for whatever it was to reach her.

Pablo came to an abrupt stop as he emerged from the trees. Seeing her ragged body standing before him, his concerned face relaxed in relief. "We've been looking for you."

Unsure of what to say, she remained silent.

"What happened?" he asked as he looked her over.

Her clothes were still wet, her pants torn and bloodied, and she was covered in dirt.

"I fell in the river," she replied, her throat scratchy.

Pablo nodded. "Come on. Benito's waiting."

Although she was afraid to sleep, the next couple of nights passed uneventfully. She figured her sleepwalking was from too much suma root so she didn't touch it again, deciding to avoid the tea as well, even though her bruised body constantly throbbed with pain. She slept, but only lightly and for short periods, waking every couple hours as if to make sure she was still under the lean-to.

One night, after a few weeks of barely sleeping, the fatigue and discomfort were too much to take and she gave in, drinking a small cup of kamalame tea before falling into a fitful sleep. She didn't remember much from that night, only the sensation of moving, but when Ivanna forcefully shook her awake a few hours later, she knew it wasn't the tea. As she stood there over Benito, gun ready and aimed at his head, she knew it was her. She was the problem.

Chapter Four

It had been a few days since they found her standing over Benito gun drawn, but Adi still couldn't bear to be near him. The guilt of what she had done crushed her, and every time Benito came close, she would pretend not to see him and walk away. She knew it hurt him, but she was afraid of herself and didn't know what else to do.

At night while everyone slept, Adi would go into an empty lean-to and lock herself in, tying her wrist to one of the poles. More often than not, she just laid there, staring at the leaf roof as sleep eluded her. But when it did come, she would lurch awake in pain, the rope biting into her skin as her body fought against its imprisonment.

One morning, as she drifted in and out of a light sleep, she woke to Benito quietly entering the lean-to, a plate of food in his hand. Adi said nothing as she fearfully watched him, his eyes wide as he looked at her wrist bound to the pole.

"What are you doing?" she asked when he moved to sit down beside her.

Benito hesitated. "I thought you might be hungry."

"You shouldn't be here." Adi sat up and scooted away from him.

A mixed look of hurt and confusion passed over his face and he looked down at the ground, biting his lip as he avoided her gaze.

"Go," Adi said, trying to ignore the pained expression. "Get out of here."

"I'm sorry," he replied, tears filling his eyes. "Whatever I did, I'm sorry. I won't do it again, I promise."

The guilt was too much to handle and Adi felt nothing but contempt. Unable to hide her anger, she yelled, "Go! Leave!"

Benito's face scrunched up as the tears fell freely down his face and he turned and ran, dropping the plate of food on the ground.

Adi had never hated herself so much and she tried to shove the disgust down, but it was no use. Quickly cutting her wrist free, she ran out of the lean-to.

She fled through the jungle, tripping on rocks and roots as she put as much distance as she could between her and the camp. Low hanging branches and vines whipped her face but she tore through the trees feeling nothing, stopping only when her legs gave out, sending her crashing into the ground. She laid in the dirt, fighting for air while pain bubbled out of her chest. Not willing to return and face him, she reached up and grabbed onto the branch above her. Her weary arms shook as she pulled herself into the tree and began to climb, moving faster as the wood limbs sprouted out in clusters. She couldn't remember the last time she had done this, but as she moved further up, she was reminded of how much she loved it. Each step towards the sunlight seemed to soothe her and once she reached the top, she was calm.

Adi inhaled deeply as her head emerged above the canopy, the breathtaking view of untouched earth before her. Lush jungle spread out as far as she could see in all directions, the green terrain only disrupted by rivers as they snaked their way through the trees, the water sparkling in the sunshine. Closing her eyes, she heard nothing but the familiar sounds of the jungle: the loud squawks of neo-coloured macaws and toucans, the howls and screeches of monkeys as they moved in packs below, the distant thunder of large rapids and nearby waterfalls. Up here by herself, the world was at peace. No one was sick, no one was dying, and no one was pointing a gun at anyone else. Up here she was safe; *he* was safe.

The thought broke her from her concentration and she opened her eyes, staring back out across the tree tops. At first the idea seemed unthinkable—she could never do that—but the more she thought about it, the more she became convinced that she didn't have a choice. By the time she climbed down from the tree, she knew what she had to do.

Over the next few days, Adi avoided everyone as she collected the things she needed. She found a couple discarded shirts and tied them into a small sack, filling it with dried fruit, roots, and leaves. Stripping off some tree bark, she managed to make a small water container, sealing it together with sap and attaching a thick vine for a strap. There was only one thing left to get and she knew exactly where to find it.

That night, she quietly left her shelter and walked into the main hut. Besides the table and stools, two wooden chests furnished the room off to the side against the shelter wall. Carefully removing the books stacked on top, Adi set them onto the table and opened the first box. While she wasn't exactly sure where the map was, she knew it was in here somewhere. Salvador had pulled it out a few times when they were discussing patrols. Every time he learned something new, he would mark it on the map before returning the drawing to the chest. Not only was it full of geographic information such as waterfalls, large unnavigable rapids, and ravines, it also had the locations of the villages in the area. If she wanted to get out of the jungle, she needed that map. She was sifting through a pile of papers when she was startled by a voice behind her.

"What are you doing?"

Almost jumping out of her skin, Adi turned around. The darkness hid his face but she didn't need to see it to know he wasn't pleased.

Rodrigo walked forward and stopped about a foot in front of her, grabbing the papers out of her hand. "What are you doing?" he repeated.

Knowing there was no way she was getting out of this, she quietly said, "I need the map."

He hesitated. "Why?"

Adi awkwardly shifted her weight onto her other foot. She hadn't planned on telling anyone until the moment she left, not wanting them to try and stop her. She was thinking of how to explain it when his voice interrupted her.

"Why?" he asked again, more demanding.

"I'm leaving." The confidence in her voice surprised even her. Rodrigo's brow furrowed in confusion and she continued. "I don't know the way so I need the map."

Adi looked at his bewildered face. She wasn't surprised he didn't understand—no one did. It was more than just the camp. It felt like the jungle was closing in and she could feel the pressure as it grew heavier by the day.

"I can't stay here," she said. Her voice cracked. "I just can't."

The confusion left his face. The entire camp knew what she had done, and she was certain they heard her screaming at night. Whenever she walked by, she could feel their mistrusting and judgemental looks.

"What about Benito?" Rodrigo asked, his agitation returning. "He loves it here. You can't just take him away." As soon as he saw the look on her face, he said, "No, you can't do that. You can't leave him behind."

Adi remained quiet, knowing there was nothing she could say to make it better.

"He's your brother," he said.

"It doesn't matter." She could no longer hide her frustration. It wasn't like she hadn't tried to think of another solution. This was the only way she could keep Benito safe.

"Of course it matters!" Rodrigo said. "You're his family. You can't just abandon him."

Adi cringed at his words, the memory of her mother sending a spike of guilt through her. "I can't take him with me."

"Why not?"

While it was the last thing she wanted to say out loud, she knew she had to. "Because," she said, her voice barely audible, "I'll kill him." Her words hung in the air like thick humidity and even though she didn't think it was possible, she hated herself a little bit more.

"You won't."

Adi shook her head in resignation. She had had this conversation with herself many times and she always came to the same conclusion. "He's safer here without me."

Unable to take the condemning silence, she turned and walked out of the hut.

ψ

She didn't sleep a wink that night, trying to find a solution to her problem. She needed that map and without it, she would never get out. She was sitting beside the river the next morning when Rodrigo walked up.

Adi ignored him and continued washing her face, the water cooling her tired eyes.

"Where you gonna go?" he asked.

She said nothing as she looked across the river, the early morning sunshine making the water sparkle and dance. "Why does it matter?"

He sighed in annoyance. "Because maybe I can help you."

41

Surprised, she looked up at him warily. "How?"

He ignored her, staring straight ahead and so she stood, giving him her full attention.

"Tell me where you're going."

Adi relented. "The city."

"Why?"

"My aunt lives there."

Rodrigo nodded and looked out across the river. "I'll make you a deal," he said eventually, looking back at her. "If you swear to come back for Benito after you find her, I'll give you what you need."

Adi considered his offer. While the thought of returning terrified her, never being able to leave was worse. "I swear."

Rodrigo reached into his pocket and took out a piece of paper.

Unfolding it, a surge of happiness rushed through her. While it wasn't the map Salvador had, it was almost an exact copy, complete with directions on how to get out of the jungle.

"When are you leaving?"

Adi carefully folded the map. "Tomorrow."

"What are you gonna tell Benito?"

She hadn't figured that out yet. While she knew she would have to tell him something, she didn't know what she was going to say. The last time they spoke, she had yelled at him and she wasn't sure how he would react to her. "Will you look after him for me? 'Til I get back?" she asked, ignoring his question.

Rodrigo nodded. "I'll watch him."

The day passed faster than Adi wanted. While she was desperate to get out of there, she dreaded talking to Benito even more. When the sun set, a vivid display of yellow and orange, she knew she was out of time.

She found him near the edge of the camp and as she approached, she watched as he scampered up a tree.

"Did you see?" Benito asked the small girl on the ground.

The girl nodded eagerly as he climbed back down and when his feet hit dirt, he spotted Adi.

"Adi," Andressa said with excitement, following his gaze. "Benito's teaching me how to climb."

She couldn't help but smile. Andressa was nothing like she had been when Rodrigo placed her limp body into her arms that day. She was unafraid of anything and as soon as she had recovered, she became Benito's little shadow.

"Watch," Andressa said. She began climbing the tree enthusiastically, mimicking Benito.

She climbed higher and higher into the tree, but as soon as she was out of sight, Adi turned to her brother.

He didn't acknowledge her, instead looking up at Andressa in the tree.

"I'm leaving tomorrow," she said, knowing there was no other way to tell him.

He was quiet for a moment. "Where are you going?"

"The city."

"Why?"

She hesitated. While she didn't want to lie, the truth was too complicated for him to understand. "Our aunt lives there."

"I don't want to live in the city. I want to live here."

The jungle was all Benito knew as he had been a baby when they moved here whereas Adi had grown up in the city. Even though she only vaguely remembered it, it seemed like a dream.

"That's why you're not coming," she said. "I'm going by myself."

Adi stood and waited for him to say something—anything. While she knew she had treated him badly, she hoped he would just brush it aside like he had done so many times before. But when he said nothing else, she knew that this time it was different so she turned and walked away.

It was barely light out when Adi stepped from the lean-to and into the sticky morning air. Her bag packed and her water container full, she gripped the map in her hand and silently made her way east through the trees. While she had been out on her own before, she never went far, staying close to camp. But as she walked farther away from what was familiar, all her old forgotten fears returned and she could feel her anxiety rising, the uncertainty of what was lurking out there building up in her mind. She was about to step onto a rock that formed a ragged pathway across the river when a hand grabbed her arm.

Adi whipped around, eyes wide with fear. Benito's small frame stood before her and she swallowed hard, forcing down the large lump in her throat.

"Will you come back?"

Hearing the concern in his voice, she felt relieved. "Yes," she replied.

His brow furrowed and he nodded.

"You'll be safe here with Rodrigo," Adi continued. "I'll be back soon."

Benito nodded again and then suddenly stepped forward, wrapping his small arms around her. He held onto her tightly for a moment before he let go and disappeared into the trees.

ψ

She walked for days, starting and ending with the light as she followed the map, hiking over mountains and navigating her way through rivers. It wasn't the fastest route, but it was the safest as she avoided difficult terrain and most importantly, the villages between her and the city.

Five days had passed and Adi was beginning to think that she had taken a wrong turn when she heard a noise in the distance.

The closer she got, the louder it became, and as soon as the trees thinned out, she saw it.

The city loomed before her, the heat rising with the clatter and commotion. She saw nothing but brick and mud as the shanties piled on top of each other, the sun glaring off their tin roofs. Dirty and exhausted, she walked down the sloping hill and into the city.

She was so happy to be there, she almost cried in relief. There were people everywhere; walking along the roads, hanging out on corners, and moving in and out of the stores. Music blared from the rooftops, the songs gently floating down into the streets, weaving into the continuous hum of the neighbourhood. As she inhaled, she almost choked, the sharp smell shocking her nostrils. She had forgotten what it smelled like here—fruit and asphalt baking in the hot sun, overcrowded slums, and humidity that made everything sweat—but she didn't care. She was out of the jungle and she was free.

A loud horn broke her from her trance as a car came barreling up behind her, screaming at her to get out of the way. She was in the middle of the street and jumped to the side, the driver swearing at her as he passed. Eager to get where she was headed, she stopped gawking and began walking through the city.

She had no idea where she was, only that she needed to go north. Approaching a man leaning against a door frame, Adi opened her mouth to ask for directions but before she could get a word out, he went inside and shut the door.

Over the next hour, she tried to find someone who would help her, but everyone she went up to would tell her to get lost the moment she looked their way. At first she didn't understand, but when she saw her reflection in a window, she got it. She looked like a street kid, covered head to toe in dirt and sweat. Even her parents had told her to avoid them. "Nothing but trouble," her mother would say. Not used to the sun's unrelenting glare, Adi found a shady spot in between two buildings and sat down as she tried to figure out what to do.

She was resting there, head against the wall, when she spotted something oddly familiar. Jumping up, she ran across the street, pausing only to let a speeding motorcycle pass, and stopped in front of a small store. The building was old, dwarfed by the ones around it, and the bricks were no longer a bright red. But that wasn't what grabbed Adi's attention. Two feet above her was a small yellow window, almost unnoticeable as the sun-baked paint was badly peeling off the frame. She remembered that window, having passed it many times on her way to the market with her sister. Finally, she knew where she was.

Filled with excitement, she headed west towards her old neighbourhood. It took her less than twenty minutes to reach it, but she almost walked straight past, barely recognizing the place she grew up in. Her school was gone, replaced by slums and make-shift houses. Even the empty lot where she used to play football had been developed, the area crammed with as many apartments as possible. When she reached her old home, she couldn't believe how unfamiliar it looked, the small house now divided into four, with more stacked on top. It was as if her old life had never existed.

She was looking around the block, unsure of what to do, when she smiled. Running to a house that sat at the end of the street, she knocked on the door and waited.

As soon as it opened, the smile disappeared and she stood there, staring at the unfamiliar woman in front of her.

"Yes?" the woman asked irritated, holding a crying baby on her hip as she suspiciously looked Adi up and down.

"Is Pia here?" she asked meekly, the disappointment coming through her voice.

"Who?" the woman asked, growing crosser by the second.

"Pia Diaz."

"I don't know any Pia. Go ask the old woman on the corner." The door slammed shut.

Her hopes dashed, Adi walked over to the woman sitting behind a small table of produce on the sidewalk. The woman's hair was almost completely white, small shimmers of brown barely peeking through, and as Adi approached, she could feel the woman's watchful eyes.

"I'm looking for Pia Diaz," Adi said once she stood in front of her. "Do you know where she is?"

"Who wants to know?" the old lady asked.

"She was my friend. She used to live there." Adi pointed to the house with the woman and the baby.

The lady nodded. "I remember. They moved out two years back, not long after the explosion."

"What explosion?" Adi asked, alarmed.

"At that factory, just south of here," she replied. "If I remember right, both Mr. and Mrs. Diaz died in the fire."

Adi was quiet, her heart heavy.

"Wasn't long after that they got kicked out," the old woman continued. "Couldn't pay the rent. Last I heard they were living in the northeast part of the city."

Adi frowned as she looked at the ground. She would never find Pia now.

"Where are your parents?" the woman asked, her sharp voice interrupting Adi's thoughts.

Caught off-guard, Adi couldn't hide the pain on her face and the lady nodded, as if she understood. Quietly reaching down beside her chair, she grabbed a small cloth bundle and handed it to her.

Tears sprung into her eyes when she saw the homemade food inside and she clutched the fabric to her chest.

"Where are you going?" the woman asked.

"My aunt's," Adi replied, her voice small. "She lives in the north end."

"Here," the woman said. She slapped some money into her hand. "The bus for the north stops across the street. Next one will be by in a few minutes."

Adi didn't know what to say. It was more than she could ever ask for and so she simply stood there, unsure of how to properly thank her.

"Go on," the old woman said, smiling.

Ψ

By the time Adi arrived at her aunt's, it was almost dark. The bus had brought her north, but not far enough, and it took her over an hour to walk the rest of the way. She had only been to her aunt's house once before but she found it easily. Unlike the rest of the city, the north end had barely changed at all. Walking onto the familiar street, she smiled. She was finally safe.

She was about to press the buzzer on the gate when a large security guard came out from the building.

"Scram," he said. "You can't beg here."

Startled, Adi cleared her throat. "I'm here to see my aunt."

"And who might that be?" he asked.

"Joselin Soto. She lives in number eight."

He hesitated for a moment and then said, "Come with me."

Adi followed him behind the gate and into the building where she was seated on a chair against the wall.

"Stay here," the guard said. He left and entered a small room off to the side.

Adi watched as he talked on the phone, smiling as he spoke while a second guard sat inside the room, looking at her with suspicion. A few minutes later, the guard came out.

"What's your name?" he asked, standing in front of her, hands on his hips.

"Adelita Alvarez."

"And your parents'?"

"Mateo and Esperanza."

Without another word he turned, went into the room again, and picked up the phone. After a minute, he came back out and simply said, "Wait."

About half an hour passed and Adi was curled up in the chair when she woke to the sound of high heels clicking sharply against the concrete floor. Looking up, she saw the security guard walking towards her with her aunt, who was speaking to him quietly. Unable to contain her excitement, Adi stood and ran towards them, wrapping her aunt into a big hug.

She immediately felt pointed fingernails dig into her arms as they pried her off and pushed her back. Watching her aunt straighten and brush off her clothes, Adi suddenly felt self-conscious. Although she wasn't tall, Joselin Soto was an intimidating woman. Her hair was perfect, large dark curls falling softly down onto her shoulders, and her face was flawless, lips full and red. Her neatly-pressed clothes hung from her body like they were made only for her and Adi could see that even her feet were impeccable, brightly painted toenails peeking out from her white high-heels. Looking at her made Adi feel gross and so she quickly tucked a loose strand of hair behind her ear.

"It's me, Adi," she said. Her aunt remained silent, looking at her intently.

"Miguel," Joselin said finally, addressing the guard. "Is there somewhere we can talk privately?"

"Of course, Mrs. Soto. Please, come with me."

Adi followed them down the short hallway and into a windowless room that contained only a table and two chairs.

"Sit," the guard instructed.

Adi did as she was told and waited as her aunt sat across from her, the guard closing the door as he left.

"Do you remember me?" Adi asked when her aunt said nothing. "We came to visit you after Benito was born."

Joselin was quiet, a strained look on her face. "Why are you here?"

Adi didn't understand why her aunt was acting so unfriendly. "I have nowhere else to go."

"You should go home," Joselin said. "Your parents will be wondering where you are."

"They're dead," Adi said bluntly. Why would her aunt say such a thing? Why else would she be here?

Her response caught Joselin by surprise and Adi watched as a mixed look of shock and pain passed over her face for a brief moment before it disappeared.

She sighed deeply. "I told your mother what would happen if she went into the jungle," she said, more to herself than to Adi. She turned her attention back to her. "Actions have consequences. You can't run off playing revolutionary without expecting repercussions."

Confused by her aunt's response, Adi remained silent.

"Now I'm left to pick up the pieces," Joselin was mumbling to herself, arms crossed as she looked at the wall. When she finally returned her attention back to Adi, she was angry. "What am I going to do with you? I mean, look at you. You're filthy and look like you haven't washed in months. Do you even know how to behave properly, in a civilized manner?"

Hurt by her words, Adi sat there, her eyes hot and welling with tears.

"What am I supposed to do?" her aunt continued. "Just let you into my home and run rampant over my life?"

By now the tears were running freely down her face, but Adi didn't bother wiping them away. This was not what she expected. She thought her aunt would be happy to see her.

"There's no need to be dramatic," her aunt scolded. "Tears never helped anyone."

It was more than Adi could take. "Why won't you help me?"

Joselin said nothing for a minute as she avoided Adi's gaze. "It's not that I don't want to," she said eventually. "I just can't. You don't belong here. You should go back to wherever you came from."

In silent despair, Adi struggled to understand, but there was nothing to confuse; her aunt wanted nothing to do with her.

"I know this may be hard to accept right now, but I'm doing you a favour. You need to learn how to survive on your own, like everyone else."

Chapter Five

Not knowing where else to go, Adi took the bus back down to her old neighborhood. She hoped that the old woman on the corner would still be there, but when she arrived, the lady and her stand were gone.

The city felt different as the daylight faded away. She had never been out on the streets at night and as she walked, her father's warning to be home before dark rang through her head. Seeing a group of boys coming towards her, she turned and went the other way.

Adi wandered through the city for a while, not knowing what to do or where to go. Her feet ached from walking, but too afraid to sit down on the street, she kept going. She continued on for a few more hours before she stopped in an alley, the throbbing in her legs too painful to ignore.

Tucking herself into a small corner against the wall, she was happy just to sit, not caring that the ground was hard and cold. Unwrapping the cloth bundle, she devoured the food and before she knew it, she drifted off to sleep.

Hands running all over her body jarred her awake, but as she sat up from her slumped position, the feeling of steel biting into her throat stopped her instantly.

"Hold still," the boy said as he crouched beside her.

Adi tried to keep calm as she watched two others rifle through her bag.

"Holy shit!" one of them exclaimed as he stood up. "Look at all this money!"

She had forgotten about the bills her aunt had shoved in her pocket.

"How much?" the boy holding the knife asked, clearly in charge.

"Like $60!"

"You got any more?" he asked Adi, his eyes staring at her from underneath his hood.

"No."

Once they were done, the knife was removed from her throat and the three of them stood there looking at her.

"Whadda we do with her?" one of them asked.

"Nothin'," the tallest boy answered. "She doesn't know us."

"We could sell her to El Monstruo," the other one suggested.

"Look at her. She's ugly and smells funny. Not even El Monstruo would want her." His answer sent them into a fit of laughter.

"Most of its just dirt," the small one replied, taking a step closer towards her. "Besides, I seen what he does with ugly girls. Cuts 'em up and makes 'em pretty. We could get somethin' for her."

"No," the tall boy replied, his tone final. "Let's go."

As soon as they left, Adi stopped holding her breath, the air rushing from her mouth. She didn't know whether she should be shocked or mad. She should've known better than to sleep on the ground. If she was going to survive, she needed to be smarter, no matter how tired she was. Not wasting another minute, she grabbed her now empty pack, shoved it under her shirt, and walked out of the alley and back into the street.

She moved quickly, trying to be as unnoticeable as possible as she went farther into the city. While the streets weren't busy, they were still active as shadowed figures slunk around, often not making a sound. While the odd shout or burst of bottles breaking would cut through the silence, Adi didn't stop for anything. By the time daylight began to seep between the buildings, her body shuddered in relief.

She was looking for a safe place to sleep when a familiar smell grabbed her. Her stomach grumbled as she followed the delicious aroma, winding eagerly through the streets. She didn't have to go far to find the small local market just opening for the morning.

She hadn't realized how hungry she was but as she stared at the basket of hot empanadas sizzling on top of the table, her stomach growled so loudly she was afraid someone might hear. She stood there for a moment, her mouth watering with anticipation, when she remembered she didn't have any money. Dejected, she turned to leave, but as she did, her gaze landed on a group of kids entering the square.

From a few feet away, Adi watched as they ran through the thickening crowd, darting in and out as they stealthily grabbed some food here and someone's wallet there.

You could do that, a small voice inside her suggested.

Adi shook her head. She wasn't a thief.

Just this once, the voice prodded, louder this time. *How else are you going to eat?*

Adi was trying to come up with an answer when her eyes landed on the empanadas again. Her mouth was watering so much she had to swallow, making her stomach clench unhappily. She couldn't take it anymore, the pang of hunger overwhelming, and she walked towards the tables.

Having never stolen anything before, she tried to mimic the kids, quickly moving in and out of the crowd, but as she approached the empanadas, she heard an angry voice behind her.

"Hey!" a man shouted, making her spin.

Adi's eyes widened in fear as a policeman barrelled towards her, a threatening hand on his stick. Frightened, she ran off, the man right behind her. She was glancing back trying to see how close he was, when she stumbled into a table full of fruit, sending oranges, mangos, and pineapples flying in all directions. She was in trouble now.

Darting behind the overturned table, she snuck along it and out the other side, the mess distracting everyone around her. As she ran from the market and back towards the street, she looked and saw that the empanadas were sitting right beside her, and no one was watching. Before she could think, she had already grabbed two of them and, terrified of being caught, she shoved them down her shirt and fled into the streets.

Adi didn't stop running until she could no longer take it, the empanadas warm against her skin. Carefully taking one out, she bit into it hungrily, the savory taste of beef dancing on her tongue. Unable to pace herself, she devoured the second one and as she licked the sauce off her fingers, she couldn't help but wish she had taken more.

She continued to move, the city sloping upwards as it spread across the mountainside. She wasn't sure where she was going or what she was looking for; all she wanted was to sleep somewhere safe. She walked for hours, climbing hill after hill, passing colourful cantinas, busy barrios, and whitewashed churches, when she finally found some large buildings grouped densely together.

Adi stopped and jumped up, grabbing onto the bottom rung of the stairs that hung off the side of the building. She climbed the metal bars all the way to the top and stepped out onto the roof, more buildings towering around her. Only pausing to catch her breath, she found the next ladder and continued to move upwards with the buildings.

She climbed as high as she could, reaching a large, flat roof that sat directly below the last layer of buildings set against the hillside. She was walking around, looking for somewhere to sleep when she found a small rooftop tucked away in a corner, surrounded by cement walls and hidden from view. She had finally found it: her new home.

ψ

It was a Sunday, church bells resonating throughout the city. Sundays were good days because if she went down to the river just south of her rooftop home, she could get food for free. She discovered it by chance one day when she went to get water. As she splashed around in the murky current, she watched as families walked around, handing out food to the kids who sat along the cement curb. She had gone back to the river every day to see if it would happen again and seven days later, there they were, in their clean clothes and brushed hair, giving away food.

The river was her favourite place in the city. No one tried to chase her away and the water was always filled with so many different people that she never felt lonely. Most of all, she loved it because it reminded her of home.

A pang of sadness passed through her as a group of girls approached the water, flicking off their flip-flops at the edge. Adi had seen these girls before and every time she did, she thought of her sister. Like them, Leti had long brown hair that shone in the sunlight and she was just as pretty without makeup as these girls were with. Adi missed her laugh. It took a lot to get Leti to even crack a smile, but when she laughed, it filled the air with so much warmth that Adi couldn't help but feel happy. She would give anything to hear her sister laugh just one more time.

Consumed with thoughts of her family, she made the long journey back to the rooftop. As she walked by a window, she caught a glimpse of her reflection and looked down at her shirt, the faded material stretched thin and full of holes. It would've lasted her a few more weeks, but when she saw a clothing rack sitting unattended outside a store, the opportunity was too good to pass up. Snatching a couple shirts off their hangers, she darted down the street.

Adi smiled as she put on the shirt, the soft, clean fabric feeling nice against her skin. She had only been in the city a few weeks, but already she was getting quicker at swiping things. While she was ashamed of stealing at first, it became clear that if she wanted to survive, she would have to do things she didn't like.

Feeling better about herself in her new shirt, she almost missed noticing the boy causally walking towards her. Focused on him, she failed to see the one coming up from behind and as she cautiously slowed, a hand slammed over her mouth.

She kicked and screamed, but it was no use. There was nobody around and the boy was much stronger than her, effortlessly dragging her into an alley as the first one nonchalantly followed behind.

"Make a sound and you die," the boy holding her whispered. He took a gun from his waistband and pressed it against her face. "You're gonna be real quiet now, aren't you?"

Outnumbered and alone, she had no response.

Sitting her down against the wall, he released her from his grasp as the first one approached. Crouching on his haunches in front of her, he watched as she steadied her breathing.

"You're new here," he said, his tone calm and even, "so you don't know the rules."

"What rules?" she asked. Her question was answered with a slap across the face and she touched her stinging cheek, unsure of whether she felt pain or anger.

"Quiet," the other boy warned.

"We're gonna take you somewhere," the boy continued, ignoring her question. "If you try to run, make a sound or even look at someone, he will shoot you dead."

She glanced at the boy with the gun as he stared back at her.

"You're no one," he continued, "so no one will care if you die. We could shoot you in the middle of the street, in front of the entire neighbourhood, and no one would give a shit. Understand?"

Adi didn't know what to do. If she went with them, she would probably die, but if she ran, she was dead for sure. A second slap woke her from her thoughts.

"Understand?" he asked more menacingly.

She nodded.

"Good. Let's go."

With her between them, they made their way into the heart of the southeast part of the city. She had never been to this area before so she had no idea where they were going. Looking around her as they walked, she saw that they were right: no one cared or even bothered to look her way, despite the boy's heavy hand on her shoulder, sternly steering her forward. They continued to wind their way through the streets and as the road narrowed, the boy ahead of her turned, pulled out a bandana, and tied it around her eyes.

She struggled, fighting to get it off, but when she felt the barrel of the gun press into her neck, she froze. Feeling a hand on each of her elbows, she moved forward, clumsily placing one foot in front of the other.

For the next few minutes, they continued walking, Adi completely blind. She could hear the city around her, but as the hands guided her up a set of stairs, everything went quiet. The lack of noise heightened her anxiety as they kept ascending, the smell of raw sewage wafting into her nose. Unable to take it any longer, she was about to ask where they were going, when she heard a faint noise, growing louder as they climbed.

By the time they reached the top of the stairs, she could clearly hear children even without seeing them. Their voices filled the air and the sound bounced around her as she was led forward. Suddenly stopping, her blindfold was removed and she was shoved into a room, the door lock clanking ominously behind her.

She stood still as her eyes adjusted to the dimness of the windowless room, unsure of what or who was in there. After about a minute, she looked around and saw two chairs pushed up against the wall. Finding no way out, she tucked herself into a dark corner and waited.

She was sitting on the floor, head leaned against the wall, when she heard the door open slowly. Not moving a muscle, she watched as two figures entered the room, one staying by the door while the other pulled out a chair and sat down.

"So," the boy sitting said, "you're the one who doesn't know the rules."

Unsure of what they wanted and a little frightened, she stayed silent.

"How long has she been around?" the boy asked when she didn't answer.

"A couple weeks," the one at the door answered. "Maybe a month."

Adi was shocked. How did they know this? She saw the figure in the chair nod.

"So," he said, addressing her once more, "where did you come from?"

Feeling completely outmatched, she gave in. "I used to live in the west side of the city."

The boy nodded again. "And then?"

"In the country."

"For how long?"

She swallowed, her mouth feeling dry and pasty. "A while."

The boy leaned forward in his chair. "Why'd you come back?"

She didn't know what answer to give him, there were so many. "My family died."

When the boy didn't say anything else, she began to worry. What if they never let her out?

"I'm sorry about the rules," she said, her desperation obvious. "I didn't mean to break them. If you let me go, I promise I'll leave and never come back."

"Where would you go?"

She didn't understand why that mattered but she tried to think of an answer quickly. "My friend Pia lives on the east side. I'll go there."

The boy sat up straight in his chair. "This Pia, what's her last name?"

Her brow furrowed in confusion, but she answered anyways. "Diaz."

He said nothing for a moment, but when he did, it was not what she expected. "Adi?" His voice cracked as he said her name and she sat there confused, trying to understand how he knew her.

"Adi, it's me," he said, leaving his chair and walking towards her in the corner.

As soon as his skinny face came into view, she couldn't believe who was in front of her.

ψ

Pulled up onto her feet, she was wrapped in a hug.

"I can't believe it," he said, smiling as he looked at her. "I can't believe it's you."

Adi couldn't help but smile back. She had first met Omar when she was five and had just gotten into trouble for speaking back to her mother. Sent to bed early with no dinner, she decided to get her own food and snuck out of her bedroom window. Omar found her wandering the streets as the sun was setting, her tear-stained cheeks giving away that she was lost. He had helped her find her way home and after that, he started checking in on her, making sure she went to school, inviting her to play football, and eventually teaching her how to climb buildings. Whenever he was around, Adi always felt like she'd be okay. "Where am I?" she asked.

His smile widened and he clasped her shoulders. "Come. I'll show you."

She followed Omar out of the room and back into the hall.

"Welcome to the Complejo."

She couldn't believe what she saw. Inside an abandoned and partially crumbling building was a tower full of kids.

"Pretty cool, huh?" Omar said.

Adi walked up to the railing, staring down at the multiple floors below. She had never seen so many kids and she watched in amazement as they occupied every floor, some playing while others slept. "What are they all doing here?"

"They live here," he replied. Seeing the confusion on her face, he continued. "I found this place a while ago. It was supposed to be an apartment building but half of it collapsed so no one wanted to live here. Plus," he said with a smirk, "it smells like shit."

"And you brought them here?"

"You know me," he said. He playfully tossed her hair. "I'm a sucker for a sad face."

Adi smiled, but it quickly faded. "You said I don't know the rules. What does that mean?"

Omar pushed himself off the railing and began walking down the hallway. "Before we came here, there were only a few of us. But then we got bigger and so did our problems. Cops started hanging around and some of the younger kids got roped into working for the drug dealers in the slums. So as soon as we came to this place, we made rules."

"What rules?" she asked as she followed him.

"We have a system," he replied, leading her up the stairs to another floor. "Each person is allowed to leave the Complejo, but only on certain days, and everything is shared. If all of us went out at the same time, we'd get a lot of unwanted attention."

She listened intently as he led her farther up the building.

"Once you're older, you can't steal anymore, so you gotta find a way to make money. But no drugs or sex. And you have to go on lookout." Omar stopped, standing in front of a short stairway that led to a grey door.

She couldn't help but notice that there was no one else on this floor, the sudden silence giving it an eerie feeling.

"So," he said, turning to face her, "you wanna come live with us? Or would you rather stay on that shitty rooftop you call home?"

It wasn't a hard decision and as soon as Omar saw the look on her face, he said, "Good." Walking up the stairs, he flung the door open.

The sun blinded her as she stepped out onto the roof. The building was one of the tallest in the area, allowing her to see all the way to the ocean. She stopped, distracted by the view.

"Ready?" Omar asked, bringing her attention back to him. He was standing behind her with a glove on one hand, holding a small, skinny piece of metal.

Smirking at her confused face, he explained. "Everyone who lives here is marked. It's how you get in. Without it, you won't get close."

As he expectantly held out his hand, Adi grimaced, knowing what was coming next. He took her arm, turned it over, and grabbed the back of it, pressing the hot metal bar tightly against the skin on the inside of her elbow.

She squirmed in pain, the metal burning her skin as the pungent smell stung her nostrils. When Omar finally removed it, an angry red line stared back at her.

"What are those for?" she asked when he used the end of the bar to burn two small dots underneath the line.

"Those are your strikes." He finished, placing the metal back on the ground. "One more and you're out."

Adi looked down at the marks seared into her arm, lightly touching them with her fingers. "What do you mean I'm out?"

"You're gone," he repeated, arms crossed over his chest. "You're out of the Complejo."

She was about to ask why when a boy burst through the door.

"We got a problem."

As soon as they were back inside, Omar told her to go downstairs. She hesitated, watching them walk down the empty hallway, and before she knew it, she was following them.

The only sound she heard as she crept through the hall was the faint echo of voices wafting up from the floors below. The air around her seemed thin and the farther she went, the less sure she felt about what she was doing. She stopped to turn around when she heard muffled voices coming from a room just ahead of her. Cautiously tip-toeing up to the door, she pressed her head against it, trying to hear what was happening inside.

"You just don't get it, do you?" she heard a voice saying.

"Please I...," a girl replied, but the sound of a dull thump interrupted her and Adi instinctively took a step back.

She knew she shouldn't be there, but she couldn't bring herself to leave. Instead, she moved back up to the door and listened. She could hear the girl crying, her voice barely audible.

"I can't be out there," Adi heard her say. "They'll kill me. Please." But Adi didn't get a chance to hear the rest as a strong hand latched onto her arm and yanked her away from the door.

Spun around, she looked up into the face of one of the boys who had caught her on the street.

"What the fuck are you doing?" he asked. His jaw clenched as his face twisted into an angry snarl.

She opened her mouth to reply, but unable to think of anything, she stared back at him as she heard the door open behind her.

The boy looked over her head. "We found another one."

"What's she doing here?" As soon as Adi heard Omar's voice, she cringed.

The boy shrugged. "Found her listening."

When Omar didn't reply, she knew she was in trouble.

"Wait here," he said to the boy as he walked in front of her. "You wanna see?" He turned her around, not waiting for a reply. "I'll show you."

Unsure of what was happening, she tried to move away, but Omar's firm grip held her in place as he walked her by the shoulders into the room. As the door slammed shut behind them, she found herself staring into the bruised face of a girl.

"Please," the girl whimpered as she looked up at Adi from her knees. "Give me another chance."

Speechless, Adi looked back at Omar but he stood still with crossed arms and a blank expression.

"Help me," the girl cried. She grabbed Adi's leg, latching onto her. "I promise I won't do it again."

When she reached out towards her, Adi saw the line with the three dots underneath and understood. The girl was out.

"Please, please," she begged.

The despair on her face was too much for Adi to take and she turned around. "She won't do it again," she said to Omar. "Can't you give her another chance?"

He moved towards her. Although his face was calm and steady, she could see the anger underneath. "Let me show you what happens when we break the rules."

Not saying another word, he grabbed her by the arm and led her out of the room. The boy waiting in the hall followed as they made their way back down the stairs to the main floor.

Adi could tell by the strained looks on the faces they passed that something was wrong, but when Omar pushed open the door to a room in the back of the building, she was not prepared for what was inside.

On the table lay a girl, maybe five or six, covered in blood.

"Give me those," an older girl instructed. She hovered over the small body, her shoulder-length black hair swaying as she wiped off the blood.

Adi watched in shock as three of them tried to stop the bleeding, but couldn't. It was gushing from everywhere.

"You want me to give that girl upstairs another chance?" Omar asked, reminding Adi he was still there. "This is what happens."

She said nothing as Omar turned and left the room, leaving her standing by the door. She had seen blood before, and lots of it, but this was different. This was something else.

"You," the older girl said, looking back at her. "Come here."

Adi swallowed hard and walked forward, the girl's battered frame becoming more visible. She was still alive, but the front of her head was matted with blood and there was a small trickle making its way down her forehead and into her ear. One side of her face was sunken and smashed in, blood pooling beneath the skin. Her shirt had been almost completely torn from her body, scrapes and bruises covering her chest as it moved up and down ever so slightly.

"Hold this," the older girl instructed, drawing Adi's attention to where she was standing.

Adi walked over to the end of the table, took the rag from the girl's hand and watched as she began cutting away the blood-stained shorts.

"As soon as these are off, you have to stop the bleeding," she said as she cut through the worn fabric. "Find the bloodiest part and press against it. Got it?"

Adi nodded and the girl removed the shorts, the blood rapidly oozing out of her and onto the table. Ignoring the hard knot in the pit of her stomach, she quickly pressed the rag against the steady flow, but within seconds, it was soaked.

"You're not close enough," the girl said as she handed Adi another rag. "You gotta get inside."

"What?" she asked, unsure if she heard her right.

The girl put the tools she was cleaning down and took the rag from her hand.

"Inside," she said. She inserted the rag into the girl without hesitation. "You'll never stop the bleeding if you don't."

As Adi watched the girl feel around for the bleed, it took all her willpower to fight the vomit forming at the back of her throat.

"Here," the girl said, interrupting her concentration. "Hold the rag right there."

Adi shakily put her fingers inside and held the rag tightly against the bleed, the little girl letting out a small moan.

"We're gonna have to do this quickly," the girl said. She brought several tools over to the table. "We gotta make sure there's nothing in there before I stitch it up. And that means you have to be fast. Otherwise the blood will fill it back up."

She nodded, understanding what she had to do.

"Ready?"

Adi quickly removed the rag, watching the girl peer inside as she held it open. A few seconds later, she moved out of the way and Adi shoved the rag back in, soaking up the leaking blood.

"I need another look," the girl said. They tried again, moving as quickly as they could.

"Anything?" Adi asked as she pressed against the bleed.

"Not that I could see," the girl replied, a needle pursed between her lips as she unwound some thread. "We're gonna do the same thing; I'll stitch for as long as I can and then you have to get in there."

They worked in sync, stitching up the gushing cut as best they could, and by the time they were finished, Adi's arm cramped from pressing so hard. She looked down at the little girl, her breath becoming increasingly shallow, and knew they had to keep trying.

For the next hour, they examined the girl's body, treating as many cuts and bruises as they could. They wiped her down, changed her clothes and washed the table.

"What do we do with these?" Adi asked as she threw the bloody rags into a bucket.

"We burn them," the girl replied. She picked it up and led her outside the room.

"Don't you have any epazote?" she asked after a moment, ignoring the stares they were getting as they walked down the hall.

"Any what?" the girl asked.

"Epazote. It's a plant that kills bugs. If you wash the rags in it and then lay them in the sun, you can use them again."

The girl shook her head. "We don't have any plants."

A few minutes later, they arrived at a metal door.

"Here," the girl said, handing Adi the bucket. "There's a bin and a lighter just outside. Burn the rags. I'll wait."

Adi grabbed the bucket and opened the door, the midday sun glaring down on her as she stepped into the heat. Finding the lighter, she dumped the rags into the bin and burned them, the smoke stinging her eyes and the smell burning her nose. As she stood there, her mind drifted back to the girl on the table, her injuries moving through her mind in vivid detail. She didn't understand it: how could someone do that to a person so small and defenseless? As soon as she was back inside, she couldn't help herself.

"What happened to her?" she asked. She followed the girl back through the hall.

"You know what happened," the girl replied.

Adi was silent for a moment. "Will she live?"

The girl shrugged.

They didn't have to wait long to find out. When they woke the next morning, the girl was dead and Adi couldn't shake the feeling that she had just entered a world she didn't want to be in.

Chapter Six

Not fast enough, her head snapped back as the fist hit her face, the sound of her nose cracking echoing through her skull. Looking at her attacker, Adi saw the smirk and lunged forward angrily, knife in hand. Focused on her target, she didn't see the second one until her feet were kicked out from under her, causing her to stumble forward uncontrollably. Distracted for only a moment, it was enough for her assailant to strike, swinging her arm out across Adi's chest and sending her backwards onto the hard ground below.

She lay there dazed for a few moments as she waited for the ringing in her head to stop. Gingerly propping herself up on her elbows, she touched the back of her head and winced.

"You okay?"

Adi looked up into the dark face above her. When she had asked Catalina to teach her how to fight, she didn't think it would take this long or be this painful. Ignoring her extended hand, Adi pushed herself to her feet.

"What the hell was that?" she asked angrily, standing directly in front of her.

Catalina shrugged. "I'm doing what you asked."

"Bullshit," she replied, spitting a wad of bloody saliva onto the ground. "That was dirty. You didn't tell me there'd be someone else."

Catalina smirked, making Adi angrier. "How exactly do you think it works?" she asked. "They're not gonna tell you shit."

Adi took a deep breath and exhaled, trying to calm herself down. She *had* asked for this, it just felt like she would never be good enough, she would never be ready.

A sharp whistle interrupted them and Adi looked up at Renan's head hanging over the railing a few floors above. Nodding, she turned to leave but Catalina stepped in front of her.

"I did it cuz you're getting good," she said. "You're quick and stronger than you think." She smiled. "You might even beat me one day."

Adi smirked. Catalina was one of the best fighters in the Complejo, and with a knife in her hand, she was unstoppable. The first time Adi saw her fight, she wanted to be just like her.

"I doubt it," she replied before walking past. She was almost to the stairs when Catalina's voice stopped her.

"Oh. You might wanna get Nayara to fix your nose."

Adi's hand went up to her face. She didn't notice how crooked her nose was until she hit a small bump near the top. Swearing under her breath, she looked back to give Catalina a piece of her mind, but she was already gone.

By the time Adi made it to the main floor, the lineup was already winding down the hall.

"What took you so long?" Renan asked irritably. He was one of the boys who had plucked her off the street and it was immediately made clear that he didn't like her.

Adi didn't bother answering and walked into the room, the early morning light making her squint as it streamed through the windows. Shaped like a rectangle and the biggest on the fifth floor, the room was full of kids lying on mats and make-shift beds that lined the walls.

"There's a lot today," Nayara said. She opened the supply chest and pulled out some tools. From the moment they tried to save that little girl covered in blood, Adi and Nayara had clicked. It was like they were meant to be together; whatever one of them couldn't do, the other one could.

Adi nodded and looked around. Only a couple beds were empty. Something in the river was giving the kids a rash. Not knowing if it was contagious, they were keeping them in the room until they were better.

"What happened to your face?" Nayara asked, getting her attention.

"Catalina."

Nayara smirked. "Right."

The door opening interrupted them. "Ready?" Renan asked.

"Just a sec," Nayara said as she walked up to Adi. "Hold still."

Nayara's hands moved so quickly that Adi didn't have time to take a breath. One minute she felt pressure and the next she was hit with a sharp wall of pain, the intensity of it making her eyes water.

"There," Nayara said as she stepped back. "Try not to move it."

They spent the rest of the morning treating the sick and injured kids waiting to see them. They set broken bones, stitched cuts, treated infections, and administered medication for malaria, fever, bites, and colds. While Nayara knew more about bones and muscles, Adi could heal wounds, reduce pain, and stop sickness with remedies she made from the plants, roots, and flowers she collected at the edge of the city.

When she wasn't working with Nayara or selling extra medications at the market, she spent most of her time on the roof, watching the sun set deep behind the mountains. It was there, in the darkening sky, that she thought of Benito, sometimes only for a moment. When he would still be on her mind as she lay down next to Nayara

73

on the mattress they shared, she would whisper the lie she told herself more times than she wanted to admit: *just a little longer.*

ψ

The unrelenting sun dried the water in her hair as she pushed her head up and out of the river. Adi couldn't remember a longer dry season and the water was full of those trying to escape the heat.

All different types of people came to the river. Married couples and their children swam next to wrinkly old men, kids her age dressed in fancy school clothes sat on the shore beside the homeless, and handfuls of kids launched themselves into the water, their excited shrieks filling the air.

With her feet barely touching the sand and the water lapping against her chin, Adi watched as two kids wrestled on top of a rock. She smiled when the loser was pushed off a few seconds later and into the river below, the laughter of their friends traveling out across the water. Three short, sharp whistles grabbed her attention and she looked over at the group she had come to the river with. Maresol and Caio waved her over and she nodded, dunking her head in once more before she climbed out.

Moving towards the shore, she wrung the water out of her clothes as she walked, her shirt clinging to her tightly. Her feet were almost out of the river when she heard a voice faintly say, "Adi?"

She stopped and turned, searching the riverbank for the person who said her name. As she looked over to the right, she saw a girl about her age standing along the edge.

"Pia!"

Adi splashed through the shallow water as she ran towards her, but when she was less than two feet away, a strong hand grabbed her arm and she was jerked back, her body hitting the sand.

From her position on the ground, she saw a large man standing above her, his head blocking the sun as he glared at her. Unsure of what was happening, she looked over at Pia, but another man was already leading her away.

"Pia," she called out, trying to stop her from leaving. The only response she got was a sad glance over her shoulder as she walked towards the street.

Scrambling to her feet, Adi tried to follow, but the man held her back by her arms.

"Let go," she said angrily as she struggled to get free.

"Don't make this difficult," he warned.

Unwilling to lose her, she stomped down as hard as she could on the man's foot. Groaning in pain, his grip loosened and Adi wiggled free and ran forward. She thought she had escaped him, but as soon as she felt her legs being yanked out from underneath her, she knew she was in trouble. Falling face first into the sand, she tried to push herself back up but it was too late. The man was already on top of her.

"I see you like to do things the hard way," he said. He easily swatted away her punches. "Just you wait. I'm gonna make things real hard for you."

She was powerless as he held her down with one hand, the other unzipping his pants. Looking around for help, she found no one as the people nearby had already moved away, leaving her utterly alone. As she felt his hand latch onto the waistband of her shorts, fear unlike any other surged through her. But as she continued to fight back, she heard a familiar voice say, "Let her go."

Looking up, Adi saw Caio standing behind the man, the barrel of his gun placed against his head. The man froze, but made no move to release her from his grasp.

"I'm not gonna tell you again," Caio warned.

As soon as the man sat up, he let go of her arms and she scooted out from under him.

"Good," Caio continued. "Now get up slowly."

Moving to his feet, the man's shirt adjusted, revealing the pistol tucked in his pants. Not hesitating for a moment, Adi grabbed the gun and pointed it at him as he glared down at her.

"You're gonna regret this, you little bitch," he said.

Whether it was the adrenaline or the rage pumping through her veins, she lowered the gun and fearlessly walked up to him. She stood and stared at him, holding his gaze with determination before she kicked him as hard as she could in the groin.

The man's face paled as he clutched his junk, dropping to his knees in agony onto the sand.

"Come on," Caio said. He grabbed her arm and led her up towards the street.

Adi looked back over her shoulder and watched with satisfaction as the man stayed on the ground, doubled over in pain. But when she heard Caio say "Shit" softly under his breath, she turned and saw that they weren't out of danger yet. Two men were coming towards them and they looked less than pleased.

"You ready?" Caio asked. She knew exactly what he meant.

As soon as she nodded, Caio ran into the busy road, Adi right behind him. Cars and motorcycles sped past, horns blaring as they darted around traffic. Not waiting to see if the men had followed, as soon as they reached the other side, they sprinted as fast as they could into the streets, zigzagging their way back to the Complejo.

It took twice as long to get there, Caio taking her the long way back as they darted and ducked through markets, walkways, and alleys that Adi didn't even know existed. They didn't dare slow down and when the area finally began to look familiar, she exhaled and caught her breath.

But as soon as they arrived at the Complejo, she no longer felt relaxed. Besides the additional lookouts she had seen on her way there, the building was oddly quiet. As they walked up to the main floor, Adi saw groups of kids huddled together, a look of fear in their eyes.

"What's going on?" she asked.

Caio didn't have a chance to reply because as soon as they stepped onto the landing, Omar was already walking towards them.

"You lose them?" he asked Caio, not looking at her.

"Think so," he replied. "Didn't see them after the river."

Adi quietly listened, unsure of how Omar already knew what had happened.

"Go tell the others," Omar said. As soon as Caio left, he turned to her, his arms folded across his chest. "Let's go."

She didn't say a word as she followed him into the room. While it was clear that the men were causing trouble, she didn't know what that had to do with her, so she simply sat down and waited.

Omar sat across from her, the anger visible on his face. "Do you know what you've done?" he asked, his voice low and quiet.

She did not, so she remained silent.

"Why would you do that?"

"Do what?"

For a moment Omar looked at her like he didn't believe her, but when the confusion stayed on her face, he explained. "Why did you go to that spot by the river? Why did you go over to that group?"

Still not understanding why she was in trouble, she replied, "I saw Pia."

Omar sat back in his chair, but then shook his head and leaned forward. "It doesn't matter. The damage is done."

"What do you mean?" she asked.

Omar sighed and looked straight at her. "Pia," he began, his voice breaking a little. "Pia isn't like regular girls. Pia belongs to someone."

He didn't need to explain further, Adi knew what that meant. Although there weren't many around the Complejo, she had seen a couple girls working on the street that were owned.

Omar rubbed his face with his hands before sighing heavily. "She belongs to La Patrona," he continued. "She lives with her on the east side."

Adi was surprised, unsure of what to say. She had heard of La Patrona and the nasty things she did, and she didn't understand how Pia could end up a prostitute, especially with her.

Omar's voice distracted her from her thoughts. "What happened at the river won't go unpunished. They're already looking for you and Caio." He paused. "You've put everyone in danger. Do you get that?"

She nodded.

"That's not the only problem," Omar continued, his voice tired as she looked up at him. "You already have two strikes..."

Knowing where this was headed, she cut him off. "But I didn't mean to," she said, her desperation clear. "I didn't know this would happen. I didn't do anything wrong."

Omar gave her a sad smile. "Some people would disagree."

"Who?" Adi asked, becoming angry. "Renan? He's hated me since I got here."

Omar put up his hands, trying to calm her down. "Nothing's been decided," he replied, "but whatever happens, you can't see Pia again. She's not your friend anymore, she's dangerous. Don't go near her."

A confused scowl covered her face. "I can't just forget about her."

"Yes, you can. And you will. You have to."

"But she's with her, with La Patrona," she said, not understanding. "We can't just leave her there."

"What do you want me to do, Adi?" His voice grew louder with irritation. "You think I can just go over there and get her out?"

She didn't reply as she looked at the floor, arms folded across her chest.

Omar stood up and went to the door, but just as he was about to open it, he turned. "I'm not kicking you out," he said, his voice much softer. "But I'm warning you: if you go near her again, you're gone."

But it didn't matter what he said. By the time she heard the door slam shut behind him, she had already made up her mind.

The streets were quiet as Adi made her way east from the Complejo late Friday night. She had prepared as much as she could over the past few days, working hard to get the supplies she needed without anyone knowing. If they found out what she was doing, they'd never let her back in.

As she rode the near-empty bus to the east side, she started getting ready. She tied her hair into a high ponytail and put on the make-up she bought from one of the girls at the market. There was only some eye shadow, blush, and lipstick, but it would be enough. Already wearing a short skirt and low-cut top, she took off her tights and shoved them into the pocket of her hoodie.

A few hours later, she stepped off the bus and started walking. She wasn't quite sure where she was going, but it didn't take her long to figure it out. The east side was still wide awake and all Adi had to do was follow the noise.

Loud music drifted out of the bars and cantinas that lined the main street, cascading over the crowd as people made their way from one place to another, drinks in hand. She had never seen such a beautiful place. The buildings were tall and made of glass and the beach was bright, lights illuminating the water. There were people everywhere, in the bars and on the street, and as she walked, she couldn't help but get lost in all the excitement. For a few minutes, she wandered around, staring at all the fancy buildings and beautiful people. But when she saw a girl younger than her emerge from an alley adjusting her clothes, she remembered why she was there. Crossing the street, Adi followed as she turned and went deeper into the heart of the city.

It didn't take her long to find La Patrona's. The girl had led her to a busy but narrow street several blocks in from the beach and Adi only had to walk along it for about five minutes before she darted into an alley, hiding against a building. There, standing on the front step of a large house, was the man from the river.

Adi watched people go in and out, trying to find a way in without being noticed. Although the make-up changed her appearance, she couldn't depend on that. If she got caught, she knew she'd never leave that house alive.

She was just about to look for another way in when a group of girls entered the street, their arms intertwined with a couple of older men. Quickly taking off her sweater, she dropped it and moved in behind them, joining the group as they walked up to the building.

Adrenaline pumped through her body as she ascended the stairs, trying to hide herself behind the others. Nearing the man at the door, Adi's hand instinctively went to the gun tucked under her shirt, ready for whatever was about to happen. But the man did nothing, barely shooting her a passing glance, and it took all her concentration to hide her relief.

As they entered the building, Adi couldn't help but stare. Fancy paintings and furniture were everywhere, and pretty girls in skimpy outfits moved around the room, flirting with men and women of all ages. A large burst of laughter drew her attention to the bar on the right and she watched as the group she had entered with walked up to it, leaving her alone in the centre of the room. Realizing that she couldn't just stand there, Adi went straight, going down a short hallway that ended at the foot of a long staircase. Unsure of what to do, she glanced around before moving up the stairs, eventually finding herself standing in a dimly lit hall lined with doors. Quietly walking forward, she approached the first door and turned the handle.

The door didn't budge and she moved to the next, trying to open each one as she went down the hallway. None of them opened. She was about to give up and go back downstairs when the last door on the left caught her attention. It was different than the others, sitting farther off to the side, and as she turned the knob, it creaked open.

Adi entered the room cautiously, unsure of what was in there before she shut the door behind her. She could hear soft groans coming from the corner, but they weren't the same type of sounds she heard in the hallway. These were ones of pain. Seeing several mattresses lined up against the wall, she walked towards them but was shocked by the sharp smell of sickness. In the beds were bruised and bloodied bodies, some bandaged, others not, and as Adi looked at them, she couldn't tell if they were alive or dead. The groaning began again and Adi followed the noise, stopping when she found a small girl lying on the floor, gripping her swollen belly. The girl whimpered louder as she approached and Adi knelt down in front of her.

"It's okay," Adi said to her softly. "I won't hurt you."

When the girl kept crying, she continued. "I can help," she said. "Tell me, where does it ache?"

"Everywhere," the girl moaned between sobs.

Adi moved beside her. She didn't know anything about having a baby but she remembered when her mother was pregnant with

Benito, she was always sore. "Try to relax," she said. She gently rubbed the girl's back, loosening up the tight muscles.

It didn't take long for the girl to calm down, the whimpering slowly subsiding as she laid her head on the floor. But as soon as Adi started massaging her shoulders, the girl began to cry. Not knowing what else to do, Adi placed the girl's head on her lap and pulled her close, saying nothing as she softly stroked her curly hair.

After a few minutes, the girl stopped crying, and they sat there in silence before Adi said, "I'm looking for a girl named Pia. She's my age, has black hair, and is a little taller than me. Do you know her?"

The girl sat up, wiped the tears off her face, and nodded.

"Can you tell me where she is?"

With a surprising amount of strength, the girl pushed herself off the floor and walked towards the door, Adi quickly following.

They went out of the room and into the hall, stopping about halfway down. Taking a pin out of her hair, the girl inserted it into the door handle, forcing it to unlock. She put a finger to her lips and opened the door.

The room was dark as they entered, but it wasn't empty. The sound of someone grunting filled the silence as they slid along the wall, hiding in a small hole stacked with clothes.

"We have to wait," the girl whispered.

Although they only sat there for fifteen minutes, it seemed like an eternity. Adi couldn't stop hearing the moaning and the more she tried to block it, the more her brain focused on it, making it louder. Desperate to get it out of her head, she looked at the other girl, but she just sat beside her calmly, hand on her belly.

When it was finally over, a touch on her arm told her it was done and Adi uncurled from the tight ball she was in. Hearing the door shut, she stood up and walked towards the small figure sitting on the bed.

"Pia," she whispered.

Unaware that there were others in the room, Pia jumped. It took her a moment to recognize her, but eventually she said, "Adi?"

Smiling, Adi walked forward and stood at the end of the bed.

"What are you doing?" Pia asked as she sat up, the fear obvious in her voice. "You can't be here."

"We have to go," the girl behind her said.

Adi didn't understand. They had waited all that time and she had just seen her.

"Come," the girl urged. "We have to leave now."

"Go," Pia insisted.

Reluctantly, she followed the girl out, sneaking back into the room at the end of the hall.

"Why did we leave?" she asked irritably once they were inside.

"Look," the girl said as she held the door open just a little.

Pressing her face against it, Adi watched as another man entered Pia's room.

"We have to wait," the girl said as she shut the door and walked back to her spot on the floor.

"How long?"

"'Til she's done."

A few hours later, Adi woke up to Pia crouching over her.

"What are you doing here?" she asked.

"I came to get you," Adi replied as she stood, relieved they could finally leave. "Come on. Let's get outta here." The confusion on Pia's face made her stop.

"Get outta here?" Pia asked, the uncertainty in her voice obvious. "And go where?"

Not expecting her reaction, Adi simply looked at her, a feeling of dread passing through her. "Does it matter?" she asked in return. When Pia didn't reply, she continued. "This is a terrible place. Don't you want to leave?"

Pia was quiet for a moment. "It's not that terrible."

Shocked, she couldn't help herself. "Why would you want to stay here and do those things? Do you like doing those things?"

Pia shrugged. "I don't know."

She stood there silent, confusion and anger filling her body. She had risked everything and Pia didn't want to leave. She should have listened to Omar.

"It's not so bad here," Pia said, more to herself than anyone else. "They protect me and give me food. When my parents died, it was a lot worse. I went hungry most of the time. Now, I don't have to worry."

"You're an idiot," the pregnant girl said from her spot on the floor, surprising both of them. Adi had completely forgotten about her.

"What?" Pia asked.

"You're an idiot," she repeated. "You think they give a shit about you, that they actually care?" She pushed herself back onto her feet. "Look around. Do you see these girls?" She motioned towards the mattresses. "Most of them were just like you 'til they got too old or someone didn't like the way they fucked. They don't care. You're just a hole."

Adi watched Pia contemplate her decision. To her, it was obvious, but she waited for her friend to decide. The girl's voice suddenly grabbed her attention.

"If she won't go, I will." She walked up to Adi and took her hand. "Please take me with you."

Looking down at her, she could see the desperation in her eyes. She wanted to say yes and take her far away from this place, but just as she took a breath to answer, the door flung open with a thud.

Chapter Seven

What was behind the door was not what Adi expected. She thought she was dead, that La Patrona had caught her, but when she quickly turned, she saw four girls standing in the doorway.

"We want to come," one of them said as they walked in.

"Take us," another begged.

Adi struggled to respond. She hadn't planned for any of this. She started to shake her head, but stopped when she saw a little girl, maybe three or four, peek out from behind the others.

"That's Evita," the pregnant girl said when she noticed Adi looking at her. "La Patrona's gonna sell her when she turns five."

Adi sighed. There was no way she could leave them now. "I can't promise you'll make it," she said, looking at the faces in front of her. "You have to do everything I say." As she watched their excited heads nod, she turned to Pia. "Are you coming?"

She stood there silently, patiently waiting for her to answer. When Pia finally said, "I'll come," Adi couldn't hide her relief.

"We stay together," she instructed. "If something goes wrong, you run."

"Where to?" one of the girls asked.

"Everyone know where the river is?"

Heads nodded.

"Go along it 'til you get to the south side. Wait there. I'll find you." When no one said anything, Adi took a deep breath. "Now, how do we get outta here?"

No one made a peep as they crept down the hallway, following the pregnant girl as she opened the back door and snuck down a dark staircase. Stopping in front of a door at the bottom of the stairs, she turned and gestured to Adi.

Adi cracked open the door and peered out into the alley. While it was still dark, the sky was beginning to lighten and she scanned the area, knowing that they were running out of time.

"We go out one by one," she told them. "Crouch down low and stay tight against the building."

As anxious faces looked back at her, she knew it was now or never. "Stay close," she said, opening the door once more and slipping into the alley.

For a moment, she heard only her own heartbeat, the sound filling her ears as she crept along. Stopping to watch the last girl leave the house, Adi cringed as soon as she saw her let go of the door, its weight causing it to slam shut behind her.

She didn't need to tell the girls to freeze as they stopped dead in their tracks, eyes wide with fear. Unsure if anyone had heard, she waited, but seeing no one, she raised her hand to motion to them when a voice stopped her.

"Hey!" a man shouted from the street, his large frame taking a step towards them.

Whipping around, Adi whispered, "Run!"

Taking off, the girls darted out of the alley and into the street, the man now in hot pursuit. Adi ran as fast as she could without losing the others, but she soon slowed, unsure of where she was going. Finding herself in a dead end, she spun around, almost colliding with the girl behind her.

"Which way?" she asked.

"This way!" the girl said. She darted down a side street.

Adi was about to follow when she noticed that two were missing. Motioning to the others to keep going, she stayed behind and waited, her anxiety growing with each second. But the relief she felt when she saw them almost instantly disappeared. The man was right behind them, and he was gaining. Tucking herself tightly against the wall, she waited in the shadows and as soon as the two girls ran passed, she stuck out her leg.

The man tripped and fell forward, landing hard onto the ground below. Adi immediately bolted, but she wasn't fast enough. A large hand latched onto her ankle and pulled her down.

She grabbed onto the road, trying to stop the man from bringing her closer, but he was too strong and she felt herself being dragged backwards. Just as his hands clutched onto her thighs, she remembered the gun and pulled it out, squeezing the trigger.

The shot made her ears ring but she didn't hesitate, crawling away the moment her legs were no longer pinned down. Pushing herself back onto her feet, she sprinted as fast as she could after the others, not daring to look back.

The streets were empty as she ran, trying to find her way to the river. She didn't know this part of the city and the roads were confusing. She was about to change direction when she saw someone leaning heavily against a wall a few feet up ahead.

"You okay?" she asked as she approached the pregnant girl, happy to have found someone she knew.

The girl only nodded as she gasped for air, her hands on her belly.

"Come on," Adi said, pulling the girl's arm over her shoulder.

Together they made their way to the river, going much slower than Adi would have liked. It took them over an hour to find it, but when she saw the glare across the water, she shivered with relief.

Although she wanted to wait just in case any of the other girls were behind them, she knew she couldn't risk it. If what people told her about La Patrona was true, they couldn't stop, not even for a minute. Quickly dousing her head in the water, she said, "We gotta keep going."

The pain on the girl's face told her she didn't want to, but she nodded, taking one last drink before following Adi down the river.

They walked south with the shore, trying to conceal their tracks as best as they could. Nothing was said as they moved, the soft croaks of frogs filling the still night air. Whenever they came across a bunch of shrubs or a pile of rocks, Adi would search it, but finding no one, they moved on. Before she knew it, they were in the south side and just as she turned to tell the pregnant girl the others hadn't made it, she heard a soft "Pssstt" coming from a clump of bushes downriver.

Cautiously approaching, a smile lit up her face and she entered the shrubs. The familiar faces of the girls stared back and she was surprised at how happy she was to see people she didn't know. But her smile dropped a moment later. Someone was missing.

"Where's Pia?" she asked, unable to ignore the feeling of alarm.

A couple of the girls exchanged looks before one of them said, "She went back."

She stood there, unsure of what she had just heard. "What do you mean?"

The girl shrugged. "She just stopped and turned around. She went back."

Adi tried to comprehend what they were telling her, but she was interrupted by the tall girl.

"We need to keep going," she said. "Pia knows where we are. She might tell."

"She wouldn't do that," Adi replied.

"She went back and you didn't think she'd do that," the girl replied. "Maybe you don't know her anymore."

Before she could say anything, she felt someone lean on her arm.

"We need to go," the pregnant girl said, the discomfort obvious on her face.

Knowing she was right, she forced herself to forget about Pia and looked out of the shrubs.

The riverside was completely still, the sound of the water the only noise as the sky prepared for the sun's arrival. Although she saw and heard nothing, she hesitated, an uncertain feeling holding her back. She was about to pass it off as being paranoid when all of a sudden, a group of men emerged from the shadows and began to slowly walk along the river. When one of the girls let out a frightened gasp, Adi knew who they were.

"What do we do?" one of them asked.

"Quiet!" another said.

Adi spun around, looking out the other side. As soon as she saw more men coming towards them, her heartbeat quickened. They were about to be trapped.

Putting a finger to her lips, Adi carefully led them through the bushes towards the street. She wasn't sure what was going to be waiting for them, but it didn't matter. It was their only option. A couple minutes later, they reached the road and just before the shrubs ended, she pulled out her gun and peered out.

Other than a few cars, the street was dead. Not waiting for the men to catch up, Adi darted across the road, the others quickly following as she led them into the streets she knew so well.

⚓

By the time they arrived at their destination, the sun was already up, shining light into the dark corners of the city. It hadn't been an easy trip, everyone weak and tired, but when Adi finally stepped onto the roof, she couldn't help but breathe a sigh of relief. They had made it.

The roof was exactly how she left it a couple days ago, a small shelter made out of cardboard tucked underneath an overhanging tin canopy. She had built it for Pia, collecting some clothes, a small mat and a couple blankets for her to use while she figured out where they would go. But as she watched the girls eagerly collapse underneath the shelter, her disappointment in her friend faded a little.

She grabbed a water jug sitting in the corner. "Here," she said.

They drank eagerly, the water disappearing as it was passed around. Her plan had been to leave Pia up here for the night and return to the Complejo, with no one suspecting a thing. Then in the morning, once she was done her regular tasks, she would return with food. But as she looked at the exhausted faces in front of her, her plan was no longer good. They had changed everything.

"Take this," she said. She stood, handing her gun to the tall girl.

The girl said nothing as she took it, looking at the shiny metal in her hand.

"What's your name?" Adi asked.

"Yumi," the girl replied.

"You know how to use it?"

Yumi nodded and tucked it into her waistband.

"I'm gonna get more water," Adi told her as she picked up the empty container. "Stay here and keep everyone quiet. I'll be back." Seeing her nod, she turned and left, climbing back down off the roof and into the streets below.

The city was already busy by the time she made her way towards the centre of the south side, passing people working in shops and on street corners. She kept to the side of the road, doing her best to blend in, not knowing if La Patrona's men were still out there.

It didn't take her long to get to the water pump and as she filled the container, she tried to think of where to get food. She couldn't go back to the Complejo. They probably already knew what she'd done, and there was no way Omar would forgive her. Unable to go back, Adi hid the jug in a side street and went to the market.

She hadn't stolen anything in a while and as she watched people moving in and out of the stalls, she felt nervous. She was just about to step out when she felt a hand on her shoulder.

"We've been looking for you."

Adi froze, feeling the sharp point of a knife pressing into the small of her back.

"Turn around slowly."

Obeying, she found herself staring into a familiar face.

Catalina said nothing as she looked at her, as if she was searching for something. After a few moments, she said, "Let's go."

Knowing where they were headed, she dreaded what was coming. She had hoped to avoid Omar's wrath, but as they approached the Complejo, she was momentarily distracted. Kids were running everywhere, packing what little they had before darting off into the streets, scattering in every direction. Arriving on the main floor, she didn't have a chance to ask what was happening because Renan immediately walked up and punched her straight in the face.

The force of the blow sent her stumbling backwards and Adi fell against the railing, the metal bar stopping her fall. Clutching her face in pain, she looked up just in time to see Renan charging at her again, but as she braced herself for the fight, Catalina stepped in front of her.

"Move," he said, anger seething out of his teeth.

Catalina simply stood there, knife in hand.

Adi could feel the tension mounting as they stared each other down. This wasn't going to end well for anyone.

"Enough," Omar commanded, his voice cutting through the hostility. "Adi, come here."

She moved away from the railing, feeling the heat from Renan's glare as she passed. But when she stood in front of Omar, seeing him visibly fight the anger boiling inside, she realized that this would be much worse.

"You really fucked up this time," he said. "Do you know what's happening out there?"

While she didn't know for sure, she could guess based on everyone's reaction. "La Patrona's here."

"Oh, she's not just here," he said shaking his head. "She's tearing up the city looking for you and what you stole."

"*What* I stole?" She knew she had caused trouble, but she did it for the right reasons and no one could tell her differently. "Don't you mean who?"

Omar let out an angry sigh. "They are not *who* to her! They're property. And you took it!"

"I didn't take anything," she replied. "They would've left with or without me. At least this way they're not dead."

"Not yet."

She glared at him, arms folded across her chest.

"You think you've saved lives, Adi," he said, "but you haven't. You've just killed more."

As soon as the words were out of his mouth, Rodrigo's voice flooded into her mind. "*How many deaths are you responsible for?*" The memory shook her, and she swallowed hard, trying to shove down the guilt clawing up her throat.

"Look around," Omar was saying. "Everyone who was safe here has to leave. You've put them back on the street. And that's where they'll die." When she didn't reply, he continued. "You might have saved some, but it cost everyone else."

No one talked to her after that, avoiding her as she walked to her old room and grabbed her bag. She wanted to speak to Nayara so she could explain, but she didn't see her anywhere. She doubted Nayara would want to see her anyways; she had just blown up her whole life. She finished collecting her things and stopped at the storage room, filling her bag with food, medicine, and a few clothes. If everyone was leaving, they wouldn't miss it and she needed all the help she could get.

Leaving the Complejo, she crisscrossed through the city, taking her time as she watched out for La Patrona. After stopping to pick up the water container, she avoided the main street and chose to go the long way around. The sun was already setting as she walked up to the shelter, but hearing a distressed noise, she burst into the lean-to.

"What's wrong?" she asked, ignoring the gun barrel shoved in her face.

"I don't know," Yumi replied. She lowered the gun. "She won't stop crying."

Adi knelt down beside the pregnant girl lying on the mat. She was covered in sweat and clutching the bottom of her belly.

"It hurts," she choked out.

"You'll be okay," Adi replied, trying to comfort her. "Take deep breaths." Shrugging off her bag, she rifled through it, searching for the coca leaves. She was having trouble finding them and as she looked back at the girl, she saw her beginning to panic. "What's your name?" she asked, hoping to distract her.

The girl let out a couple more sobs before she answered. "Talita."

"That's a beautiful name." She shoved her entire arm into the sack. She was about to ask where she was from when she decided against it. She couldn't risk distressing her even more. "How old are you?"

The girl was quiet. "Ten," she replied, exhaling loudly.

As soon as her fingers latched onto the leaves, Adi pulled them out. "Here," she said. She placed them in Talita's mouth. "Chew them a little and then tuck them in your cheek. It'll help."

With Talita finally quiet, she watched as her breathing slowed, her chest calming down to a normal pace. Waiting for the medication to kick in, she handed out the food, the rest of the girls quietly eating the cold beans and rice. As soon as she saw Talita drifting off into a light sleep, everyone breathed a collective sigh of relief.

"Are we staying here?" Yumi asked after a few minutes of silence.

When Adi turned towards her, she saw that everyone was listening. "I don't know," she replied. While it wasn't safe to stay, she didn't know where else to take them. They couldn't go north, they would just be kicked out, and there was no way they were going east. The only other option was west, but she didn't know if they would be safe there either.

"We can't stay," one of them said firmly. She said it with such conviction that Adi couldn't help but look, finding herself staring into a small, round face. "La Patrona will come for us."

As the others nodded, Adi knew she didn't need to tell them that La Patrona was still searching for them. They knew better than anyone what she was like and what she would do.

"Where we gonna go?"

She was just about to answer when someone ripped off the shelter door. In shock, she did nothing but stare at the faces in front of her.

"We're not going back," Yumi said defiantly, pointing the gun at the intruders.

"It's okay," Adi said. "They're not here for you."

As Yumi lowered the gun, Renan, Catalina, Nayara, and Caio squished underneath the shelter, the noise causing Talita to stir.

"What are you doing here?" Adi asked before a more important question popped into her head. "How did you find me?"

"You're not that hard to follow," Renan said as he glared at her.

At first she was surprised, but her astonishment turned to fear. As if she could read her mind, Catalina said, "Don't worry. No one else is coming."

"What do you want?"

Renan looked around at the girls for a moment before he answered. "The Complejo was our home. It was the only place in this fucking city where no one tried to use you for something. And now it's gone." His eyes burrowed into her as he paused. "So, you're gonna make it up to us. Make things right."

Adi hesitated, knowing whatever he wanted wouldn't be good. "How?"

"You're going to take us into the jungle. Tonight."

Stunned, it took her a moment to reply. "You want me to take you into the jungle."

"Yes."

"Why?"

"Isn't it obvious?" he asked, scoffing a little. "If we stay here, we're dead."

Deep down, she knew he was right, but the thought of returning to the forest was too much and she tried to think of another option. "You could go to a different city."

Renan huffed. "You just don't get it, do you? The Complejo was something special, it doesn't exist anywhere else. And I'm not going back to being someone's bitch. So you're taking us into the jungle, whether you like it or not."

Chapter Eight

That night, they climbed down from the rooftop into the black streets below. Adi had thought that once darkness came, she would feel better, but as dusk settled, she knew nothing would calm her fears. They had spent the rest of the evening planning their escape and preparing the girls for the trip. It wouldn't be easy, but as she watched them throw on baggy t-shirts and wash off their make-up, she felt a surge of hope that they could actually do this.

Pairing up in teams of two, Catalina led them through the streets, sticking to the quieter, less-used roads. Near the back with Talita, Adi followed the others as they headed west through the city. At first, the pace was manageable, cautiously creeping along as they looked down each street before entering. But as they exited the south side, their momentum increased and it wasn't long before her and Talita began to fall behind. Rounding a corner an hour later, Talita came to a stop.

"I can't," she said as she leaned against the building. "I can't do it."

Before Adi could say anything, she sank to a heap on the street.

"Get up," she whispered, urgently looking around.

Talita was breathing so hard she didn't even answer. All she did was shake her head.

Adi bent down and pulled her arm over her shoulder. It took all her strength to lift her back onto her feet and as soon as she stood, she knew they wouldn't get far. Not like this.

"Come on," she said, leading her into an alley.

Sitting Talita down behind a dumpster, Adi waited, hoping that with a little rest she could keep going. But when Talita continued to grimace in pain after a few minutes, she realized they were in trouble. She was thinking about what to do when Talita interrupted her thoughts.

"Just go," she said, her head leaning against the metal bin. "Leave me."

"I'm not leaving you."

"Go. I won't make it."

"Yes, you will."

As she shook her head, Adi sat down beside her. "Here." She handed her a couple more coca leaves. "Sleep. When you wake up, you'll feel better and we can keep going."

While she sounded convincing, her words did nothing to soothe her own fears, which were building with each passing minute. Unable to do anything else, she covered their bodies with a couple cardboard boxes.

The sound of voices woke her and she jerked her head up, listening intently as they grew louder.

"Boss wants us to check every alley," she heard someone say as they neared.

"Why are we out here?" another one asked. "They'd never make it this far."

"Just do it," the first one replied. "I'm fucking tired."

Moving her legs tightly into her chest, Adi turned and saw that Talita was awake, her eyes wide with fear. Putting a reassuring hand on her arm, they waited.

The footsteps came closer and Adi pulled out her gun, pointing it towards the entrance of the alley. She could hear him on the other side of the lane as he kicked at the garbage on the ground and gradually, he came to them, rummaging through the litter as he went. He was right in front of them, kicking the boxes that hid their frozen bodies, when Adi felt his foot lightly graze her shoe.

He took a couple steps forward but stopped and turned around, coming back to where they were sitting. She waited, hoping he would just go away, but when she felt him kick the bottom of her foot once more, she knew they were caught.

She pulled the trigger, the sound of the shot piercing the hot night air. Letting out a soft groan, he fell, lying perfectly still on the ground in front of her.

Adi's mind raced as she thought about what to do. If they ran out of the alley, they risked running into his friend, but if they stayed here, they might not make it out at all. But she didn't get a chance to decide as footsteps pounded towards them, coming to a stop at the front of the alley.

For the next few minutes, it was eerily quiet. When she didn't hear anything, she thought maybe they had gone, but as she peered through the bullet hole in the cardboard, she watched two men creep forward.

Adi held her breath as one of them stopped and checked the body, terrified that he would spot them. But when he stood back up and moved farther into the alley, she exhaled, watching with rapt attention. They were almost at the end when she decided she couldn't just sit there. Putting a finger to her lips, she slid out from underneath the cardboard and darted across the lane, sneaking in behind some garbage on the other side. Taking a moment to steady her hands, she aimed and pulled the trigger.

The man screamed as he clutched his butt cheek, dropping to his knees as the other one darted to the side, hiding himself in the shadows.

Her heart raced as she searched for the second man. Focused on finding him, she didn't see the first one collect himself and turn around, gun cocked and ready.

Bullets flew past her as he fired, aiming at everything and nothing at the same time. Worried about him accidently hitting Talita, Adi squeezed the trigger once more, the slug slamming into his chest. As he fell face-forward onto the ground, she heard the shot just as she felt the lead tear into her arm.

Overwhelmed with pain, it took all her concentration to lie perfectly still, knowing that if she moved an inch, the next round would kill her. But the longer she laid there, the worse it got, and unable to take the burning, she shifted, causing the pile that hid her to wobble. The moment she heard the gun fire, she knew she was dead.

She closed her eyes and waited for the end to come, but when it didn't, she watched in surprise as the man fell from the shadows, toppling over. Looking back at the entrance, she scrambled to her feet.

"Come on!" Catalina stood at the front of the alley, gun in hand.

Running over to Talita, Adi pulled her up and they followed Catalina down the street.

They made it outside the city in just under an hour and it took them another thirty minutes to find the others. Waiting for Adi to take the lead, she looked back at the city one last time before she turned and walked into the jungle.

The moment she was surrounded by trees, she was overwhelmed by the sights, sounds, and smells of her life before. While everything felt familiar, it also felt different. Back in the city, she had been too afraid of what would happen if she came back, but as she walked, her old torments did not return.

Unsure of which way to go, she decided to take them farther west, eventually finding the same overgrown path that had led her to the city. They walked until they couldn't, and as soon as they found a place to camp, Adi got to work.

They had brought as many supplies as they could fit in their packs, including food, medication, and a couple blankets. Nayara tended to Talita while Adi showed the others how to make a quick shelter out of skinny trees, cutting into the trunks about half-way up and bending them, the tops meeting in the middle. Finding a bunch of banana leaves, she used them to patch the holes in the canopy, creating a covered roof. Although the shelter didn't have sides, it would be good enough for one night and everyone settled underneath, happy to rest. She was leaning against a tree trunk when Nayara walked up.

"Let me look."

Adi extended her arm as Nayara sat down beside her and began cleaning the bullet wound. They hadn't spoken since Adi snuck out of the Complejo and as she watched Nayara work, she didn't know what to say.

"I'm sorry," she said eventually, unable to stand the awkward silence. "I know how much you loved it there. I didn't..."

"You don't need to explain," Nayara interrupted. "I get it."

She was surprised. "You do?"

Nayara nodded and looked around cautiously before she replied. "I...," she began, her voice not much louder than a whisper. "Someone owned me once."

Shocked, Adi stayed silent.

"When I was little, my mama died and her boyfriend sold me to this man." Nayara cleared her throat. "I belonged to him for a while, but he got tired of me so he beat me and threw me out. That's where

Omar found me." She smiled as she said his name. "I couldn't even walk and he just picked me up off the street and carried me home. I'll never forget it."

She said nothing as Nayara finished wrapping her arm. She was mad at Omar for the things he said, but for some reason it felt like she had left him behind. "Why didn't he come?"

Nayara sighed. "I asked him to," she said sadly, "but he won't leave. The Complejo might be gone, but the kids are still there. He belongs to them."

Adi thought about Omar and the many times he had helped her. While she didn't regret what she did, if she could redo it, she would've done it differently.

"It's not your fault, you know," Nayara said, interrupting her thoughts. "The Complejo was too good to be true. Things like that, they never last. Not in our world."

The next morning, they went farther from the city, hiking their way through valleys, across rivers and over hills. Talita's condition had improved with sleep and as Adi watched everyone interact with the jungle, some for the first time, she couldn't help but smile. Evita was running everywhere, giggling nonstop as she tried to catch the butterflies that flew past her. Even some of the older girls got excited when they spotted squirrel monkeys swinging in the trees above them.

But it wasn't all fun and games. In addition to leading the way, Adi spent most of her time trying to stop everyone from getting injured. Caio was stung by a scorpion when he didn't shake out his shirt after a swim; Lupita, an eight-year-old from La Patrona's, almost got bit by a snake while trying to climb a tree; and Nayara got a rash from touching the wrong plants. By the fourth night, things were about to get worse.

"Adi, wake up," Giovana said. Her slim figure hovered above her, giving her a firm shake. "It's Talita."

Quickly walking over to where she lay, Adi knelt next to Nayara who was already examining her.

"What's wrong?" she asked, though she could guess.

"Nothing," Nayara replied as she felt the bottom of Talita's belly. "It's just time. The baby's coming."

She had dreaded this moment. "Do you know what to do?"

When Nayara shook her head, her heart sank. She had only seen someone give birth once, and that was a long time ago.

"What do we do?" she whispered, trying to remain calm. They were days from the city and even if they got back in time, she doubted anyone would help.

"I don't know," Nayara replied. "All I know is, she's having this baby right here and soon."

Adi rubbed her face with her hands, trying to think of anything that might help. While she had some pain relievers, she knew that was the least of their problems. So many things could go wrong. As she watched Yumi gently stroking Talita's head, she suddenly stood and ran to her bag.

"What are you doing?" Nayara asked as she dug through it.

Adi didn't reply as she found what she was looking for and held it up to the moonlight, trying to see the faded ink on the worn out paper.

"I don't think we're far," she said as she examined the map, trying to calculate the distance.

"Far from what?"

"From where I came from. See this?" she said. She pointed to a small dot. "That's where the camp is, and this is the city." She pointed to another mark. "I think we're somewhere around here," she said, bringing her finger close to the camp. "If I get there by morning, I can bring help back. Think she can hold on 'til then?"

Nayara exhaled and looked back at Talita, thinking it over. "I don't know," she said. "She's not cramping a lot, but that could change." She paused. "We don't really have a choice."

That was all Adi needed to hear. She handed her bag to Nayara and slid her knife up her sleeve.

"Give her coca leaves for the pain, but not too many," she instructed.

Nayara nodded.

"And if she starts, keep her quiet," she continued. "Anyone could be out here."

Nayara nodded again. "I'll get Renan to keep watch."

She gave her a small smile and turned to leave, but stopped when she heard a voice.

"Wait for me," Catalina said as she threw on her pack. "I'm coming with."

They travelled west through the jungle, the darkness and dense trees forcing them to walk most of the time. Adi couldn't stop herself from wondering how they would react to seeing her again, but she pushed the thought away. Regardless of what happened, she had to make them help her. Talita and her baby depended on it.

After about an hour, they came upon a clearing, but spotting a village in the middle, she stayed deep in the trees and led Catalina around it, not wanting to be seen. She was tempted to ask for help, but remembered the warning about the villages east of the river, so they kept going. Not long after they passed, the forest thinned and they burst into a run, going as fast as they could through the trees. Finally arriving at the river a couple hours later, Adi worked on figuring out how to get across as they caught their breath.

Crossing the river at night was dangerous as caimans, anacondas, and other predators filled the water, hunting for their next meal in the dark. These animals didn't live in every part of the river, but she knew they were there because as she slowly walked along the shore, she could see them, their bright eyes intently watching as they sat along the water's surface. Finding what she needed, she studied the area for a minute before she walked back to Catalina, picking up sticks along the way. Her plan was in no way good, but it only had to work for a minute.

Standing next to Catalina, she asked, "How far can you throw?"

The dead bird hit the water with a splash, sending the caimans diving after it as Adi and Catalina entered the river, half-wading, half-swimming as fast as they could to the other side. Every second counted against them and as the noise downriver began to grow quiet, Adi swam faster. They didn't have much time.

She was the first one out, but as she looked back, she saw the water rippling behind Catalina. Without a moment's hesitation, she ran back into the river, pounding her fists full of sharpened sticks down as hard as she could, the ends connecting with her target. The caiman reared back angrily, its powerful tail lashing back and forth as it snapped at her. Her sticks now gone, Adi scrambled out of the water and onto the shore just as the caiman charged, darting up the riverbank towards her.

The log came down heavily with a thud, hitting the caiman directly on the head. Stunned and injured, the reptile slithered back into the water as Catalina dropped the tree, helping Adi up onto her feet.

"Let's get outta here."

They jogged through the trees, the sunlight illuminating the way as it rose higher into the sky. The jungle had grown dense again and so they slowed, carefully winding around large trees and brush. They were walking through a tangled clump of vines when Adi heard a light click.

She froze, looking back at Catalina, who had already removed one of her knives, the blade resting against the side of her leg. Turning again towards the front, she listened for another sound, but hearing nothing, she went to take a step forward when a voice commanded, "Don't move."

Looking into the wall of thick leaves directly ahead of them, Adi slowly moved the knife in her sleeve down into her hand. She couldn't see who was behind it, but when she heard the bushes rustle, she knew they were about to find out.

Two boys stepped from cover, their guns aimed and ready as they warily approached, suspiciously looking the girls over. They couldn't have been much older than her and as she looked at their torn and ratty clothes, she knew they weren't from a nearby village.

"Who are you?" one of them demanded. "What are you doing here?"

"We're here to see Salvador," Adi replied, almost certain what the answer would be.

As soon as she said his name, the boys exchanged a look, confirming her suspicion.

"We don't know any Salvador."

She ignored their denial. "We need to see him."

They didn't move for a minute, clearly conflicted as she waited for them to decide. She didn't want to seem too eager, but when the boy lowered his gun, she inwardly smiled.

They led them through the green wall and into the dense foliage, Adi slowly recognizing the area around them. It hadn't changed much—birds still chirped, monkeys still screeched, and the river still ran past them with authority—but when they came upon a large camp about half an hour later, it was not the same place she had run away from. Small huts surrounded the clearing, their round shapes forming a circle against the trees as a large fire sat in the center, its heat radiating outwards. But that was all Adi had a chance to see before they were ushered to a small, half-built shelter that sat on the outskirts of the clearing and told to wait.

By the time someone came to see them, the sun was completely up and shining, the sounds of people going about their day filling the air. As Adi watched the man approach, she stood, eager to return to the others. But, as he came closer, she wasn't sure they were going to get the help they needed.

The man was the same height as Renan, but twice as wide. He had thick brown hair that hung down to his shoulders and even through his beard, she could see the angry scowl covering his face. Grabbing a chair, he turned it around and sat down in front of them.

"What do we have here?" he began, the hostility impossible to miss. "And I thought you were long dead. But here you are, in the flesh."

Unsure of how he knew who she was and a little thrown off by his demeanor, Adi slowly sat back down.

"I gave up on you a while back," he continued. "But it's nice of you to finally show up."

Suddenly it hit her, and as she looked into his angry eyes, she had no doubt. "Rodrigo."

He glared as she spoke, the contempt radiating off him.

Knowing it would be a waste of time asking him for help, she said, "We need to talk to Salvador."

Her voice sounded much smaller than she wanted, but she waited, Rodrigo taking his time to answer. "'Bout what?" he asked. When she didn't reply, he smiled at her arrogantly. "I'm the one who decides if you see him, so if you wanna talk to him, you have to go through me."

She gave in. "There's a baby coming and we don't know what to do. We need someone who can help."

For a while, Rodrigo said nothing. He looked at her stone faced. When he finally spoke, it was clear he didn't care. "And why would we help you?"

Although she wasn't surprised by his reaction, she had still hoped for a different response.

"You don't deserve help," he said as he stood. "You deserve to be forgotten, just like Benito."

She could feel his glare from where she sat. Knowing that nothing would change his mind, she turned to Catalina. "Let's go."

She was a couple steps away when she heard her voice behind her. "What the fuck is your problem?"

Adi turned just in time to see Rodrigo pivot, his attention now fully on Catalina.

"What the fuck is *my* problem?" he asked. He stepped forward, stopping right in front of her. "Maybe your friend over there forgot to tell you what she did, but she's the last person in the world I would help."

"So?" Catalina asked, completely unfazed.

"So?" Rodrigo scoffed.

"It's got nothing to do with her." Rodrigo was about to respond when Catalina continued. "She's not asking you to help her, she's asking you to help someone else. And if you don't, they'll die. Is that something you're comfortable with?"

Rodrigo didn't respond, the conflict flashing across his face, but when he turned and left the shelter without another word, they had their answer.

They were silent as they left the camp, slowly walking through the trees. It didn't matter if they made it back in time or not; they had nothing that would help. But as they approached the river, they whipped around, pulling out their knives as they spun to face whatever was behind them.

Adi was surprised as she watched two girls emerge from the trees, one with a pack, the other with a gun.

They stood examining one another before the one with the bag said, "We hear there's a baby coming."

Chapter Nine

Less than five hours after making it back to Talita, the baby came out screaming, her loud cries penetrating the jungle around them. At the two girls' insistence, everyone packed up and left for Salvador's. Adi had tried to tell them that they would be fine on their own, but the one with the gun, Valentina, shook her head. "Salvador says you're coming back with us." That was final.

It took almost an entire day to get there, which Adi was grateful for. She was in no hurry to face Rodrigo again and she couldn't even imagine what seeing Benito for the first time would be like. But she was able to avoid it all for a little longer, because as soon as they arrived, she immediately found shelter and collapsed on the ground, the exhaustion of the last few days sending her into a deep sleep.

Adi was dreaming, her mind swirling with images of the city, when the sound of someone's shoe crunching on the ground jolted her awake. She reached for her bag, trying to grab her gun, but wasn't fast enough. Caught from behind, one arm wrapped around her body while the other covered her mouth. She struggled with all her might, kicking and flailing, but the arm held her still, carrying her backwards and out of the shelter as the sleeping faces of her friends slowly disappeared from view.

Her mind raced as she was dragged through the trees, the camp no longer visible. Determined to get free, she closed her eyes and controlled her breathing, trying to calm the panic pulsating through her veins. When she opened her eyes a few moments later, she knew what she had to do.

Stretching out her legs as much as she could, she reached for every tree that passed, trying to latch onto it with her feet. The first few she missed, but eventually she caught one and when she wrapped her legs around it, holding on with everything she had, her captor jerked to an abrupt stop. He turned, seeing what was holding him back and just as he walked forward to untie her limbs, his grip loosened just a little.

Adi thrust her elbow into his side and he dropped her, doubling over as she scrambled to her feet and ran back towards the camp. She was flying through the trees, desperate to get far away when she was hit from behind, the force of the blow knocking her unconscious.

It took a while, but when she slowly came to, she could feel herself being gently rocked back and forth as if she was in a hammock. But when she opened her eyes, her mouth gagged and her hands tied in front of her, she looked up and saw Valentina, the light of the moon falling across her face.

Valentina said nothing as she smiled, her gun resting casually in her lap as Adi lifted her head off the bottom of the boat. Looking out, she watched as two others paddled upriver. She had no idea what was happening, but unable to escape, she laid her head back down.

It was still dark when they banked on the river's edge, Valentina standing guard as the others carried the boat into the trees. As they walked back towards her, Adi saw a familiar face and her confusion instantly turned to anger.

"I'll take out the gag and untie your hands under one condition," Rodrigo said. "You won't run or make a sound. Got it?"

Adi didn't move as she glared at him, unsure if she was mad because they had gotten the jump on her or because he looked so damn smug about it. Knowing the answer wouldn't help, she forced herself to nod, having no intention of keeping her word. Her mouth and hands no longer bound, they turned and walked into the trees, Valentina shoving her forward.

They went silently, the only sounds the flow of the river and the occasional monkey calling in the distance. Adi had no idea where she was, but as the trees thinned, the landscape began to look oddly familiar and suddenly, she knew exactly where they were.

"Why are we here?" she whispered to Rodrigo, unable to hide the alarm in her voice as she looked at the village in the middle of the clearing. She had been here less than two days ago, carefully going around it, knowing what these villagers did with kids they found wandering alone.

Her question was answered with a threatening look and they crept along the edge of the village, Adi trying to figure out how she was going to escape. Stopping behind a small shack that sat partially in the trees, Rodrigo tied her hands back up and forced her to sit, Valentina standing almost on top of her. As he left them there, walking casually into the village, Adi racked her brain. There was no way she was going to let him give her to these people. If that happened, she'd end up back in the city, forced to do the same things Pia did.

Just as she convinced herself that she could take on both Valentina and the other boy, Rodrigo returned with an older man, his black hair shimmering with hints of grey. They talked in hushed voices while looking at her, sending chills all over her body. This was not happening, this was not going to happen to her.

When Rodrigo approached, she loudly said, "No," and he quickly grabbed her, his hand covering her mouth.

"What are you doing?" he whispered. "Do you want to get us all killed?"

Confused, Adi searched his face, trying to figure out what he meant.

"Come on," he said as he pulled her forward, the older man leading the way.

They moved towards the village in the dark, stopping at a large house. The older man took a moment to peer inside before he entered and Adi followed involuntarily, Rodrigo pushing her through the doorway and into the hall. For a split second, she thought about running, but as soon as she recognized the voices coming from a room just up ahead, her legs went numb.

The older man opened the door ever so slightly, carefully looking into the lit room before he stepped out of the way. Rodrigo nudged her forward, but her feet didn't move, having never felt so heavy as fear took hold. Seeing her resist, he picked her up with one arm and silently dropped her down in front of the door, giving her a full view of the room.

Although she already knew who was inside, she couldn't help but feel a renewed sense of dread when she saw them. There, sitting around the room, were La Patrona's men.

Adi felt herself being pulled away, the men disappearing as the door shut, not making a sound. Giving the older man a nod, Rodrigo grabbed her by the arm and led her out of the house through the dark. As soon as they were back underneath the trees, Rodrigo took out his knife and cut her loose.

"You know them," he stated more than asked.

She didn't have to answer. Her face did that for her, and when she looked up at Rodrigo, she saw nothing but anger.

"How could you do this?" he asked, fighting to keep his voice down. "How could you do this to us?"

She struggled to find the words, the seriousness of what was happening setting in. "You don't know why they're here," she said more to herself than to him. "They could be here for something else."

Rodrigo scoffed. "Do you honestly expect me to believe that? You must think I'm an idiot."

She didn't reply, trying to figure out how they had followed them this far.

"They're going village to village, asking if anyone's seen a group of runaway girls," he continued, his voice low. "You don't have to be smart to figure it out." He was silent for a moment. "What did you do?"

Frustrated, her fear dissolved. "I didn't do it on purpose," she said, glaring at him. "I thought we had been careful. I made a mistake."

Rodrigo shook his head. "That seems to be all you can do."

Adi knew he was mad at her for what she had done, but his words still hurt. He wasn't just angry with her, he hated her. Turning away from him, she walked back to the river.

The boat ride was silent as they made their way downriver, the sky becoming lighter as it prepared for morning. While Adi was angry and scared, she shoved those feelings aside knowing that she needed to come up with a plan. If they had tracked them this far, she knew they would keep coming. Closing her eyes, she pictured their faces and tried to count how many men were in that room. She got to seventeen before she quit. It didn't matter; they didn't stand a chance.

They arrived at the camp a few hours later and as soon as they walked in, Adi watched Catalina storm towards them. Rodrigo barely had enough time to look her way before she sucker punched him right in the face.

He stumbled backwards and caught himself as he fell, but not missing a beat, he immediately pushed himself up and charged, taking her out at the waist as he slammed her body onto the ground.

Running over, Adi tried to pry him off, but it was no use, he wouldn't be moved. As he punched Catalina in the face, she slammed her knee as hard as she could into his side and he crumpled, giving Catalina enough time to jut the palm of her hand into the bottom of his chin, causing him to fall backwards. They stood at the same time, and foolishly trying to stop it, Adi jumped in between just as their fists swung. She felt each punch as they accidently hit her from both sides, causing her to drop to the ground. As she crawled up onto her knees, Catalina took another swing at Rodrigo.

"She's here," Adi managed to get out, her voice strained. "La Patrona is here."

⚘

She didn't have to repeat herself. Catalina had stopped, a look of disbelief on her face. As Adi stood back up, Salvador approached them.

"What are you doing?" he demanded, looking at Catalina and Rodrigo's red faces.

"We got a problem," Rodrigo answered, wiping the blood from his mouth.

Noticing the growing crowd around them, Salvador nodded. "Come."

Adi didn't follow as the three of them went into the main building, choosing instead to go find the others. If anyone had to tell them about La Patrona, she wanted it to be her.

"Adi," Nayara said with relief as soon as she walked into the shelter. "Lupita saw them take you. We've been looking everywhere."

Adi nodded and tried to smile as Talita and Evita jumped up, but as she watched them look back at her with uncertainty, she knew it wasn't working.

"What's wrong?" Talita asked, her voice small as she held her newborn tightly to her chest.

There was no easy way to say it. "They're here."

It took a moment to sink in, but when Evita let out a tiny gasp, she didn't need to explain.

"How many?" Renan asked as he entered, Yumi and Giovana right behind him.

"I don't know," Adi replied. "Around twenty."

"What are we gonna do?" Yumi asked, her question echoing through the shelter.

Adi was about to answer when Pablo walked in.

"Adi," he said, giving her a strained smile. "Salvador wants everyone in the hall."

It took a while for them to gather, hushed voices filling the room, but once they were all there, Salvador didn't waste any time. "I need each of you to listen. What I'm about to tell you will not be easy, but if we do it right, we will be just fine." His speech lasted less than two minutes and when it was over the kids scattered, running off to do as they were told.

"This won't work," Giovana said, shaking her head as she tightly held Evita's hand. "She'll find us, I know she will."

Adi knew she was right. The plan was to split up and hide until La Patrona was gone, but as she watched the scared faces disappear into the trees, it wouldn't be enough. La Patrona wouldn't stop until she got what she wanted.

They left the camp, walking west through the trees, but less than a kilometre in, Adi stopped.

"Keep going," she said, handing Yumi her gun. "Don't stop 'til it's dark. Get off the ground."

"Where are you going?" Nayara asked.

"To end this." But as she turned to leave, a hand latched onto hers.

"I named her Esperanza."

Adi stood still, the name throwing her off as she looked into Talita's penetrating stare. "What?"

"My baby." Talita looked down at her daughter sleeping against her. "I named her Esperanza, after your mama."

Adi couldn't control the wave of emotion that flooded over her.

"I know how much you loved her," Talita continued. "Whatever happens," she squeezed Adi's hand, "just know, I'll never forget it."

Adi remained where she stood, unable to move as she watched them walk out of sight. But as soon as they were gone, she took a deep breath, shoving the emotions down, and sprinted back through the trees.

She ran as fast as she could, whistling loudly as she went, hoping that Catalina and Renan would hear the familiar tune. When she saw Catalina running towards her with Caio right behind, she wasn't disappointed.

Reaching the camp, Adi stopped along the edge and peered in, searching for any indication of movement. It was weird seeing it so empty and quiet, the smoldering fire the only sign that someone had been there, giving off a small wisp of grey smoke.

"How long 'til they're here?" Catalina asked.

"An hour, maybe less," Renan answered, making Adi jump. He smirked as she looked back, unaware that he was there. "They're crossing the river now."

Adi nodded, trying to decide what to do. They didn't have much time and she needed to make a decision. Dropping to her knee, she grabbed a stick and drew a line in the dirt.

"Here's the river," she said as the others watched. "Here's the camp and here's the green wall. We need to stop them there."

"We can't stop all of them," Renan said kneeling beside her. "Some are gonna get through."

"No," Adi said shaking her head. "If they get past the wall, they'll find the camp, and that can't happen."

"So we stop them at the wall then," Catalina said.

Although she was trying to sound confident, as Adi looked at the three faces around her, she saw their doubt.

Not another word was said as they walked towards the green wall. Stopping at a puddle, Adi smeared herself in mud, determined to use every advantage. Even if they didn't stop the men, the least they could do was give the others a chance to get away. Arriving at the wall, they crept through and headed towards the river.

Adi squatted down, surveying the area. She couldn't see anyone, but she could feel them, the jungle's silence letting her know that they were there. She steadied her grip on the large knife Catalina had given her and got ready.

She spotted the first group a few yards out and moved forward, trying not to be seen. Without a gun, she was forced to get much closer than she wanted, but as she slid her back against a tree, every muscle in her body flexed in anticipation.

The first man walked up without hesitation, not seeing her behind the tree as he passed. Waiting for the second man to come closer, Adi struck, stabbing him in the side of the neck as she plunged her other knife into the first one's back. Too busy to see if there were more, she instantly dropped to the ground and heard a shot ring out, the sound splitting the silence.

Renan nodded to her as he checked the dead body of the third man. Pulling her knife out of the first one's back, Adi took his gun and followed Renan as they continued on.

For a while, they saw no one else. Unsure of what they were walking into, Adi scampered up a tree and peered out towards the river. It took a moment for her eyes to spot them, but eventually she saw the dark figures slinking through the trees below. Motioning to Renan, she crouched on a low branch and waited.

As soon as the man walked underneath, she dropped, plunging her knife straight down into his neck. He fell like a block of cement, but the moment she landed, a bullet whizzed past, just missing the top of her head. Ducking into some bushes, the shots came fast and furious as she sat there trying to figure out where Renan was. Distracted, she didn't see the man until it was too late, and he knocked the knife easily from her grasp as his large hands grabbed her throat.

"Where are they?" he demanded as he squeezed, the weight of his body holding her against the ground.

Adi thrashed desperately, trying to get loose. Not strong enough, she couldn't break his hold, but as he brought his face close to hers, she thrust her thumbs into his eyes. The man screamed as she felt his eyeballs squish underneath, clutching his face as he sat up. It was enough for her to get out and as soon as she stood, she pulled the gun from her waistband and shot, pumping a bullet into his head. She was breathing hard, looking at his crumpled body, when something on her right moved and she whipped around, finger on the trigger.

"Shit," she said hoarsely as she lowered her gun.

Rodrigo slowly stepped forward, looking in disbelief at the bodies around her. "What are you doing?"

Adi was about to answer when she suddenly dropped to her knee and shot, the bullet missing Rodrigo by a couple inches. Looking behind him, he watched as a man slumped over dead before turning back to her.

"Do you know how fucking insane this is?" he asked.

Hearing a sporadic burst of gunfire to her left, Adi smiled. "Yes," she said, before sprinting towards it.

She only got about ten feet away before she saw more men coming at her. Stopping behind a tree, she steadied her breathing and waited.

"Now!" she heard Rodrigo yell. She spun out, dropping low before swinging her knife upwards in one fluid motion.

The blade bit into the man's thigh and he screamed as he fell, the blood flowing out of him faster than she could have guessed. But as she looked up, she saw the butt of the gun right before it hit her directly on the head, and she dropped hard onto the ground.

"You little bitch," the man said. He viciously kicked her in the stomach, leaving her breathless. "I'm going to gut you like a fish."

Prying the knife out of her hand, he raised it high above his head, but just as he was about to plunge it down into her, she slid the knife out of her sleeve and cut him across the inside of his arm.

The knife drove into the dirt next to her as she rolled to the side, the man's blood covering her like a warm waterfall. Clutching his limb in agony, Adi kicked him in the chest with both feet, sending him backwards. Wrenching her knife out of the ground, she pushed it into his chest with all her might before she stumbled, falling down against a rock. Her head was throbbing and she was dizzy, but once her vision finally cleared, she pushed herself back up, trying to see what was going on.

Catalina and Caio were just west of her, attacking the men coming in from the river, and she could see Rodrigo on the east side, pounding some guy into the ground. She was looking for Renan when she heard a shot from behind her and she spun, crouching as she searched the green wall. She didn't see the gun until it shot again, the bullet flying past her and into a man about ten feet away. That's when she saw her through the leaves: Valentina. Adi turned, but just as she started towards a man a few yards ahead of her, she heard a familiar whistle and sprinted towards it.

Bullets flew all around as she ducked and zigzagged through the trees, knowing what that whistle meant. Seeing a man thundering her way, she ran as fast as she could towards him before sliding on the ground at the last second, slicing his legs as she passed. He wasn't dead, but there was no time to finish as the whistle sounded again, this time more urgently.

She arrived at the same time as one of La Patrona's men, and she threw her knife as he shot, both of them missing the other. She could feel the bullets hit the tree as she stood behind it, tucking her gun into her pants. Making sure to stay out of sight, she climbed the trunk. High enough, she peeked out and watched as he made his way over to where she had been standing, oblivious to her above him. She took out her gun and squeezed the trigger, not missing this time. He hit the ground with a thud.

"Renan," she whispered as soon as she dropped from the tree, scanning the area.

"Here," she heard him croak, his voice filled with pain.

Running over to a bunch of twisted vines, Adi peered through and spotted him lying on his back in the dirt.

"Fucker caught me from behind," he said, grimacing. She examined the bloody hole in his calf, making sure the bullet went through. Taking out her knife, she cut away his shirt and ripped the fabric into strips. Knotting the first piece above the wound, she folded up the other and placed it on top, wrapping a bunch of vines around it tightly to secure it in place.

"Stay here," she said. She covered him as best she could with leaves, ferns, and moss. "Don't make a sound." Handing him her gun, she gave him a reassuring smile before slinking off into the trees.

The jungle was oddly silent as she ran, an unsettling feeling passing over her. She didn't see or hear anything and was about to think the worst had happened when she heard shots fired in the distance.

Picking a few guns off the dead bodies she passed, Adi stopped about ten feet in front of the wall and scooted up a tree, getting a perfect view of the area ahead of her. There were only a handful of men left and as they came into sight, she took a deep breath and fired, slowly dropping them one by one as they shot back randomly, not knowing where she was.

Taking the last shot, Adi stayed in the tree and waited, carefully searching for anyone else. The jungle was quiet once again, the only sound the rustling of leaves above the canopy as a gust of wind passed through. Satisfied, she climbed down but as her feet touched the ground, she heard a burst of gunfire and Catalina yelling, "He's behind the wall!"

Adrenaline rushing into her veins, Adi sprinted towards the camp as fast as she could go. Unsure of where he was, she took the most direct route, determined to catch him. If he saw the camp and got away, they'd never be safe.

She made it there in record time and crouched against a hut, scanning the open area as she tried to find him. When nothing moved, she waited and just as she exhaled, she saw him, gun aimed and ready as he entered the clearing.

There was a look of surprise on his face as he glanced around, obliviously passing Adi as she waited in a shadow to his right. Silently stepping behind him, she thrust her knife into his back, his arms dropping down as the blade entered. Falling to his knees, he dropped dead face-down in the dirt.

Adi stood there looking at his body when out of the corner of her eye, she saw something move and she spun, her knife loose and ready in her hand. She froze, recognizing the person in front of her.

His light brown eyes widened as he looked back at her in surprise.

"Benito," she said, but it was too late. He had vanished.

ψ

She couldn't move, grounded in place as she tried to will him back to her, but as soon as Rodrigo walked up, she had no choice but to break away. Something was wrong.

By the time Adi reached him, Caio was dead. Catalina didn't acknowledge her as she approached, silently holding his limp body in her arms. Staring at the two of them on the ground, Adi said to Rodrigo, "Renan's been shot. He's hiding near the river on the east side."

She said nothing else as she heard him leave, kneeling down in front of Catalina. Looking into her expressionless face, Adi placed her hand on the back of her neck and pulled her towards her, pressing her forehead against her own. They sat in silence, eyes closed and when Catalina finally moved back, Adi watched as she picked up Caio's body and carried him to the camp.

There was nothing to celebrate as Adi dragged the dead man out and into the river. Valentina had already left to round up the others and as Rodrigo helped Renan limp back, Adi watched as everyone filtered in. She was leaning against a tree, wiping the blood off her knife when she heard a voice yell, "Hey!"

Looking up, she watched a boy about Rodrigo's age beeline towards her, the anger on his face hard to miss.

"Who the hell do you think you are?"

Adi didn't respond as she looked him over. While she didn't know who he was, she had seen him before. He was the only one who cut his hair that short.

"You think you can just walk in here and do whatever you want?" he yelled.

She felt the silence of the camp, but didn't move, refusing to squirm underneath the stares.

"What the fuck is wrong with you?"

"Marcelo," Rodrigo warned.

"No," he replied, shaking his head. "She isn't allowed to get away with this. Look at what happened." He pointed to Caio. "He's dead."

Her eyes followed Marcelo's arm but stopped when she saw Catalina, a hardened look of hatred covering her face as she glared at Marcelo from the ground.

"I don't care what you did in the city, but out here, you're in my territory," he said, oblivious to Catalina's angry eyes boring into his back. "You don't get to make decisions for us."

Adi simply held his gaze. She was tired of people always giving her shit. She was doing the best she could. Didn't they see that? Unable to fight back the rising anger, she said, "I did you a favour."

He practically laughed in her face. "Please," he replied, his voice condescending. "The only person you've ever done a favour for is yourself. Just ask your brother."

The moment the words left his lips, Adi lost control, the rage too strong to contain. She stood there smiling for a second before she launched herself forward in one quick motion, her fist slamming squarely into his jaw.

Marcelo staggered backwards onto the ground as everyone flooded in between them, trying to stop the fight. Adi went to walk forward, but was held back by someone behind her and she turned around, shoving Pablo off before making her way towards Marcelo. She had to push her way through the bodies and when she felt a hand latch onto her arm, she spun just as Catalina ripped the hand off, saying, "Don't fucking touch her."

Fights erupted all around as she got closer to her target, but she didn't notice. She could see his angry face coming towards her through the pile and as soon as Giovana threw the last person out of her path, the punches began to fly.

Adi swung wide and as she missed, she felt Marcelo's fist catch her in the side, knocking all her air out. She staggered backwards and he didn't hesitate, rushing at her as he swung again. Ducking in time, she launched her body into his, slamming him hard into the dirt. Using her legs, she pinned him down and pummeled his face with her fists, not caring how much it hurt. So focused on what she was doing, she didn't notice him moving his leg.

He rammed his knee into her back and her grip loosened. He rolled her, sitting on top as he swung, punching again and again. Adi blocked most of his assault with her arms and just as he threw another one, she moved her head to the side, his clenched hand slamming into the hard earth. Shocked by the pain, he stalled and Adi jabbed upwards, her hand connecting with his throat. Gasping as he clutched his neck, she threw him off and stood, watching him cough and groan on the ground below. She kicked him viciously in the side a couple times, forcing him to roll onto his back. Dropping down on top of him once more, she watched his eyes widen as she pressed her knife against his throat.

"Listen to me you piece of shit," she said as she held him there, her voice dripping with venom. "If you ever talk about my brother again, even mention his name, I'll beat you so hard you won't be able to eat for weeks. Got it?"

The sound of a gunshot interrupted them before Marcelo could answer and Adi watched as the fighting stopped, the crowd parting as Rodrigo walked towards them with Salvador right behind. She said nothing as she sat on Marcelo, looking up as they stared down at her. Seeing the outraged look on Rodrigo's face, she reluctantly put away the knife and stood.

Marcelo angrily pushed himself to his feet, spitting a large wad of bloody saliva in her direction before storming off. Salvador said nothing as he held her gaze for a moment, the disappointment obvious, and he shook his head, following Marcelo out of the crowd.

Adi was standing there, watching everyone slowly dissipate when Rodrigo grabbed her arm and pulled her into the trees just outside the camp.

"You are fucking impossible." He rubbed his face in frustration. "You just got here and you're already fighting with everyone. You really don't like making things easy, do you?"

"He deserved it," Adi replied.

"It's Marcelo! Of course he deserved it! But that doesn't mean you get to punch in his face every time he makes you angry."

Adi said nothing as she looked out into the trees, her jaw locked in irritation.

Rodrigo sighed. "Whether you like it or not, you need to realize that everything you do either hurts or helps the people around you. None of your friends are gonna last out here if you walk around like a ticking time bomb. Forget yourself for once. It's time you started thinking about them."

Chapter Ten

Adi tip-toed through the trees, muscles taut and ready, trying not to make a sound. As she crept over a fallen tree, a green iguana stared back at her, its throat puffing as she slunk by. The bow in her hand was tightly strung, the arrow loaded and waiting as she silently followed her prey, getting closer with each minute. Suddenly, it stopped and she froze, not daring to move a muscle as the animal cautiously looked around. After a moment, it lowered its head and began searching the ground for food. Adi raised her bow and aimed, the arrow locked in on her target. But just as she exhaled and loosened her grip, a group of toucans burst from the trees, their loud croaks filling the air. Startled, Adi's fingers let go of the arrow and it zinged past the peccary, missing by a mile.

She barely had time to swear under her breath as she watched another arrow rip through the air, hitting the animal straight in the front shoulder. The peccary wavered for a moment before it eventually stopped and dropped dead onto the ground.

Looking out in annoyance, Adi watched as Giovana stepped from cover and gave her a cocky smile, bow still in hand.

"That was terrible," Rodrigo said from behind her, unable to hide his amusement. "You weren't even close."

Adi tried her hardest to be mad, but as Giovana hoisted her prey onto her shoulders, she couldn't help but smile. They had been here for about a year and already Giovana was a better hunter than she would ever be. In fact, she was better than Adi at most things, including pissing Marcelo off. After their big fight, Adi had avoided him at all costs, so when he accused her a week later of putting a nest of scorpions in his bed, she knew someone else was messing with him. Later that day, as she shovelled dirt as her punishment, Giovana had silently joined her, giving her nothing but a small smirk.

"Come on," Rodrigo said, interrupting her thoughts. "The others will be waiting."

They had a long journey back to the village. They were southeast of it, having crossed the river and then travelled down, looking for a new place to hunt. Valentina and Benito had come too, but as soon as they were out of the boat, the two of them disappeared into the trees without a sound, their bodies melting into the jungle. Benito had said little to Adi since the day she arrived, in fact she noticed that he barely spoke at all. Rodrigo had told her that Benito preferred to be alone, spending most of his time in the forest by himself, but as she walked back to their meeting place by the river, she couldn't help but wonder if he was like that because of her, because of what she'd done.

They sat beside the water, Giovana napping in the sun as they waited for Benito and Valentina to return. Leaning against a tree, Adi looked upriver and watched as a couple otters played, zipping in and out of the water after one another. Just as she smiled, something moving caught her eye and she watched in amazement as a small deer cautiously left the trees and went to the edge, slowly taking a drink.

Adi couldn't believe her luck. She hadn't seen a deer in forever and as it disappeared back under cover, she turned to Rodrigo. "I'll be right back."

Not waiting for a reply, she ran north, trying to catch up to it. If she could snag a deer, they would never make fun of her hunting skills again.

Spotting the animal through the trees, she slowed down, carefully following along as the deer moved farther east. Adi tracked it for quite some time, trying to get close enough for a clear shot, but knowing the others would be waiting, she was just about to turn around when the trees finally thinned. Adi lined up her target, the deer in her sights. But as she lifted her bow, the animal suddenly paused, ears twitching with uncertainty as it looked ahead. Distracted by its alarmed behaviour, Adi hesitated just long enough to lose her chance, the deer bolting south faster than she could make a move. Frustrated, she lowered the bow, dropping her arms to her sides. It took her a moment to notice, but as she looked at where the deer had been, she saw a lightly-worn path ahead of her. Adi stepped out onto it, curiously peering through the trees. She didn't see anything out of the ordinary until she crouched down, suddenly spotting a village less than twenty feet away.

Surprised, she didn't move, unaware that there were others living so close to them. But as she crept forward, stopping at the edge of the trees, she could see why they didn't know. The village was eerily quiet, nothing moving in or out. She was about to walk into the clearing when something came up behind her.

Knife in hand, she spun, coming face-to-face with Rodrigo. By his expression, she knew he was pissed, but when he looked past her, his anger faded.

"What the hell are you doing?" he whispered, not taking his eyes off the village.

"I saw a deer."

"We should go," Giovana said behind them. Her face scrunched in concern.

"Something's wrong," Adi replied, and as she looked at Rodrigo, she could tell he thought so too.

He was quiet for a moment. "Wait here," he said.

She was about to protest, but he was already out of the trees.

They watched as he sprinted up to a house, walking carefully alongside it towards the centre of the village. As soon as he reached the end of the building, he turned and disappeared from view, leaving Adi and Giovana waiting with baited breath. The next thing they heard was the sound of a single gunshot cutting through the air.

Adi's heart pounded as she ran into the clearing, Giovana right beside her. Giovana turned left so she went right, sliding herself along the house before peering out. Nothing moved so she walked forward and entered the first house, as quietly as she could.

It took her eyes a minute to adjust to the darkness, but her nose didn't need any time. The stench of rotting flesh hit her like a brick wall and she took a step back, gagging. Her vision clear, she stood there in shock, looking at the dead bodies piled on top of each other, flies buzzing eagerly around them. Seeing it seemed to make the smell worse and as Adi lifted her shirt up over her nose, she felt a shaky hand touch her shoulder.

Turning, she shuddered in relief when she saw Giovana, her stomach already twisted into a hard knot. "Find him?" she asked.

Giovana shook her head, her eyes lingering on the bodies.

"Okay," Adi said. "Let's go."

They moved to the next house, eager to get out of there, but when they opened the door, they found the same thing: dead bodies rotting in piles. House after house they searched until they checked every one, finding nothing but death. Adi sprinted across the clearing to the houses on the other side, panic building in her chest. Flinging each door open, she desperately searched for Rodrigo and when she finally found him, crouched down on the floor, a small relieved sob escaped her throat.

"Rodrigo," she whispered, seeing the recently dead dog beside him.

Hearing her voice, he turned his head, eyes full of tears.

"We need to go."

"I can't," he said, choking on the words. "I can't leave her."

Adi looked at the small girl in his arms. She had been shot in the head, the bullet tearing off part of her skull and she was missing a couple fingers, her skin punctured with teeth marks. "She's dead. You can't save her."

"Adi," Giovana said as she entered the house. "You need to come."

She didn't want to leave, but knowing it was important, she followed her into the next house. What she saw stopped her in her tracks. There, on the floor, was a baby.

"It's alive," Giovana said as they stared at it.

"Go get Rodrigo," Adi said as she knelt. "We need to get outta here."

Hearing Giovana leave, Adi slowly removed the baby from its dead mother's grasp, the child not making a sound as she lifted it. Green-brown eyes stared back at her as she held it in her hands, not knowing what to do. The baby wasn't very old and she didn't even know if it would survive. All she knew was that she couldn't leave it there.

A low rumble interrupted her thoughts. At first, she didn't recognize it, but as it grew louder, the sound was unmistakable. Pressing the baby tightly to her chest, she burst out of the house.

"Gio!" she screamed as she ran.

Hearing her, Giovana stepped from the house. "He won't move."

"Trucks," she said desperately. "Trucks are coming."

It took a second to sink in, but when it did, Giovana's face filled with fear.

"Here," Adi said as she reached her, shoving the baby into her arms. "Don't stop 'til you're across the river. Go!"

Giovana hesitated for a moment, obviously torn about leaving, but eventually she turned and ran for the trees.

Sprinting into the house, Adi grabbed Rodrigo by the shoulders. "We have to go," she almost yelled at him, her voice pleading. "They're coming. You have to let her go."

He numbly shook his head.

"Rodrigo!"

He didn't move. Knowing it would be a matter of seconds before they arrived, she hurriedly closed the door and crouched down low in a corner.

It was quiet for only a moment before she heard the trucks drive in, Adi jumping as they slammed their doors shut.

"Burn it," she heard a voice say. "Leave nothing behind."

Footsteps moved in all directions and it didn't take long for the smell of smoke to reach her nose, her desperation heightening.

"Rodrigo," she whispered quietly, trying to snap him out of it. "We need to go." As she looked at him, she saw nothing but pain. "You can take her with us," she said, willing to try anything. "We just need to go."

When he didn't reply, she could feel the fear clawing up her throat and she shakily inhaled, trying to keep calm. Looking around her for anything that might help, she suddenly saw it: a way out. Climbing over the dead bodies, she tried to get to the door at the back of the house, but as she made her way towards it, her foot slipped and she fell, landing on top of the decomposing body of an elderly woman. Freaked out, Adi quickly scrambled off, but as she did, she disturbed the stack and she could do nothing but watch as a body rolled off, the weight of it slamming into the wall with a thud.

She didn't move a muscle, hoping no one had heard, but when a voice said, "Check it," she knew she was in trouble.

Clamoring to her feet, she grabbed a body and pulled it up against the door, trying to block it. She was dragging a second one over when she saw the doorknob turn. Lunging forward, she pushed all her weight against the door, trying to keep it shut.

"It won't open," she heard the man say, but her relief quickly evaporated when she realized what would come next.

She dove behind an overturned table at about the same time the shooting started, the bullets ripping through the walls with force. The sound seemed to snap Rodrigo out of his daze and his head jerked up, suddenly aware of the danger. But as he stood, the rounds came fast and heavy, and Adi could do nothing but watch as he got hit from behind, the shot forcing him back onto his knees.

The little girl tumbled from his arms and he dove on the floor, covering his head as the assault continued. Adi kept perfectly still, her muscles tense as she waited for her moment. She closed her eyes, listening intently to the rhythm of the gunfire and the second she heard the chamber click empty, she launched forward, pulled Rodrigo up onto his feet, and sprinted for the back door.

Adi kicked it open and ran for the tree line, the bullets narrowly flying past as they left the clearing. Blood was gushing out of his abdomen but she ignored it, keeping him upright as they ran through the trees. They headed straight for the river and as soon as they reached it, Adi plunged them into the water, letting the current take them down and away as she watched the shore behind. The river snaked back and forth through the jungle, creating an endless amount of curves and bends, so it didn't take long to float out of sight. Hidden from view, Adi turned and began the difficult task of swimming to the other side.

Beating her to the water's edge, Rodrigo helped pull her out before collapsing back down onto the dirt, his chest rising quickly as he gasped for air. They stayed there catching their breath before Adi forced herself back up.

"Come on," she said, holding out her hand.

They arrived at the camp a few hours later, Valentina and Pablo rushing forward to help. As soon as they lifted Rodrigo off, Adi saw Marcelo storming towards her.

"What happened?" he asked angrily, the permanent scowl on his face deepening.

His tone was always accusatory whenever he talked to her and as Adi watched Rodrigo being carried to the shelter, she tried to think of how to explain.

"Gio told us about the bodies and the trucks," he continued before she could reply. "Did they see you?"

"Adi!"

Recognizing Nayara's panicked voice, she turned and saw her calling from the shelter.

"The blood," Nayara said as soon as they ran up. "It won't stop."

She looked at Rodrigo on the table as Pablo pressed against the wound, the rag so soaked it was beginning to drip on the floor. The paleness of his face reminded her of the bodies and her mind flashed back to the village, a tingling sensation running over her as she felt the clammy skin of the old woman once more.

"Adi!" Valentina shouted and she jumped, breaking from her daze. "Do something!"

Expectant faces around her waited and she forced herself to focus on the problem in front of her. Walking up to the table, she took the rag away from Pablo and looked at the wound. It was the largest bullet hole she had ever seen, the ammo tearing straight through his side and out the other end with little resistance. Knowing that neither red sap nor thread would close the gaping hole, she could only think of one other solution. "Bring him to the fire."

They obeyed without hesitation, carrying Rodrigo out of the shelter to the middle of the camp. As they laid him gently on the ground, Adi held the knife in the flames until it burned hot, the handle becoming almost too warm for her to grasp.

"Hold him down," she said as they crouched beside him, each person hovering over a corner of his body.

"Have you done this before?"

Nayara's question made her hesitate and she tried to remember the one time she had seen it done. While it was risky, as she watched more blood stain the dirt around him, she stopped delaying and pressed the red-hot blade forcefully against the wound.

Rodrigo's body jerked as the smell of searing flesh filled the air. Though he was weak, he still had enough strength to fight back and Adi had to lean all her weight against his leg, forcing him to keep still. Again and again, she placed the metal against the wound, burning the ripped skin until it eventually closed, an angry red blotch staring back at her. By the time she finished, Rodrigo had passed out cold and they placed him back underneath the shelter.

"Now what?" Nayara asked.

ψ

A light rain fell and everyone hid in the huts, the trickling moisture too gentle to break the unrelenting humidity. Adi sat in the chair, staring at Rodrigo on the table, his body covered in blankets. They had sealed the wound, but she wasn't sure he'd make it. If he was still bleeding on the inside, he would eventually fill up with blood and die.

She sighed and sat slumped in the chair, unwilling to think about that possibility. She told herself she was concerned because Benito was close to him, but that wasn't exactly true. Since her return to the jungle, she and Rodrigo had been almost inseparable. It was like she had never left. He meant something to her, something more than she expected, almost as if he was...

Family. The thought entered her head at the same time Valentina walked in, the surprise from her realization fading as she watched her from against the wall. The look on Valentina's face perplexed her, but as she observed her gently caress Rodrigo's head, she realized it shouldn't have. It made sense now, all the times Valentina stayed close and helped him. It wasn't because she liked him—she loved him.

She watched them for a moment before she suddenly felt tired, her eyelids drooping, and she pulled her blanket close. But just as quickly as sleep came, so did the nightmares, and she was back in that place, surrounded by broken, decomposing bodies, their cold and clammy skin grabbing and pulling her down. She struggled to get free, flailing with all her might as they held her firmly, and just when a hand gripped her ankle, she kicked as hard as she could.

The force of the jolt jerked her awake and she sprang up, searching the shelter for danger. The only thing that was there was Giovana, curled up in a tight ball in a chair beside her, fast asleep.

She sat back down, listening to the rain fall as her mind returned to the village, the bodies etched in her memory. She thought about the dead, going over it again and again, but she couldn't figure it out. Why did it happen?

The sound of someone gasping interrupted her, and she watched Rodrigo slowly wake up on the table. She could tell that he was struggling to remember where he was, but when his eyes finally found hers, it clicked.

"What'd you do to me?" he groaned as he pulled off the blankets, looking down at his side.

"I..." Adi began, standing beside him, but then she stopped. "How do you feel?"

He exhaled loudly. "I feel like I've been lying on a table."

He moved to sit up but her hand stopped him.

"Don't," she said. "Stay. We don't know yet."

"Don't know what?"

She didn't reply as she felt along his side, pressing down every inch or so, feeling for any liquid underneath. The closer she got to the wound, the more she felt Rodrigo tense, but he said nothing as he waited for her to finish.

"That bad, huh?" he asked when she was done.

She wanted to say something that would reassure him, but she came up short. "I don't know."

Rodrigo said nothing else.

Unsure of what to do, she said, "I'll get you some water."

The news that he was awake spread quickly. Over the next couple of days, the shelter was crowded with kids wanting to see him. While Adi checked his wound daily, she wasn't sure if it was getting better or worse. It just stayed the same.

Several nights later she went down to the river, wanting nothing more than to cool off. After dunking her head in the water, she pulled herself into a tree, climbing a few branches up before sitting down on one that gave her an unobstructed view of the river. She rolled her neck around, trying to get the tension to leave, but it stayed tight, unwilling to relax. She sat there enjoying the silence, when all of a sudden, a faint sound split the early morning air.

She sat up straight, closing her eyes as she listened. About a minute later, she heard it again. Gunshots.

She scrambled out of the tree, barely landing on the ground before she sprinted up the path and into the camp. Grabbing the gun and knives from her bag, she ran into the main shelter.

"Where's Salvador?" she asked as she entered, seeing Valentina and Marcelo sitting with Rodrigo.

Marcelo glared at her. "He's sleeping."

"Wake him up," she replied, tucking the gun into her pants.

"Why?"

Knowing that telling Marcelo off would get her nowhere, Adi fought back the frustration. "It's important."

Marcelo didn't move and had just opened his mouth when Rodrigo cut in.

"Marcelo," he said, adjusting uncomfortably in his chair. "Just do it."

By the time he returned with Salvador, she already regretted her choice. She had wasted too much time. She should have just gone by herself.

"What is it?" Salvador asked as he smoothed down his ruffled hair.

"Gunshots," she replied. "South of the river. Near the Morro Rio village."

"You're sure?" Salvador asked, frowning.

She nodded.

"It's probably a hunter," Marcelo said, his arms folded across his chest. "With bad aim."

Although she knew she couldn't, she wanted nothing more than to beat the living crap out of him. He irritated her like no one else. "It's not a hunter," she said, forcing herself to sound calm. "It's something bad. Trust me."

Salvador paused. "Alright. So, what would you like me to do?"

It was not the response she expected.

"If it's anything like what you and Rodrigo encountered," he continued, "we should stay away."

"And what about the people there?" she asked. "You're just gonna leave them?"

"We're not responsible for them. We're responsible for those who live here."

Adi shook her head. This wasn't right. "I'm not just gonna let them die like the others."

Salvador studied her for a moment. "That's your choice, but unless you can promise me that whatever's out there won't follow you here, you can't come back."

It was as if the shelter suddenly shrunk, the air feeling thick and heavy.

"You got lucky last time," he continued. "And the time before that a group of gangsters almost destroyed the camp. I'm sorry, but I will not risk our safety again."

Adi looked at him, trying to understand his decision, but she couldn't. Before she even walked out of the shelter, she already knew what she was going to do.

Running down to the river, she searched for the boat, but didn't know where it was hidden.

"Going somewhere?" a voice asked, startling her.

"I would be if I could find the stupid boat."

Catalina smiled and walked over to a pile of shrubs, pulling the boat out from under cover. "Where we going?"

"*We're* not going anywhere," Adi said as she dragged it to the water. Climbing in, she sat down and pushed off with the paddle but stopped as soon as she felt Catalina jump in behind her. "Get out," she said. "You can't come."

Catalina didn't reply. She sat down and picked up the other paddle.

"Catalina."

"I'm not leaving, so just accept it. Where you go, I go. That's how this works."

While she wanted nothing more than for her to come, she knew she couldn't ask her to, not with the potential consequences.

"So," Catalina said, interrupting her thoughts, "where we going?"

She was about to protest again when a voice answered behind her.

"The Morro Rio village," Rodrigo said. He threw his guns into the boat and pushed off, sending them downriver and on their way.

Chapter Eleven

Unlike the section of river north of Salvador's camp, the area to the south was much wider, the boat gliding easily across the water in the lightening sky. Docking the boat on the other side, they ran towards the village, hoping they weren't too late. His injury slowing him down, Rodrigo motioned for Adi and Catalina to go on without him and they sprinted through the trees, trying to get there as fast as they could. But when Adi looked up and saw a light trace of smoke creeping through the sky, she knew they were too late.

The heat of the fire radiated out as they ran into the village, not stopping to check for danger. Sprinting for the closest house, Adi pulled out her gun and kicked in the door.

"Anyone here?" she yelled. Flames and dead bodies answered her.

They searched house after house, but as they neared the last few, they couldn't even get close, the fire completely engulfing them. Defeated, Adi sank to her knees and watched the houses burn, the air filling with ash and the smell of burning flesh. She didn't know how long she sat there, but when she felt Catalina touch her head, she sighed and got back onto her feet.

There was nothing to say as they walked back to the river, finding their boat and paddling across. Giovana and Renan were waiting for them, but when they landed, Adi watched their hopeful looks fade. It wasn't until they reached the campfire in the middle of the clearing that someone spoke, Rodrigo voicing what they were all thinking. "What the fuck is happening?"

She wished she had an answer, but as she watched Salvador come out of the shelter and motion to them, she sighed. The pain wasn't over yet.

Adi sat beside Giovana and Catalina as they waited. She didn't feel like being there and she could tell the others didn't either. They had just watched an entire village burn and no one was in the mood to talk.

"You should've told me you were going," Valentina said, her voice rising as she spoke to Rodrigo at the side of the shelter.

"Why?" he asked. "So you could talk me out of it?"

Adi couldn't help but look and she watched as an unimpressed expression covered Valentina's face.

"You're injured," she replied. "You shouldn't have gone."

"You're right," he said. "But someone had to. Maybe if we hadn't wasted so much time talking, they wouldn't all be dead."

"You didn't know..." Valentina started.

"I knew," he said, cutting her off. "And so did you. Adi was the only one willing to do something about it."

At the mention of her name, she looked away, but found herself meeting Marcelo's gaze. He stared back at her for a few seconds before he turned away.

"Alright," Salvador said as he entered the room. "I want to discuss what's happening at the villages. It's been made very clear that not everyone agrees on how to approach this, so we need to make a decision."

"They have to be related..." Pablo started, but Marcelo cut him off.

"We don't know that," he insisted. "It could be nothing."

"They murdered everyone in those villages and then burned them," Rodrigo replied, his tone low and firm. "That's not nothing."

The room was quiet, as if his word was final, and when no one else said spoke, Salvador began again. "So, what do we do?"

People started talking all at once and Adi listened as ideas were tossed around. Some wanted to leave while others didn't and there were a couple who still didn't understand why they had to choose.

"We should help them." The voice was small, but it was strong enough to cut through the noise.

Adi turned towards Giovana, unsurprised by her suggestion. She suffered the same nightmares Adi did, and there were many nights when Adi found her curled up beside her, hand clutched tightly onto her arm.

"How?" Marcelo asked. "We can't bring them here. We don't have the room or the food."

"That's not what she's saying," Catalina said. "We just need to go there, make sure they're okay."

Marcelo sighed. "What's the point?"

"To warn them," Nayara said. "Give them a chance to leave."

This time he huffed in annoyance, but he didn't get to reply.

"How many villages?" Salvador asked, clasping his hands behind his back.

"Four," Rodrigo said.

"Four," Salvador repeated, thinking it over.

"It'll only take eight of us to do it," Rodrigo continued. "Nothing more."

Salvador stayed quiet for a while before he looked over at Marcelo.

"I still don't think it's a good idea," Marcelo replied. "There are too many risks. We have no idea what we're walking into. Everyone we send out there could die."

Adi didn't realize that she had huffed out loud until she looked up and saw everyone staring at her.

"Would you like to say something?" Marcelo asked irritated.

She hesitated for a moment. "If this is happening at the other villages, losing eight people will be the least of our problems." She paused. "You think that people don't know where we are? You're wrong. No one's safe. Not out there and not in here."

Ten minutes later, everyone left the shelter, their plan in place. As Adi lay down that night, she hoped it wasn't what she thought it was. She hoped she was wrong.

ψ

She woke up just before daylight to meet Marcelo at the centre of camp. When they were deciding on who would go to which village, she was just as surprised as everyone else when Marcelo volunteered to go with her.

"I've got something for you," he said as he walked up.

Adi followed him across the camp and into the supply shed. He began rummaging through a wooden box.

"Here," he said as he stood back up.

She was quiet as she examined the oddly shaped knife. It was long and curved, but the inside edge had jagged teeth along the ridge. While it was big, it was lighter than a machete and had a comfortable grip.

"We found it a couple years ago," Marcelo explained as she turned it over in her hands. "It came with this."

She looked up and saw the knife case in his hands. "What's the strap for?" she asked.

"It goes over your shoulder," he replied. "Here, I'll show you." Marcelo placed it over her head and underneath her left arm. "Give me the knife." Sliding it into the pouch, he said, "Reach back."

As soon as Adi put her hand behind her head, she felt the handle of the knife slip easily into her grasp. She pulled it straight up and out in one fluid motion, slicing the air in front of her. She smiled.

"Come on," he said as he walked out of the shed. "Let's try not to die today."

They made their way north, travelling to the second farthest village. Marcelo knew the terrain well, leading them strategically across rivers and around hills. They had been running almost all morning when he stopped at the base of a steep slope.

"It's just up this hill," he said as he sat down.

Adi drank some water, the noonday sun beating down on them through the trees.

"The village sits against the mountain. It won't take us long."

Climbing the hill, they were forced to circle around the edge of the field in order to stay hidden, the trees becoming sparser the closer they got. Adi spotted the village as they neared and seeing people walking around, she breathed a sigh of relief.

Leaving the trees, they approached the village, Marcelo tucking his gun under his shirt and Adi adjusting her pack so it covered most of her knife. As they entered, she noticed that there were only young children and elderly people there, just like all the others.

"Can I help you?" an older woman asked as she walked out of her house, a wary look on her face.

"We're from a nearby village," Marcelo began but then stopped, unsure of how to say it.

"We're here to warn you," Adi finished for him, blunt and to the point.

The woman was quiet for a moment, her brow deepening. "About what?"

She opened her mouth to answer when she heard a faint sound. She hesitated, unsure if she was actually hearing it, but needing to be sure, she sprinted towards the road and scaled a tree, looking out into the jungle.

The moment her head passed the thick leaves, she heard it. "Trucks," she said, the word barely escaping her throat. "Trucks!"

"Run!" Marcelo yelled, trying to sound somewhat calm. "Hide in the trees! Go!"

At first no one moved, looking at Marcelo oddly, but when they saw Adi's face as she dropped back onto the ground, they started running.

Adi darted into the houses and pulled people out, urging them to leave. Picking up two small children, she ran with them across the clearing to the tree line as Marcelo helped an elderly man over. They ran back and forth, bringing people under the safety of the trees and when they finally crouched down under cover, Adi could feel the tension building.

"What's going on?" someone asked.

"Quiet!" Marcelo answered firmly, his eyes focused on the village in front of them.

Time passed slowly as they waited in silence for the trucks to appear, but nothing happened. Adi could feel the villagers' impatience growing and even Marcelo was beginning to doubt her.

"Adi," he said, turning his head, "are you..."

A collective gasp went up from the group, and when he looked back out, he saw them: six black trucks.

No one moved as they watched the armed men step warily from their vehicles, their guns aimed at the houses. They searched the village but finding no one, they gathered in the centre, cautiously looking at the forest around them.

"We should move farther back," Adi whispered to Marcelo, "in case they come looking."

"Okay," he replied softly. "Keep watch."

She surveyed the men as Marcelo moved the villagers deeper into the trees. By the time almost everyone was down the hill, the men had lit the houses on fire, the flames licking up into the sky as smoke billowed around them. As she studied the men, one in particular caught her attention. He was looking around when he abruptly stopped and started walking in her direction.

Reaching behind her, Adi gripped her gun. She didn't want to use it, but she would if she had to. Her heart beat faster the closer he came, and just as she inhaled, she suddenly froze, the air almost choking her as his face came into view. There he was, right in front of her. The man with the scar.

She had to slam her hand over her mouth to keep the cry from escaping, her chest moving up and down uncontrollably. Gulping it down, her hand shook as she pulled out her gun, the metal feeling slippery in her grasp. Aiming it at his head, she took a deep breath, but it only caused her to shake more and as he continued to walk towards her, tears streamed down her cheeks as fear ran rampant over her body. Just when it felt like she was going to collapse, he suddenly turned and walked away.

Adi didn't take her eyes off him as he went back to the burning village. Unable to move, she stayed in place, gun drawn, and watched as he climbed into the truck and drove out of sight. When Marcelo placed a hand on her shoulder, she jerked so hard her tense muscles screamed in anger.

"Let's go."

She didn't move and he walked in front of her, the tear-stained cheeks impossible to miss as she continued to look past him.

"Come on," he said. "We need to go."

Still not getting a response, he reached out and placed his hand on top of the gun, gently pushing it down. The movement seemed to snap her out of it and she quickly wiped away the tears, took one last look at the village, and walked down the hill.

"Who were they?" someone asked as they approached.

"We don't know," Marcelo said.

Adi passed around what little water they had.

"Why would they burn down our homes?" someone else asked.

Marcelo shrugged. "We don't know that either. But they've done this twice before."

A murmur went up in the group and her mind began to churn. If they had gotten here just in time, the men might already be on their way to the next village.

"We need to go," she said. "Now."

He shot her an irritated look so she continued, lowering her voice.

"What if they're going to the next one? The one that Gio and Renan are at." As soon as she saw the realization in his face, she knew it made sense.

"What do we do with them?" he whispered to her. "We can't just leave them here."

"Go," an elderly woman said, overhearing their conversation. "Save as many as you can."

Adi didn't need to hear another word, immediately running east with Marcelo right behind. Even though they had a direct route to the village while the jungle roads were slow and difficult to navigate, the trucks had left a while ago and she wasn't sure if they would make it in time. Forcing the thought from her head, she dug deep and pushed herself harder, flying through the trees at a pace that even Marcelo couldn't keep up with.

"Go," he yelled behind her, breathing hard.

"I need you," she replied, refusing to slow down. "I don't know where to go."

"You're almost there," he said, his voice growing fainter. "Go straight 'til you reach the river then follow it south. You'll run right into it."

She sped through the jungle, her heartbeat pounding in her ears as the man with the scar filled her head. It took longer than she wanted to reach the river, but when she finally did, she turned south, jumping over large rocks and logs that crowded the bank. She didn't know how close the village was, but not smelling any smoke or hearing any gunshots, she took that as a good sign and kept going. Suddenly, the village appeared in front of her and she ran straight into it, not bothering to look for danger.

"Get out," she said as she leaned over, gasping for air. "Get out!"

She got nothing but odd stares.

"Adi!" Giovana said as she ran up. "What happened? Where's Marcelo?"

Adi was relieved to see her. "Get everyone out. They're coming."

Without another word, Giovana returned to the house while she stood there, trying to catch her breath.

"You okay?" Renan asked as he approached, Giovana right behind him.

"I'm fine," she snapped. She didn't understand why people weren't moving. "We need to get them out."

Renan gave her a disappointed look. "Gio told them what you said. They don't want to leave."

Adi shook her head in frustration. They didn't understand what was coming. *He* was coming. "They'll die," she said. "Don't they get that?"

"Yes," an elderly man replied as he walked up. "We do."

She turned to face him. "So why won't you leave?"

He smiled at her. "Our community has lived here for generations. We have survived every tumultuous regime change, dictatorship, and military takeover. This is our home. Whatever happens, we will live on, right here, where we belong."

Adi shook her head in frustration. He didn't understand.

As if sensing her internal struggle, he continued. "You cannot predict death, just as we cannot leave this land. It is a part of us. We are lost without it."

The words were barely out of his mouth when the force of a bullet hitting her right thigh crumpled her like a falling skyscraper. Grenade explosions, gunshots, and screams filled the air and Adi's ears rang, deafening her to all other sounds. From her stunned position on the ground, she watched as the man she was just talking to fell dead in front of her, a bullet hole centred in his head. Flipping over, she crawled towards the trees, pushing herself forward with her one good leg. She desperately needed cover but as she looked back, she saw a man casually following her, AK-47 pointing towards the sky. She didn't need to see his face to know who it was.

She tried to crawl faster, but it was no use. It was like he was waiting for her to give up, totally unconcerned with the chaos around them. Exhausted, she turned over onto her back, propping herself up onto her elbows as she watched the face and the scar that had haunted her materialize before her eyes.

"Adelita Alvarez." He smiled and crouched, so close he was almost on top of her. "Now this *is* a surprise."

She said nothing as she stared back, her fear vanishing with the knowledge that she'd soon be dead.

"When they told me I had to kill every single person in that village, I didn't realize how serious they were." Withdrawing a knife from his side, he flicked the edge of the blade with his thumb. "But now I understand what a pain in the ass one rat can be. It was you at the other village, wasn't it?"

She remained silent.

He chuckled. "Of course it was! Not to worry though. We'll find and kill them just like the others." He shifted his gaze from the knife back to her. "I have to say, I am thoroughly impressed with your ability to run through the jungle. You are fast!" He laughed again before the smile dropped from his face. "Your father was fast too, but not fast enough. Let's see if you share his tolerance for pain." Lifting the knife, he plunged it into her hand.

Adi screamed in agony as he twisted it, the blade digging into her flesh. She grabbed at the handle, but he held her down, his body hovering over hers.

Leaning forward, he whispered into her ear, his breath hot against her face. "Your father screamed just like that when I tortured him over and over again."

As quick as she could, she withdrew the knife tucked up her sleeve and slashed, the blade slicing across his throat. It took a moment to register, but when it finally did, a stunned expression fell over his face. Sitting back on his heels, he touched his neck with his hand. Seeing blood, he looked at her with a surprised smile.

She didn't waste a second, wrenching the knife out of her hand as she launched her good leg forward, kicking him squarely in the chest. He fell onto his back, grasping at his throat as he tried to stop the gushing blood.

Using a tree, she pulled herself off the ground and hobbled as fast as she could into the forest, the sound of gunshots continuing in the village behind her. Finally finding a trail, she limped along it for a while before losing consciousness and hitting the ground with a thud.

She drifted in and out, feeling like she was floating beneath the trees as the sunlight sporadically hit her face. She wondered if she had died and this was what heaven was like. She heard a muffled sound but didn't go towards it. She was so tired, and being here was so wonderful, she never wanted to leave. She smiled as she closed her eyes and gave in to the exhaustion.

Pain unlike any other jolted her awake as it coursed through her body.

"Hold her still!" she heard a voice say.

Not knowing where she was, Adi struggled as the agony increased. Something was forced into her mouth but she violently spit it out as she fought to get free. She wiggled one hand loose and swung at the blurry figure closest to her. But when her punch connected, the intensity of the pain shocked her so much that her arm went numb, dropping uselessly beside her. She screamed as another spike of pain thrusted through her body, knocking her unconscious once again.

Chapter Twelve

A light breeze made its way across her body, tickling her skin as it travelled through her hair against her scalp. Shivering at the sensation, she slowly woke and opened her eyes. Her vision was blurry, but it eventually cleared, blinking sluggishly as the ceiling came into view. While it looked familiar, she couldn't place where she was and as she pushed herself up, she stopped, a wave of dizziness slamming into her, making her gasp.

Looking down at her side, she saw that her pants were ripped and covered in blood. She moved her hand down, grimacing as she touched the wound below her right hip, the hole about the width of a sugarcane stalk. Examining the rest of her body, she felt numerous bruises all over but stopped when she touched the front of her head, her hair matted with blood. Distracted by the soft spot in her skull, she almost didn't notice that her left hand was tightly bandaged. She was about to unwrap it when someone touched her arm.

"Benito," she managed to say, her voice weak and raspy.

He said nothing as he looked at her, his eyes beginning to well up. Unexpectedly, he stepped forward and laid his head on her stomach.

Adi fought to hold back the tears, her throat thick with emotion as she held him tightly. She couldn't remember the last time he had touched her and as she felt his small chest move up and down, she closed her eyes and tried to absorb every second of it. When he raised his head, she wanted nothing more than to stay there forever, but knowing she couldn't, she reluctantly let go.

"Here," Nayara said softly beside her.

Adi reached out and took the cup, draining it. The liquid felt good against her dry throat.

"Sleep," she said, gently placing a hand against her forehead.

Adi nodded, but noticed that Benito was still there. She studied him for a moment, the exhaustion on his face making him seem much older than he was, before she patted the spot on the table beside her. She didn't know if he would do it, his hesitation making her doubt, but just as she was about to say he didn't have to, he climbed up beside her and fell asleep.

The next time she woke, it was light and Benito was no longer there. Able to withstand the pain this time, she pushed herself up and dropped her legs down off the table. Heavy throbbing reverberated through her head, squeezing her eyes shut. But once she slowly started to relax, the tension eased and when she opened her eyes again, the pain had weakened to a bearable ache.

She looked around the shelter, seeing Catalina quietly getting up from where she sat, Lupita sleeping soundly in a chair beside her.

"Nayara says you need water," she said, handing her a cup. "And eat if you can."

Adi slowly drank, the liquid hitting her empty stomach. While she was hungry, she was still nauseated and the thought of food made her gut clench. But when Catalina handed her a soft papaya, her sad face unmistakeable, Adi knew there was something she wasn't telling her.

"What's wrong?" she asked, watching her carefully.

Catalina tried to smile, but it dropped off her face. "Nothing," she said. "Just tired."

Adi didn't believe her, but decided not to press it. Catalina would tell her when she was ready. "What happened to your eye?" she asked instead.

"You don't remember?"

Adi shook her head.

"You decked me, hard," she said. "I was helping Nayara and you started freaking out. You punched me right in the face."

"Oh," Adi replied, unsuccessfully hiding her smirk. While she didn't remember much, she couldn't help but find it funny that she had been able to catch Catalina off guard. It was practically impossible.

"You were really messed up," Catalina continued. "When Gio got back and told us what happened, we thought you were dead. But then Marcelo showed up with you later that night. He carried you the whole way."

Adi cringed as the memory of what happened slowly came back to her. She remembered the attack, but more importantly, she remembered *him*, and her muscles instantly tensed, sending bolts of pain through her body. She was about to tell Catalina about it when she realized something.

"Wait," she said, her brow furrowing. "You said Gio got back. What about Renan?"

When Catalina paused, Adi knew it was bad, but as she watched her softly shake her head, her face filled with pain, Adi understood. Renan was dead.

This time when she woke, it was night and she was thankful for the darkness. But when she looked over to the side, she saw that it was Rodrigo's turn in the chair and he wasn't sleeping.

He said nothing as he looked at her, Adi barely able to make out the silhouette of his face. She opened her mouth to say something, but then closed it. There were only two things she wanted to know. "What happened at the village? What happened to Renan?"

His silence annoyed her.

"Tell me. I deserve to know." Getting no response, she sat up and swung her legs down. "Rodrigo." Her irritation turned to anger and she jumped off the table, ignoring the pain as she stormed towards him. "Answer me!"

So shocked by the paleness of his face, she stopped and stared at his red eyes, the lids noticeably swollen. Looking at the rest of him, she saw that his clothes were more wrinkled and dirty than normal and as her gaze drifted down, she saw his knuckles, cut up and bloodied.

"You don't remember me much from our village, do you?" he asked.

She didn't answer, unsure of where this would go. She wanted to talk about Renan, but when he continued, she realized she wasn't going to get her way.

"When your family first got there, I was eleven years old." He stopped talking and looked up at her. "Leti was twelve, you were seven, and Benito was just a baby." He smiled, a sadness filling his eyes that Adi had never seen before. "I remember the first time I laid eyes on Leti. I'm pretty sure I loved her the moment I saw her."

She took a step back, afraid of the words coming out of his mouth. Her breathing increased against her will as she stood there, fists clenching anxiously.

"I had the biggest crush on her," he continued, a soft laugh escaping his throat. "But by the time I worked up the guts to tell her, she was already dating Luis." He exhaled. "I won't lie, it hurt like hell, but I tried to be happy for her. He loved her, just as much as I did. You could tell by the way he looked at her." He cleared his throat. "But then that day came when Commander Martinez said we had to fight."

The tension gripping her body was so strong it was everything she could do just to breathe.

"The night my mama convinced me to leave, I didn't want to go, but she begged me to. I went to your house to tell Leti and I found her outside crying. I tried to get her to come with me, but she wouldn't." He paused and looked up at her again. "She wouldn't leave you behind."

Adi slowly exhaled, her lower lip trembling.

"She asked me not to go," he said, his voice quiet. "She wanted me to stay and watch over you and Benito, but I told her I couldn't. So she made me promise that once I found someplace safe, I would come get you." His voice cracked. "But I broke that promise. I left and never came back."

Adi silently watched the tears run down his face.

"When you and Benito showed up at the camp a few weeks later, I thought I was getting a second chance. But then you left and it became this sick joke. No matter what I did, I just kept losing you over and over." He stopped and looked down at his broken hands. "So when Gio got back and told us what happened, I lost it."

He went quiet, the pain obvious, but when he looked back up at her, she suddenly understood. She wasn't just family to him; she was to Rodrigo what Benito was to her: purpose. Without it, there was no point to any of this.

She knelt in front of him, gently wiping the tears off his face.

"I can't lose you," he said as his voice broke, his eyes welling up again. "I can't."

She had always thought Rodrigo was invincible, but as she looked at him, she realized that he was fighting to stay afloat, just like her. Refusing to leave her friend, they stayed there until he sighed deeply.

"Come on," she said as she stood. "Let's fix up your hands."

They sat outside next to the fire, Adi cleaning his knuckles as best she could. Her left hand was useless, the bandage wound around it tightly. She didn't doubt it was ugly and afraid of how damaged it was, she was scared to unwrap it.

"Renan died at the village," Rodrigo said quietly as she worked. "They shot him in the head."

She could feel the sadness creeping in, but as she nodded, she recognized that it was a better death than most. "And the village?"

When he didn't speak, she looked up and watched as he shook his head. She inhaled slowly, trying to stop the exhaustion from overwhelming her. After all they had done, no one had survived. Finished with his hands, she let go and leaned against the log, a pocket of wind dancing through the air. She sat there for a few minutes, enjoying the quiet of the night before she sighed and lifted her bandaged hand.

She slowly unwrapped it, knowing that she might as well look at it now. It's not like she could feel any worse. She expected Rodrigo to try and stop her, but he said nothing. The closer she got to her hand, the bloodier the bandage became, and when the last few layers wouldn't budge, Rodrigo handed her a knife.

Cutting the cloth away, Adi sharply inhaled, her mangled hand impossible to miss even in the dull light of the fire. There was a diagonal laceration about two inches long that went straight through the middle of it, the centre ballooning out through her palm. As she stared at the splotchy mark, her mind drifted back to the feeling of the knife being twisted into her.

"Nayara says you're lucky," Rodrigo said as she examined it. "She thinks you can still use it."

Adi bit her tongue, knowing there was no point in saying that she was the last thing from lucky. She tried to wiggle her fingers, but only the first three moved, her fourth and pinky fingers staying completely still. She swore she could still feel every inch of them, but they refused to budge. Lowering her hand, she swallowed back the angry disappointment and looked up at the sky.

"Did you kill him at least?" Rodrigo asked, shattering the silence.

She was quiet, willing the tears away. It was a simple question, and as much as she wished she knew the answer, she didn't. "Maybe," she replied, her voice small.

"What do you mean?"

She sighed, not wanting to think about him, but eventually gave in. "I cut his throat."

Rodrigo didn't say anything for a minute. "How is that a maybe?"

"I didn't see him die."

He smiled. "Not many people survive having their throats slit."

"He can."

Rodrigo hesitated. "You knew him?"

"Yes."

His confusion melted into concern. "Who was it?"

It was her turn to pause and she looked back up at the sky. If she said it out loud, it would make the nightmare real again, but as a spike of pain shot through her hand, she knew it was real whether she said it or not. "It was him."

"Him who?"

She stayed quiet as she looked at him, holding his gaze as she watched it sink in.

His mouth fell open in shock. "Did he recognize you?"

She nodded.

"How do you know?"

As Adi opened her mouth to reply, her mind flashed back to three years before. "He knew my name. He called me by my name."

※

Rodrigo hadn't stopped pacing as he continued peppering her with questions, trying to understand. Adi told him everything; how she had seen him at the north village, how he had followed as she crawled on the ground, what he said about her father.

"Like I said, I cut his throat, but I didn't see him die. And if he didn't, that means..." her voice trailed off, unwilling to say it.

"That means he could still be out there."

She nodded. "What happened at the village you and Yumi went to, the one in the southwest?"

"Nothing," Rodrigo replied. He walked the loop around the fire pit. "It was fine."

"And the west village?"

"Same. Catalina told them what was happening, but they weren't concerned."

She was quiet for a second. "How long have I been lying on that table?"

"Six days."

"Has anyone gone back?"

"To which village?"

"Any."

Rodrigo nodded. "Marcelo and Ivanna went two days ago. Everything was fine."

"Okay," she said, thinking it through. "So the villages north, east, and south of us are gone but the ones in the west are still there."

"For now," Rodrigo said.

She nodded. "So, either he doesn't care about them or he just hasn't gotten there yet." She sat up suddenly. "I need a stick."

Rodrigo found one and handed it to her as she knelt in the dirt. Her leg throbbed in pain, but she ignored it, a sense of urgency coming over her.

"He's been working his way west from the city," she said as she drew a rough map of the area. "The first village was east of where we are," she said, marking that village with the number one. "The second was south, the third north, and the fourth northwest."

"Why would he go west?" Rodrigo asked. "That's where he's from."

"Because," Adi replied, the realization hitting her, "if he pushes east and people escape, they could warn the others. But if anyone gets away now, they would run right into the area he already controls."

"No loose ends," Rodrigo said.

She looked at her map on the ground as he began to pace again. Suddenly, he stopped walking.

"He's gonna find us, isn't he?"

Glancing up, she could see that he already knew the answer, but as he patiently waited for her to say it, she nodded. "Yes."

Before she could say anything else, he disappeared into the dark.

Chapter Thirteen

Even the sun wasn't up as twelve of them left the camp heading south. Two days had passed since Adi and Rodrigo's revelation by the fire, and although they tried to convince everyone that the man would come for them, few wanted to leave.

"You're overreacting," Valentina had said as heads nodded in agreement. Even Salvador said it was unlikely the man would find them, but when Marcelo walked up to her the night before they left, bag in hand, Adi knew she wasn't crazy.

It was the morning of the fifth day and they moved off the mountain into a wide valley, travelling southwest in a tired line. They had been hiking up hill after hill since they left the last familiar section of jungle days ago, and as she stepped onto the flat ground, she was thankful for the break. The air was beginning to warm as the sun rose, sending sporadic sparkles of sunlight through the thick leaf ceiling and illuminating the dirt ahead of them. Adi couldn't help but feel relaxed as they made their way through the trees, the sound of birds and monkeys calling to one another overhead. She always enjoyed this part of the day and the animals seemed to agree, chirping and squawking as they passed by.

She was walking behind Talita when she felt the air around them go still. Not thinking much of it, she casually turned her head, just in time to see a harpy eagle swoop underneath the canopy, flying straight towards them.

"Get down!" she yelled, pulling Talita onto the ground.

She scrambled over her, shielding the baby with her torso. As the others crouched low, Adi watched as the large bird, undeterred by their sudden movements, simply adjusted its target and locked onto something ahead. Whipping her head around, she saw Evita standing all alone.

Lurching to her feet, she ran as fast as she could for the girl, knowing that the bird would be right above her. As its shadow moved past, she threw herself forward, sending Evita sprawling into the dirt.

Almost instantly, Adi felt the harpy's sharp claws dig into her shoulder, muscle and skin ripping as it tried to pick her up. Shocked by the piercing pain, she froze and simply lay there as the bird jerked her body back and forth, trying to fly away. She barely heard the angry screams as the others attacked it, trying to force it to release her. But when the sound of the gunshot cut through the noise, silencing everyone around her, Adi crumpled to the ground, the weight of the dead bird's body pulling her over.

"Get it out of her!" Nayara sounded frantic as Catalina rolled her onto her side.

"Hold still," Rodrigo said.

Although she knew it would hurt, she wasn't prepared for the amount of pain that seized her right shoulder as he pulled out the first set of talons, tears springing into her eyes.

"One more time," she heard him say as they moved her again.

As if in protest, her body tensed, every muscle rigid as she prepared for the incoming pain.

"Adi," Catalina said as she knelt beside her, her face coming into view. "You have to relax."

"I can't," she replied, finding it difficult to even breathe.

Catalina picked up her hand. "Squeeze."

Although she felt weaker than she had ever been, she gripped Catalina's hand tightly and squished it as hard as she could, her teeth clenching angrily. As soon as she stopped, the tension left her muscles and Rodrigo pulled out the claws, a small sob bursting from her throat.

"Sit her up," Nayara said. She knelt beside her, ripping away what remained of her shirt.

Even though she was sweating, she felt cold and her muscles clenched again. She was still as Nayara inspected her wounds, her mind occupied with the sole task of breathing. It hurt to inhale and every time she exhaled, her muscles shook, sending painful jolts up her shoulder.

She could feel every inch of the six talon-sized puncture marks in her shoulder as she attempted to stand, her heart urgently pumping blood through her body. She was so lightheaded that she wobbled a bit and Giovana caught her by the arm, sending a new wave of pain into her. Doubling over, she gasped, cradling her arm tightly against her body.

It took a few more minutes, but eventually she stood up straight, multiple hands guiding and holding her firmly in place. While the others wanted her to rest, Adi knew it was going to hurt regardless, so she wrapped her arm in a sling, stuffed several coca leaves into her mouth, and started walking.

The next few days dragged for Adi. While the group had slowed down to make it easier for her, every step she took sent pain through her shoulder. Nayara gave her everything they had to lessen it—sarsaparilla root, guayacan leaves, and even suma root—but it still wasn't enough and at the end of each day, she was always pale and drenched in sweat.

"You need more sleep," Nayara told her as she sat down, handing her a couple small pieces of fish. "Otherwise it won't heal."

Adi didn't reply as she ate, listening to the others around the fire talk about what they wanted to build in their new home. She knew Nayara was right, her body needed to be still, but she also knew that they weren't far enough away yet to stop. She wasn't sure how much longer it would take, but she trusted that when it was time, she would know.

A burst of laughter distracted her and she looked up, watching as Lupita playfully threw a handful of dirt at Benito. He was smiling slightly and as she looked at him, a surge of determination ran through her. Nothing was going to happen to him, not if she could help it. She was adjusting the sling around her shoulder when a large hand slid silently over her mouth.

Adi woke to the feeling of being bounced up and down, the sound of water lapping against her head. Looking up, she could see nothing but an empty sky, the wind whipping against her skin as they moved at a fast pace. She tried to push herself up, but couldn't, her hands tied to the side, so she gingerly crawled onto her knees and peered over the edge.

She was in one of three boats travelling upriver, the pale morning light guiding their way as they slipped effortlessly along the water. Looking over into the boat beside her, she could see her friends lying on the bottom, several men dressed in black and green camouflage sitting around them. She was straining to see into the other one, searching for Benito, when the rope on her wrists reached its limit and she was jerked back down onto the floor.

"The more you struggle, the more it hurts," a calm voice said to her left.

Adi rolled over and looked at the man in front of her. He was in the same black and green outfit as the others and a bandana on his face covered everything but his eyes. She said nothing for a moment as she studied him, his body relaxed as he casually sat near the front of the boat, slowly peeling a green guava.

"What do you want?" she asked.

He said nothing.

"Are you bringing us to him?"

Finished eating the fruit, he rinsed his hands off in the water and said, "Rest. You have a long journey ahead."

An hour later, they landed on the riverbank and were directed out of the boats. Tied in a row along a single rope, they were led into the jungle, the terrain turning into a straight climb up the mountain. For hours they pushed, struggling up the hills as the men forced them along, giving them a shove forward whenever they slowed down. Adi's leg and shoulder throbbed with pain from the pace and just when she thought she couldn't take another step, they stopped at the top of a hill.

She collapsed onto the ground, blood pounding in her ears.

"Get up," one of the men said as he took a few steps towards her.

Struggling to regain her breath, she pushed up with her arms but her muscles were too weak and they gave out, sending her back down to the ground.

"Get up," the man repeated, but this time more angrily.

"Give her a minute," she heard Marcelo say from somewhere behind her.

The man turned and the next thing she heard was a groan. Looking back, she saw Marcelo doubled over and watched the man walk back up to her.

"Get up."

It took everything she had to stand back on her feet and as soon as she did, they were marched forward once more.

They climbed again, but this time they moved slower, unable to ignore the fatigue of the group. Finally reaching the top of a steep hill, they stopped and Adi's body pounded with exhaustion. Then she saw the men pulling black hoods out of their bags.

"No," was all she managed to say before she was shrouded in darkness.

She forced herself to breathe, trying not to panic as she stood there blinded, unsure of what the men were going to do. But when she felt the rope pull her forward, she swallowed the lump in her throat and carefully took a step ahead.

Their journey in the dark was by no means easy or quick. Someone at the back must have fallen because she heard a couple of surprised grunts before she was pulled down from behind, the rope taking everyone out. Helping each of them back onto their feet took a while and Adi could hear the men cursing in frustration as she stood there, waiting to be moved along again.

They continued once more, climbing higher as they wound their way up the mountain. She was beginning to think that the hills were never going to end when suddenly, it flattened out into what felt like a well-worn path. They hadn't been walking for long when she heard it, a familiar yet foreign sound drifting through the trees towards her. At first it was quiet, but as they kept going, it grew louder and by the time she rounded a corner, she had no doubt. There was a village, somewhere in front of them.

They stopped and someone said, "Separate them."

Unsure of what that meant but unable to do anything, Adi waited for her fate. She felt a hand on her shoulder directing her over when the same voice said, "No, not her. Bring her to the room."

As she was led away, she could hear Evita whimpering behind her. She struggled against her constraints, but the man took her by the shoulders and walked her ahead, the strength and pain from his grip too much to overcome.

They walked about a hundred feet before they turned and Adi was shoved forward, hitting the floor with a thud as a door clicked shut. Groaning as she rolled onto her back, she reached up and removed the hood.

She was in a small room with only a chair and a blanket set off to the side. She leaned against the wall and tried to think. While this could be the man with the scar, she didn't believe it was. He wouldn't have known what direction they had gone in and even if he had, he would've come from behind, not in front. Besides, he never would've gone through all this trouble to keep them alive.

Remembering the knife up her sleeve, she cut away her restraints, looking for a way out. With no windows and only the one door, she crouched along the wall beside it and waited. Eventually, someone would come and she'd get her chance.

It took longer than she expected, but someone did come. Hearing the door unlatch, she readied herself, knife in hand. As soon as the man entered, she lunged, stabbing him in the side. He groaned in pain, slouching as she ran past, avoiding his outstretched arm as she darted out of the room.

Stepping past the door, she found herself in a hallway, the sunshine seeping in through the windows. Although it wasn't fancy, the building and its size stunned her. It was a permanent structure, made of rocks and cement, and while it was well-maintained, she could tell it had been here for a while. Taken aback, it took her a second to refocus. Pushing her many questions to the back of her mind, she started running down the hallway, but as she rounded the corner, she skidded to a halt. Three men were walking towards her and it only took them one look to know that she wasn't supposed to be there. She spun and sprinted the other way, but didn't make it far before she felt several strong arms latch onto her and drag her back to the room.

ψ

Adi had been left tied to the chair for the rest of the day. She woke up the next morning to two men entering, one standing against the wall while the other gave her some water.

"That's enough," the man at the door said firmly. The other one left.

After a chair was placed in front of her, she watched as a woman entered and casually sat down, saying nothing as the man shut the door. He eyed her suspiciously from his position against the wall.

Adi studied the woman in front of her. She had long dark hair, the bulk of it twisted into a braid that laid against her shoulder, and her skin was smooth, a few wrinkles surrounding the lightest green eyes Adi had ever seen. She was dressed in clean clothes that fit her comfortably and as far as Adi could tell, she carried no weapons. The woman looked at her with a smile, and seemed incredibly relaxed.

"You and your friends are causing quite the stir," she said finally. "No one wants to talk." When Adi didn't reply, she continued. "By the number of weapons you carry and what you can clearly do with them, it seems you're not particularly friendly." She paused. "But I suppose those are important traits to have when you're wandering around by yourselves in the middle of nowhere." She waited but got no response. "We won't hurt you," she said after a moment. "All I require is a few answers. Then you'll be free to go."

Adi thought about what to do. While she wanted to believe the woman, she wasn't sure she should. They had been kidnapped and forced to come here. Who does that for a bit of information? But as she sat there in her restraints, she knew she didn't have a choice.

"I want to see my brother," she said finally. "Then I'll answer your questions."

The woman smiled. "What's his name?"

"Benito."

The woman turned and nodded at the man waiting by the door. A few minutes later, he returned and as soon as Benito saw her, he ran up and placed a hand on her shoulder.

"You okay?" she asked quietly.

He nodded.

"The others?"

"Fine."

Adi looked him over. He seemed alright; in fact, he looked cleaner than before. She was about to ask another question when the woman interrupted.

"Time to go."

Benito gone, the woman adjusted in her chair. "What are you doing in this area?"

Taking a moment, Adi focused on the question. While she would answer, she wouldn't give any more than she had to. "Looking for a place to live."

"Why?"

"Our old one wasn't safe."

"Where was that?"

"Northeast of where you found us."

The woman nodded slowly. "Was it a village?"

"Sort of."

"Explain."

Adi thought for a minute before she replied. "There was a bunch of us that lived together in a camp."

The woman nodded. "Where did you come from?"

Adi hesitated. It was a straightforward question, but her answer was more complicated than she cared to share. "The city."

"Is that where your friends are from?"

"Some. Others we met here."

"Are there others?"

"At the camp?"

The woman nodded.

She hesitated again, unsure if she should tell the truth. There was no way the woman would know if she was lying, but then again, the woman didn't know where the camp was either. "Yes," she replied.

"And they didn't come with you." It was more a statement than a question.

"No, they wanted to stay."

"Even though it wasn't safe?"

She nodded.

"What made you leave, instead of staying with the others?"

Adi squirmed in her chair. She was stiff and sore from sitting so long and the questions were beginning to make her uncomfortable. But deciding that the answer wouldn't risk anything, she said, "People in the villages around us were dying. So we left before it happened to us. Not everyone wanted to come."

The woman was silent. When she spoke again, her voice was different. "Where are your parents?"

Not expecting the question, her body tensed. "Dead."

She studied her. "And the others'? Where are their parents?"

Adi shrugged. She honestly didn't know.

"So, this village you built is made up of children and no adults?"

While the question was simple enough, it irritated her. She had been on her own for years and others even longer. It happened all the time and she didn't understand why people were shocked. Her irritation was obvious. "Why is that so hard to believe? Do we look like children to you?"

The woman gave her a sad smile. "No, you do not." She silently observed Adi before she spoke again. "Roberto, take her to Señorita Perez."

Adi sat there in confusion as the man forced her from the chair. Was that honestly all the woman wanted to know? But when she was led down the hallway to another room, she forgot all about it.

She sat still as the woman began examining the wound in her shoulder, unable to pretend that the infected claw marks didn't hurt like hell. When a plate of food was placed in front of her, she tried to ignore it but eventually gave in, the hunger overtaking her determination. After drinking her weight in water, she had her first hot bath in three years. The water stung at first, but her wounds slowly soothed, her body relaxing in the warmth. She told herself she would figure everything out once she was done with the bath, but as her chin dropped heavily down onto her chest, she never got the chance. She was fast asleep.

ψ

Adi woke almost two days later. She found herself in a bed in a small room, her wounds bandaged and her hair washed. Dressing herself in the clothes she found draped over the back of a chair, she walked out of the room.

The sun was bright on her face as she exited, cautiously going down the hallway, unsure of where she was. People passing by didn't give her a second look and as a small group of children ran ahead of her, Adi quickly followed.

Less than a minute later, she was in a large opening, the midday sun beating down on her. Looking around, she watched as people played football, washed clothes, and sat around in groups, their happy voices filling the air. The yard was surrounded by buildings that formed a circle, and as she looked past them, her eyes landed on a large wall that surrounded the village. She was watching two people at the wall, guns casually slung over their shoulders, when she was startled from behind.

"You look lost."

She turned, recognizing the voice but not the face.

"I'm Kaue," he said.

Realizing he was the man from the boat, she examined him. He was tall—taller than even Rodrigo—and had a muscular build, shockingly similar to that of her father's. He wore a relaxed smile and there was something about his eyes that made Adi feel like he wasn't there to hurt her, something kind and reassuring.

"Adi," she replied, her voice hoarse. When he said nothing else, she couldn't help but ask, "What is this place?"

He smiled at her question. "It's a village, like any other."

"No," she replied shaking her head. "It's not."

He gave her a knowing smile. A loud cheer distracted her and she watched a couple people run around the yard, celebrating the goal they just scored.

"How many people live here?"

"Hard to say," Kaue replied. "Seventy or eighty."

"What do they all do?"

He smiled again. "What regular people do."

"Why do you live out here?"

Kaue laughed. "Full of questions, aren't you?" When she didn't join in his humour, he said, "Come on. Let's go get you some answers."

She followed him back into the building, down the hallway, and out the other side, coming up to the wall. Motioning to the man at the gate, it opened and they walked out into the jungle.

Kaue said nothing as she followed him down a well-worn path through the foliage.

"Where are we going?" she asked, hoping for any information. She didn't have her knives and she felt naked without them.

"To see Helena," he replied.

"Who?"

"The woman you spoke to when you first arrived."

After a few moments, she asked, "When do I get my stuff back?"

"You mean your weapons?"

176

She didn't bother answering.

"What makes you think you deserve them?"

She thought it over. It wasn't a matter of deserving them; she needed them.

"You'll get them back when Helena decides you're trustworthy enough to have them," he said when she was quiet. "Besides, you don't need them in the village. You're perfectly safe."

Although Adi doubted that very much, she knew saying so wouldn't get her what she wanted.

"Where did you learn how to fight anyway?" Kaue asked. "Emilio didn't even see you coming."

She quietly stepped over a rotten tree stump, remembering the man she had stabbed. They didn't trust her and the feeling was mutual. Until she knew what they wanted, she wasn't going to share anything she didn't have to. "I'll tell you when I get my stuff back."

She didn't have to see his face to know he was smiling, but as she looked up into the trees above her, it took everything she had not to jump. A camouflaged man sat on a branch watching her below.

"How many men do you have out here?" she asked, happy that she sounded so confident.

Kaue looked back and followed her gaze up into the tree. "You spotted him. Impressive." He continued walking. "We have people all over. How do you think we found you?"

Adi tried to process what he was saying, but found it difficult. "You have people all the way out there? Why?"

He smiled again. "I'll let Helena explain that."

Looking ahead, she could see that more light was beginning to filter in around them and when the trees suddenly stopped, she saw Helena standing near the mountain's edge.

She smiled as they approached, but Adi barely noticed, staring at the view in front of her. They were on top of the highest mountain range in the area and as she looked around her, she saw nothing but untouched jungle moving up and down the hills surrounding them. Rivers snaked along the valley floor, bending and twisting to the will of the mountains, and hearing the faint sound of a waterfall nearby, Adi looked down but stepped back in alarm. The earth ended directly in front of them, a cliff plummeting straight down for longer than she cared to look.

"Peaceful, isn't it?" Helena said.

Adi nodded, opting to look straight ahead.

"I come here when I need to think," she continued. "It gives me perspective."

Not knowing what she meant, Adi said nothing as she looked out into the open sky.

"Walk with me."

Adi moved beside her in silence as they went down a trail that wove along the clifftop, Kaue following casually behind.

"So," Helena started after a minute, "how do you like our village?"

She didn't know what to say. She had only seen a small part and still wasn't sure what they wanted. "It's different," she replied.

Helena smiled. "It is different. Kaue tells me that your name is Adi. Is that short for Adelita?"

"Yes," she replied, wondering why that was important.

Helena said nothing else and they walked for a few minutes, eventually stopping alongside the cliff once more.

"Why did you ask me all those questions before?" If they weren't going to give her any information, the least she could do was ask.

Helena smiled. "I needed to know who you were."

She didn't understand. "And now you know?"

"No, but I know who you are *not*, and that is more important."

Her answer confused her further, so she pressed on. "And why's that?"

"We live a peaceful life here. Our village is safe, our people are protected and we plan to keep it that way. Anyone who wanders into our territory is considered a threat. The answers to those questions tell me who you are and who you are not."

"But we weren't anywhere near your village. How could we have been in your territory?"

Helena turned to face her, her green eyes focused. "Tell me, how many people did you encounter after you left your last home?"

"None," Adi replied, feeling a bit vulnerable under her stare.

"Exactly," she said. "No one comes this way. There are no trails, the river system is almost impossible to navigate, and yet, there you were with your friends, walking through the forest where no one should be."

"So your land goes past this mountain and into the valley where you found us?" She didn't quite believe her. She would need hundreds of people to watch it all. When Helena didn't reply, she asked, "How is that possible?"

Helena smiled. "Have you ever been alone in the trees before? With no one else around?"

"Yes."

"And what do you hear?"

"The jungle."

"Right. The jungle and all its sounds. And what happens when a foreign presence enters, an unfamiliar event occurs?"

She hesitated before answering. "It goes silent."

Helena nodded. "It goes silent. And what happens to a sound when everything else is silent?"

"It travels," Adi replied, the answer suddenly dawning on her. "The gunshot. You heard the gunshot."

Helena smiled. "We don't need to be everywhere at once because the jungle watches for us. It tells us when something is there that shouldn't be, and it tells us when everything is alright. When that gun went off, the jungle told us that something was wrong, that something was there that didn't belong. And there you were."

Adi thought it over, wondering exactly how far the sound travelled. If someone had been following them and they heard the shot, could they find them here? Her thoughts were interrupted by Helena moving again.

"Tell me about the deaths at the villages," she said as she walked down the path. "Do you know who did it?"

Adi hesitated. She had already told her more than she cared to. While she seemed trustworthy, there was something she wasn't telling her. They were too well armed and had too many look-outs. Something was going on and she needed to know what. "I'll tell you if you tell me why you guard your village so well."

Helena said nothing for a moment as she walked ahead of her. "It is simply the smart thing to do," she said eventually. "We are protecting ourselves from the many threats that might occur."

"I find that hard to believe," Adi said, surprising them both. She didn't mean to say it out loud, but it was too late.

"That's unfortunate," Helena replied, not missing a beat.

They went back to the village in silence. As soon as they got to the wall, Helena stopped. "I hope you choose to stay here, Adelita, you and your friends, but it is ultimately up to you. If you want to leave, you will exit the way you came in, blindfolded and bound. But if you decide to stay, I can offer you safety and protection. It's your choice."

Adi had to find the others and ask, but when she looked up at the village gate, she already knew what their answer would be.

Chapter Fourteen

The only thing she heard was the sound of her own breathing, each inhale under control. She could feel a small trickle of blood slowly making its way down her forehead as the vision in her right eye began to blur, unable to stop the swelling. Ignoring the pulsating pain in her jaw, her lips curled into a smile.

She swung wide with the stick she held in her left hand, hoping it would distract from the stick in her right. But her opponent saw through it, easily blocking both attempts before coming at her aggressively. Forced backwards, Adi tried to stop the attack, struggling to keep up with the pace and strength of the blows. So occupied with what was coming at her, she didn't see the hole in the ground behind her and she stumbled, almost dropping to her knee as she fought to keep her balance.

The opportunity wasn't missed by her adversary and she charged, swinging hard and fast. Adi thought she had gotten through the worst of it until she felt the stick slam into her left side, the wood biting into her bones, sending waves of pain through her torso. Knowing she couldn't falter now, she rushed forward, pushing her attacker back with everything she had. Widening her stance to re-stabilize herself, she prepared for the next charge. Her opponent advanced and Adi took a deep breath as she carefully watched her movements, eyes focused on her hands. The first blow came high, aimed straight at her head, and as Adi lifted her stick up to block it, she only caught half of it, the wood cracking down onto her arm.

Momentarily stunned by the pain, she almost failed to see the second swing and lurched backwards just in time, the stick grazing her cheek. She was gathering her strength to go on the offensive when a strong kick to the chest caught her off-guard and the next thing she knew, she was lying flat on her back.

Adi stayed on the ground, trying to figure out where it had all gone wrong when her opponent calmly walked over. Staring down at her in the dirt, she held out her hand. Adi reached up and was pulled onto her feet.

The moment Kaue had introduced her to his wife, Mariana, Adi knew she liked her. But once Mariana started training her how to fight, Adi *loved* her, and training was by far her favourite part of the day, even if she got her ass kicked every time.

"You did well," Mariana said. She gently brushed the blood off her cheek. "You're starting to anticipate my moves."

She stood still as she let Mariana look at her eye. It didn't feel like she was doing well. It hurt to breathe and the ache in her arm was bone deep.

As if sensing her disappointment, Mariana said quietly, "You're faster than Kaue."

Surprised, Adi jerked her head back and saw the twinkle in her eye.

Mariana grinned. "Don't tell him I said that. Otherwise he'll pout."

She couldn't help but smile. When they first arrived, she thought Kaue was nothing but kind, but when she went out hunting for the first time, she saw a completely different side. He was competitive as hell. So much so that when Rodrigo came back with a peccary *and* a caiman, Kaue refused to return to the village until he had caught more.

The smile stayed on her face until Mariana pressed down on the cut on her scalp, making her grimace.

"You'll live," she said as she stepped back, patting her cheek just a little too hard. "Now go before you're late."

Adi nodded and turned, putting the sticks back in the pile before she made her way towards the building. Not having time to wash, she quickly dumped a bucket of water over her head and changed her clothes. By the time she walked into Señorita Perez's clinic, Nayara was already there. The moment she saw Adi, she burst out laughing.

Adi rolled her eyes as she walked up and carefully sat down in a chair, gingerly holding her side.

"Let's have a look," Señorita Perez said. She patted the table that sat on the right side of the room.

Doing as she was told, she laid down, slowly exhaling as her head hit the pillow.

"Come here, Nayara," Señorita Perez instructed. "Carefully, feel along her side."

Nayara pressed her fingers up her torso, Adi gasping in pain as soon as she hit the spot.

"Keep going," Señorita Perez encouraged. Nayara continued, causing her to whimper a few more times.

"Anything broken?" Señorita Perez asked.

"No," Nayara replied, carefully going back over them.

"Good," she said with a smile. "Now, get off my table."

They spent the next two hours with Señorita Perez, like they did every other day, helping her with anyone who was sick or injured. When no one needed treatment, Señorita Perez would teach them everything from how to properly set a broken bone to how to treat a cold. While Adi thought she already knew a lot about the plants in the jungle, learning from her made her realize that there was so much more she didn't know. Sarsaparilla vine could be used to treat arthritis and skin conditions, guayacan tree leaves helped to treat weakness and fatigue, while the calabash tree was used to induce labour. As she listened to Nayara name off plants and their healing properties from memory, Adi couldn't help but think about the first time they met. Nayara was different—everyone was—and as she watched the joy in her face, she knew they had made the right choice by staying.

On most days, Adi would spend the afternoon with her friends while the younger ones were attending the small school near the centre of the village. Rodrigo and Giovana would be finished hunting, Catalina would be done working on the house in the corner and Marcelo would be ending his shift with Kaue on the wall. But today was a Tuesday, which meant that Helena would be waiting for her. Late from lingering at Señorita Perez's, Adi grabbed a mango and a piece of dried fish from the kitchen before walking to the gate.

As soon as she passed through the wall, she slowed down, seeing who was waiting on the other side. Adi said nothing as she ripped off a piece of fish and ate it, staring into the angry face in front of her.

"Where's my abuela?" he asked after a moment, his glare unwavering.

The first time she met Thiago, it hadn't gone well. She had been walking with Helena when a man a bit older than her suddenly appeared on the trail ahead of them. Having no weapons, she immediately picked a stick up off the ground ready to fight when Helena wrapped him in a hug. She said nothing as she watched them, seeing the happiness on Helena's face and the concern on his.

"Who's this?" he had asked, looking at Adi.

"Adelita," Helena said, turning back to her. "Come meet my grandson."

As she came towards them, she watched as his face changed from concern to confusion, his bright brown eyes intently studying her.

"What are you two doing out here?" he asked, looking back to his grandmother.

"Adelita and I are discussing the importance of purposeful work in the community," Helena had answered. The look on his face darkened.

When he spoke, his voice was low, causing her skin to prickle with uncertainty. "You've chosen *her*?" he asked, his tone incredulous.

While she hadn't known what he meant, and still didn't, she knew it was bad. Every time they passed through the same space, he looked at her with absolute disdain. Looking into his face now, she could tell nothing had changed.

"Don't know," she replied as she continued to eat the fish.

When she said nothing else, he huffed haughtily. "Do you even care about any of this? About any of the things she does for you?"

Adi remained silent, knowing nothing she said would be good enough for him.

"You have no idea, do you? How important this is?"

"What's going on out here?" Rodrigo's voice cut through the tension.

A dark frown covered Thiago's face as he folded his arms across his chest, unhappy about being interrupted. "Nothing," he replied, focusing his irritation on Rodrigo.

Adi could feel Rodrigo looking at her, but she refused to turn her head, opting to keep staring out into the trees.

"Doesn't look like nothing," Rodrigo replied, reading her defensive body language like the back of his hand. While she didn't care what Thiago thought of her, it clearly bothered Rodrigo. "What's your problem with her exactly?" he asked.

Thiago smiled condescendingly. "It's none of your fucking business."

Rodrigo laughed, taking a few steps closer to him. "Oh, I think it is."

Although she could feel the testosterone-riddled tension fill the air around them, she was in no mood to stop a fight. Her body hurt from training and her mind was trying to figure out what Thiago's words meant. There was something she didn't know and it was beginning to bother her.

"Hey!" someone shouted from on top of the wall.

She looked up at Vagner standing above them.

"Cut it out," he commanded. When neither Thiago nor Rodrigo moved, he said, "If you stand there for one more second, I'm gonna come down and beat the piss outta both of you."

Adi hid her smile as Thiago angrily went back into the village and as Rodrigo approached, she turned and watched the frown drop from his face.

"Shit," he swore under his breath as he reached up and gently touched her eye. "Mariana?"

She smirked and nodded as she dug her fingers into the mango's skin.

"You're the only person I know who enjoys that," he said as he leaned up against the wall beside her.

She shrugged as she handed him a chunk of fruit. "Catalina and Gio seem to. And don't forget Lupita."

Rodrigo huffed in response as he chewed on the mango. "Gio will shoot anything and Catalina is obsessed with knives. And Lupita..." his voice trailed off. "Lupita is something else."

She chuckled softly at the seriousness of his tone. Ever since Lupita had been shown how to fight at Salvador's camp, she took to it like a bird to flight. Although she was only nine years old and small for her age, it was like the floodgates had opened and out poured years of rage and frustration. At everyone's insistence, Adi had made her promise to stick to a few rules and in return, she would teach her everything she could. While the others were afraid of her, she knew that fighting was Lupita's way of dealing with her past.

"What are you doing out here?" he asked. "Waiting for Helena?"

She nodded as she threw away the pit and wiped the juice off her hands and onto her pants. She was about to say something when a sharp whistle from inside the village drew her attention. Turning, she saw Emilio waving her over.

"I'll see you later," she said to Rodrigo as she jogged back in through the gate. Stopping in front of Emilio, she asked, "Yes?"

"You're wanted in the room," he replied.

"What room?" she asked, but she got no response as he was already walking away.

A few minutes later, they entered a hallway Adi had never been in, stopping in front of a simple, brown door. Opening it, he waited for her to walk through before shutting the door loudly behind her.

All alone, she looked around, noticing the large table in the middle, a low-hanging light centered above it. The room was dim and as her vision adjusted, she saw something she couldn't take her eyes off of: a map. It had everything on it—rivers, villages, towns, mountain ranges—but as she walked towards it, she saw that it was so much more. So captivated by it, she didn't hear her come in.

"Interesting, isn't it?" Helena said as she walked up to the table, causing Adi to jump.

Turning, she saw the small smile on Helena's face. "What do the red x's mean?"

Helena looked at her for a moment. "I have something for you."

She was wondering why she wasn't answering her question until she saw what Helena was holding. She smiled, taking the bundle from her outstretched hands.

"I get to keep them?" she asked as she examined her knives, the familiar feeling of the handles sending excitement through her body.

"Yes." Helena smiled. "They're yours."

She looked each blade up and down, checking for wear. Finding none, she gently slid them back into their covers, placing them in various positions around her body. She could feel Helena watching and when she looked up, she could tell that there was something she wasn't saying. "Why are you giving these to me now?" she asked.

Helena sat down on the stool beside the table. "You're ready."

"Ready for what?"

"For your trip out."

While she knew that there were people who left the village to get supplies, she also knew that only a select few went. Since they arrived, she hadn't gone more than a hundred feet from the wall and although going deeper into the jungle didn't frighten her, travelling to a strange town and meeting unfamiliar people did. As doubts flooded her mind, she instinctively touched the knife up her sleeve and Helena continued.

"There'll be a group of you going," she said as she studied her face. "You'll meet them just outside the gate, one hour before sunrise."

Adi couldn't help but feel like there was more riding on this than just a supply run. She wasn't sure what, but perhaps this was what Thiago was talking about. Perhaps this was a test for something. But regardless of what she felt, and however uncertain she was, she needed to prove that she could do this. Pushing her fears aside, she forced a smile. "Okay."

Adi woke up much earlier than she needed to. She lightly caressed the hair on Benito's head one last time as he slept, grabbed her bag, and headed to the gate.

"Ready to go?" Vagner asked as she approached, his dark silhouette emerging from the wall's shadow.

"Think so," she replied, hoping her voice sounded more confident than she felt.

She could see his smile through the darkness. "Everyone's nervous on their first run," he said. "But don't worry, you're in good hands."

Adi nodded and walked through the gate, wondering whose hands exactly she would be in.

As the darkness began to thin, she waited for the others in silence, thinking about what they were being sent off to do. When she told Benito she was leaving, he had tried to hide his disappointment, but she saw it, a pang of guilt shooting through her as she looked at his worried face. Even though she promised she was coming back, she could tell he didn't completely believe her. Feeling a shiver run down her spine, she reached into her bag and pulled a second shirt over her head.

"You won't need that."

As soon as she heard the voice, she froze and inwardly groaned, trying to ignore the feeling of dread passing over her. If this was a test, Helena sure wasn't making it easy.

"Please tell me you're not coming with," she said as she pulled the rest of her shirt down over her torso and turned around.

Thiago smirked as he walked up, answering her question as he placed his bag on the ground.

"Unfortunately," the man beside him began, his tone light, "we need him." He gave Adi a warm smile. "I don't think we've met," he said. "I'm Miguel."

Adi nodded, surprised by how young he was. She had heard people around the village talking about him, but had never seen him. All she knew was that he was the runner Helena chose when no one else could get what they needed. Hearing footsteps behind her, she turned and watched Catalina and Marcelo walk up.

"Alright," Miguel said as he stood in front of them. "Before we leave, we need to go over the rules. First, you'll do exactly as I say the moment I say it. No arguments, no hesitating. Second, we leave with five, we return with five. We don't leave unless we have everyone. And third, under no circumstances will you give out any information to anyone—ever. No names, no places, not even what kind of flowers you saw blooming the other day. Nada. If someone asks you a question, you lie and keep your answers short. I don't care what you tell them, but you are not to reveal any information about our life here. That is the only way this works. Understood?" Seeing everyone nod, Miguel clapped. "Good. Let's go."

They followed him silently into the trees single file, the sky just light enough to see where they were going. The jungle was thick and tangled, forcing them to walk, but when it finally opened up that afternoon, they ran.

Running through the trees was one of Adi's favourite things to do. It made her feel untouchable and as the air gently caressed her face, she smiled, the worry lifting from her shoulders. They ran until they no longer could, stopping only when it became too dark to see and starting again as soon as the morning light sifted in. Other than almost being spotted by a few people on a trail on the second day, they continued like this for the next two days, going up and over mountains, crossing rivers, and passing through valleys. Just as Adi was about to ask when they would get there, Miguel suddenly changed direction.

"Why are we going east?" Marcelo asked the same question in her head. They had been traveling in that direction for almost two hours and it was beginning to make Adi uncomfortable. She had no desire to go even remotely close to the places she had fled.

Ignoring the question, Miguel finished eating his orange and used his shirt to wipe off his hands. "Put these on," he said. He pulled some long-sleeved shirts out of his bag, throwing one to each person. "Make sure your knives and guns are hidden. If you can't hide it, it goes in your pack."

Taking off her shirt, Adi threw the new one on, the dull, shapeless fabric going almost to the middle of her thighs. With most of her knives already hidden in strategic places around her body, she only had to readjust her largest and favourite knife, taking it off her back and shoving it into her pack, the handle peeking out of the top. She tucked the large shirt into her pants, leaving it a bit loose at the back so she could access her gun, and threw her bag back on.

"We're going east," Miguel finally answered as they finished changing, "because that's the direction we want to be seen entering the town."

It took them another hour to reach the road, Miguel explaining the plan as they walked. They needed to make two stops once they arrived. He would go to the store with Catalina and Marcelo while Thiago would take Adi to meet his contact. When they had what they needed, they would meet back in the trees.

Adi's heart pounded as they stepped onto the empty road. They walked along in a small cluster but as soon as she heard a vehicle, she had to force herself to stay calm. It had been a while since she had heard or seen a truck and as she carefully watched it drive past, she exhaled and removed her hand from her gun. A few more went by and the closer they got to the town, the more people they encountered. By the time the first few buildings came into view, Adi had relaxed.

They had been walking through the town for about five minutes when Miguel suddenly turned right, Catalina and Marcelo following. Remembering the plan, Adi quickly caught up with Thiago as they continued down the main street.

She had planned on asking him who they were going to meet, but as she looked around, she forgot all about it. She had never been to a place like this before; it was smaller than a city but much bigger than a village. It was quiet and yet had a distinctive hum to it, one that she couldn't place. While there were people out on the street, it wasn't overcrowded and everyone casually walked along, some of them even nodding as they passed.

They continued for about twenty minutes before they reached the other end of town, the stores thinning out as warehouses began to take their place.

"This is how it's going to work," Thiago said as he stopped and turned towards her, refocusing her wandering attention. "Once we get in there, you don't say a word. I've been working this contact for two months straight and I won't have you screwing it up."

Adi said nothing as she crossed her arms, waiting for him to finish.

"This package is important and it requires a certain type of..." He struggled to find the word. "Charm. So I'll do the talking."

She wanted to tell him to shove it, but she knew nothing about this, so she glared at him before finally nodding.

Satisfied, Thiago turned and walked up to a building ten feet down the street, Adi slowly following. As she approached, she couldn't help but notice that it had no name, sign, or windows, but that was all she had time to see as Thiago was already halfway through the door.

She blinked a couple times as her eyes adjusted to the dim light, the dinginess of the room becoming apparent as she looked around. Besides the tables and chairs that filled the room, there was a bar to their left, a long counter with stools lined up alongside. The room was empty except for three men who sat around a table, tucked into the back corner.

"Stay here," Thiago said. He left her by the bar, walking towards the men.

Sitting on a stool, she watched as they greeted Thiago, welcoming him to sit as soon as he approached.

"Wanna drink?" a voice asked. She turned towards it.

The bartender smiled at her, his yellow teeth filling his thin face as he stared down at her. His eyes were a soft brown, but there was a hardness in them that she didn't like, sending a small shiver down her spine. He smelled like the cheap cigarettes they used to steal in the city.

"No," she said simply. She looked over at Thiago, wishing she was there instead.

She was twisting a napkin in her hand when Thiago turned and waved her over. Thankful to get away from the stench of body odor, she walked towards the group.

She was thinking about how happy she would be once they were back at the village when the faces of the men suddenly came into view. The impact of who she saw sent a numbing sensation through her body. It took every fibre in her being to keep moving forward and hide the shock on her face. She could see their mouths moving, but didn't hear a word. By the time she reached the table, her back was drenched in sweat. Sitting in front of her, with broad smiling faces, were the men who murdered her sister.

ψ

Never in her life did she think she would be in this position. Her heart was pounding, but she could hear them, their voices sounding like nails on a chalkboard as Thiago listened intently, nodding at all the right times. She was holding onto the chair in front of her, perhaps too tightly, and as she looked at them around the table, Toro's intense gaze met hers. She turned away, finding herself focusing on Pedro Martinez's fat mouth as he spoke, a smile on his lips. Oscar Fuentes said nothing, his small hand casually wrapped around his cup as he watched Thiago attentively.

Unable to take it anymore, Adi suddenly said, "I'll be outside," cutting Martinez off mid-sentence.

Her back burned from the intensity of their stares as she left the bar as fast as she dared, almost crying in relief when she burst outside, the fresh air clinging to her face. Hearing the door slamming shut behind her, she leaned over and gasped, her body numb. She stayed there for a few moments, trying to simply comprehend what, *who*, she had just seen, but as a couple tears dropped down into the dirt, she clamped a hand over her mouth, struggling to muffle the painful scream that was attempting to escape.

She pushed herself back up, needing to move. Every cell in her body felt like it was about to burst from her skin. She started walking down the street, oblivious to the odd glances she was getting. A million thoughts ran through her head as she tried to comprehend what was happening and when her mind eventually moved past the shock, only one question remained: How the hell were they still alive?

The last time she had seen the three of them, they were driving away from the village, hauling children and old men off to fight, leaving Adi and what was left of her family to cry over Leti's dead body. She remembered seeing the trucks drive out, her eyes so full of tears that her vision blurred. It was the first time in her life that she had been completely consumed by rage, its effect almost calming as she swore she would kill them the moment they returned. But they never came back to the village and as she walked up and down the street, that familiar feeling rushed to life inside her once again, caressing her bones like an old friend. By the time she made her way back to the bar, she knew what she had to do.

She was leaning against a post about twenty feet away when Thiago exited the building, his eyes narrowing the moment he spotted her. He didn't say a word as he walked up, grabbed her by the arm and pulled her into an alley.

"What the hell was that?" he asked, fighting to keep his voice down.

"Nothing," Adi replied, her tone measured and even.

Thiago looked like he wanted to kill her and he took a moment before he said, "That's bullshit. You almost tanked the deal. They weren't going to give it to me until I convinced them that something was wrong with your brain."

She bit down hard on her lower lip, the thought that she was mentally unstable making her laugh. With what she was dreaming about doing to them, he probably wasn't far off.

"Even after that, they seemed skeptical," he continued. "They're probably never going to sell to me again."

"So you got it?"

He glared at her for a moment. "Yeah, I got it."

"Good," she replied. "Let's go."

Their walk back through the town and down the road was silent, the sun gently warming her face. She didn't know how it was going to happen, but for the first time in a long time, she felt as though she had purpose, like her life had been leading up to this moment. If she had met them at any other time, she doubted she would've been ready but, here, now, she was more than capable of doing this. Carefully looking around before stepping off the road and into the trees, Adi smiled. She was finally going to get some justice.

It took the others about an hour to arrive, their bags full. Without a word, Miguel led them deeper into the woods, stopping only once it was dark. By her calculations, they were less than ten kilometres away from the town and as she took off the baggy shirt and slid her knife onto her back where it belonged, she knew she had to leave soon if she was going to finish before morning. Resting on the ground, she carefully watched the others as they fell asleep, Marcelo's soft snores filling the air. Even when she was certain that no one was awake, she waited a few more minutes, unwilling to chance it. Not making a sound, she picked up her bag and snuck over to where Catalina was sitting.

"Shit," Catalina said when Adi sat down next to her. "You scared me." It took Catalina a minute to see the bag in her hands, but when she did, a cross look passed over her face. "What are you doing?" she asked warily.

Adi hesitated before she answered. She hadn't planned on telling anyone, but when Miguel put Catalina on watch, she knew she couldn't just leave. She couldn't do that to her.

"There's something I need to do," she said, her voice steady. While she wanted to tell her everything, she knew it would be better if she didn't.

Catalina didn't reply as she searched Adi's face, trying to find answers, but when their eyes locked, her face softened and she looked away for a moment. "What do you need me to do?"

Adi smiled and looked down. With everything they'd been through, she never felt more grateful for Catalina than she did in this moment. "Keep watch 'til morning. Go back to the village without me. I'll return when I'm done."

Catalina was quiet for a minute before she nodded.

Having no words to express how she felt, Adi turned to leave when at the last second, Catalina grabbed her arm.

"Promise me you'll come back," she said, staring directly into her eyes. When Adi hesitated, she shook her arm. "Promise me."

Adi exhaled slowly, unsure if she could say such words. But as she looked at Catalina, she reluctantly said, "I promise," and disappeared into the darkness.

She went back the same way they came, but instead of walking along the road, she continued under the cover of the trees, sneaking behind the warehouses that lined the street. As she watched the bar from an alley, she twisted her ponytail into a bun and strapped her pack tightly against her. She had no idea if the men were still there, but knowing that it was her only lead, she casually walked across the street, past the bar to the back. Sliding up against the building, she spotted the backdoor and waited, knowing someone was bound to come out of it sooner or later.

She didn't have to wait long as a little while later, she watched as the skinny bartender walked out, leaning against the building with a cigarette dangled between his lips. She moved as close as she dared, hidden by the darkness, and waited as he finished, his fingers squishing the butt and flicking it onto the ground. As soon as he opened the door, she ran forward.

She could hear the noise from the bar as she approached, grabbing the door right before it closed, its squeaky hinges masked by some laughter as she slipped inside. She walked through the short hallway, stopped at a second door, and peered through the window.

While the bar wasn't packed, it was busy and Adi carefully scanned the crowd, looking for her target. She spotted them in the same spot as before, sitting at the table in the back watching the crowd as people milled about, drinks in their hands. There was no way she could get to them with this many people around. While she might manage to kill one, she'd be stopped before she finished the others and that couldn't happen. She needed to get them alone. She needed to get them out.

She walked back down the hallway, searching for anything that might help, when she found the storage room and entered, locking the door behind her. As she looked at all the alcohol sitting on the shelves against the wall, a plan slowly formed. Shrugging off her pack, she took out the shirt Miguel had given her and threw it on the floor, looking around for more flammable items.

She grabbed cardboard boxes, cleaning rags and even found a couple large stacks of napkins, piling it all together in the centre of the room. Next, she ran over to the shelves and scanned the bottles, finding one without a label. Opening the jar, she was immediately overwhelmed by the smell of alcohol, the sharp odor stinging her eyes. Taking the jars of chirrite, she emptied them onto the floor and soaked the pile. She knew as soon as she lit it, the fire would be quick and hot so she poured a generous line of booze towards the door, stopping about a foot in front. Grabbing her bag, she removed a small metal container and took out a match. She wasn't sure if it would be enough to force the men outside, but as she struck the match against the floor, there was no turning back.

It took less than ten seconds for the fire to travel down the line and reach the pile, the force of it making a whoosh sound as it hit the napkins, the heat stunning Adi as she quickly unlocked the door and ran out, leaving the building. She was running back down the alley towards the street when she stopped, a terrible feeling passing over her. She had planned on watching the front entrance, but what if they came out the back?

Spinning on her heel, she ran back, grabbing a large stick off the ground as she went. She jammed one end of the wood underneath the door handle, kicking the other end tightly into place in the dirt. She was slowly backing away, unsure if it would hold when a loud explosion ripped through the air.

The speed and force of the fire that tore through the building surprised her. She had figured it would take much longer and as she ran back towards the front of the building, she hoped she hadn't made a mistake. If they died in the fire she wouldn't get what was hers, what she was owed. But as soon as she rounded the corner, she saw them, running out of the building with the others, the bartender looking terrified as he screamed at everyone to get back.

A second explosion erupted into the night sky, lighting it up as flames snaked through the roof. The bar patrons stood in stunned silence, watching it burn for a moment before someone sprang into action, sending them all into a flurry of activity.

Adi watched from her hidden position as they tried to salvage as much as they could and prevent the fire from spreading. Distracted by the commotion, she almost missed her three friends walking towards her.

She crouched, hoping the shadows were enough to cover her as Martinez, Fuentes, and Toro walked past, talking as they went. Her heart was pounding so hard that she didn't hear what they were saying, the fright of almost getting caught morphing into anger. Her carelessness had just about cost her. It wouldn't happen again.

She waited a few more moments before she followed, keeping a significant distance between them. They walked for about ten minutes before they turned right, the road sloping up and away from the town. With no other buildings around, Adi lost her cover and she snuck in behind a pile of bricks, watching as they approached a warehouse at the end of the road.

Adi stayed put, her gaze focused on the building as they entered, trying to see if there was another way in. Other than the door, she spotted a couple small windows on the second floor, but they were out of reach and there was no way she could climb up. But when her eyes landed on the large tananeo tree growing close to the side of the building, she smiled.

Convinced no one was watching, she slipped back under the trees, concealing herself as she ran towards the warehouse. As soon as she got close, she sprinted forward and launched herself up the trunk, climbing as fast as she could. High enough, she inched out onto a large branch, feeling it sag under her weight. Although she was hanging above the roof, she was not quite over it and so she swung her body back and forth. After the third swing, she let go, landing on top of the roof with a thud, and quickly dropped down in front of the windows. She searched for a way in, feeling along the edges, but there was none. She was about to give up and return to the ground when another explosion rippled through the air and she didn't hesitate, smashing the glass with the butt of her gun.

Squeezing through the window, Adi landed softly on her feet as she surveyed the room around her. It took her a minute to realize what she saw, but when she finally did, she didn't know what to think. She was in a room full of bullets. Shelves upon shelves of bullets. This was what Thiago was getting.

Her fingers softly touched the shells as she passed. While it didn't surprise her, it made her sick knowing that Helena would buy from people like them. But just as soon as the thought entered her head, she shook it out. Right now, it didn't matter; she was here for something else.

Creeping up to the door, she opened it and looked out, hearing voices coming from below. She pulled out her gun as she stepped into the hallway, carefully making her way down the stairs and towards the noise. Although she was calm, her pulse quickened and she could feel her heart pounding steadily as she passed several tables, walking silently down the wide corridor. Just as she saw the light seeping out from beneath the door, she felt the cold barrel of a gun touch the back of her head and the familiar voice of Toro say, "Don't move."

Adi gritted her teeth, willing herself to remain calm as the metal pressed against her skull, threatening to unleash the panic bubbling at the surface.

"Show me your hands," Toro instructed. "Show me your hands!"

Adi did as she was told but the moment she felt Toro rip the gun from her grasp, in one fluid motion she dropped to her knees, grabbed the knife off her back and spun.

The sound of Toro's shot piercing the air above her head broke away any fear holding her back and she sliced upwards, the blade cutting into his thick leg muscle. She stayed put, watching the shock and fear on his face as he bled out, but as soon as she heard the sound of a door opening, she dove behind his convulsing body.

She barely felt the bullet bite into her calf, the adrenaline pumping heavily as the shots continued, their rapid concession hitting Toro with deadly force. Hearing the comforting click of an empty clip, she sprang up and ran down the hallway, diving into a room as the barrage of bullets began again, her body slamming down hard onto the floor.

Adi gasped as she tried to push herself up, the pain from her shoulder resonating through her upper body. She wasn't sure if it hurt because she landed on it or because there was a bullet lodged tightly in her flesh, but knowing they would be closing in, she scaled a nearby shelf in the corner, and one-handedly lifted herself into the open ceiling.

She could hear someone enter the room, methodically searching around as she hid along a beam. When she looked down, she saw Fuentes right below her. Not wanting to waste her chance, she dropped on top of him, the blade of her knife pointed downwards as she let the weight of her body and gravity do the work. The metal easily and fatally plunged into his neck, his body crumpling to the ground in a heap, taking Adi with him. As she scrambled to her feet, she heard a voice call out.

"Fuentes!" Martinez shouted, his voice betraying just a hint of fear. "Fuentes, you there?"

"No, he's not," Adi answered for him, picking up his gun. But as soon as she reloaded it with the clip from his pocket, she heard Martinez running down the hallway.

She took off after him, refusing to let him escape. He was fast but the warehouse floor was wide open, and she watched as he ran towards the back, ducking into a room at the end just as she closed in. Not hesitating for a second, she emptied the gun into the room, sweeping it back and forth as it kicked repeatedly, jerking her arms forcefully.

"Wait!" he called out the moment she paused, his voice filled with pain. "Stop, for the love of God, please stop."

Unsure if it was a trick, Adi kept the gun trained towards his voice. "Come out," she said, watching cautiously as his figure emerged from the shadows.

Blood was oozing from several places as he came into view, clutching his arm to his side.

"Please don't kill me."

The moment the words were out of his mouth, she fired a single shot, the bullet ripping through his leg. As he dropped screaming onto the ground, Adi found a chair, dragged it into the middle of the room, and grabbed a fist full of his hair, pulling him up onto it.

"Just take it!" he screamed at her, spit flying angrily from his mouth. "You bitch! Just take it and leave!"

She said nothing as he cried, leaning back against the wall in front of him. It surprised her not only how much she was enjoying this, but also how pathetic he looked, bubbling and crying like a fool, as if anything he said could save him. He had been a monster, tormenting her memories, but as she stared at him, she realized that he was just a pathetic, dead man.

"I don't want your guns," she replied quietly, watching the confusion register on his face.

"What then?" he asked, a wave of fear passing over him. "What do you want? Why are you doing this to me?"

Adi stood up straight and took a step towards him. "I'll give you three guesses," she said, not looking away.

"What happens if I guess wrong?"

She smiled. Clearly, he had played this type of game before. More than likely, he had been the one in control, the one dishing out the punishment, and as she stared at the coward in front of her, she couldn't help but feel like this was exactly how it was meant to happen.

"I shoot you," she replied calmly.

"And if I get it right?"

She smiled again, entertained by his optimism. There was no way he would guess right. "I'll let you go," she replied. "Sound fair?"

Martinez nodded.

"Alright then." She leaned back against the wall. "First guess."

Martinez watched her for a moment, trying to read her, but failing. "You came in the bar with that kid," he replied cautiously. "The one who bought the ammo. You didn't like what he got," and before Adi could open her mouth to reply, he quickly added, "and you didn't like the price. You want your money back."

She looked down and smiled, chuckling. He was a smart fucker, she would give him that, but no matter how many guesses he crammed into one, he wouldn't be able to save himself. She looked up and watched the hope on his face fade. "No."

Before he could blink, she pulled the trigger, the bullet slamming into his shoulder. He doubled over, screaming in pain.

She walked up and crouched down so that he could see her face. "This isn't going to end well for you." She pushed his torso back up with the barrel of her gun. "Come on, you can do better than that."

He sobbed as she stood, his cries filling the warehouse. "Just do it," he said. "Just kill me."

While his offer was tempting, Adi wanted more than just revenge for her sister. It was one thing to simply kill those responsible for Leti's death, but another to have them realize why. Out of all the crimes he had committed, all the families he was responsible for breaking, she wanted him to know that it was Leti's death that would be the end of him. That the moment he ripped the life from her beautiful, pure soul was the moment he guaranteed his own, violent death.

"Next guess," Adi said. When he didn't answer, she drove her gun into the wound, making him scream. "Next guess."

"I don't know!" he yelled back, his voice filled with rage. "I don't fucking know!"

She studied him for a moment, waiting for some sign of deception to reveal itself, but when it didn't, she relented. "I'll give you a hint. Your name is Pedro Martinez, but I know you as *Commander* Martinez."

Adi watched it sink in, a faint look of disbelief falling over his face.

"You were part of the movement?"

Adi smiled. "I was. Along with my family."

"But the village was massacred," Martinez said almost to himself. "There were no survivors."

Adi laughed. "Yes, that's interesting, isn't it?"

The sound of her voice broke his concentration and he looked back up.

"There were no survivors and yet, here I am and here you are."

Martinez eyed her suspiciously.

"Tell me," Adi said, knowing she finally had him where she wanted. "How exactly did you and your two worthless dogs escape the death that came for the rest of us?"

Martinez said nothing as his face turned hard, as if he was stiffening his resolve.

"Come on," Adi warned. "Don't make this any more difficult than it needs to be."

He remained silent.

"Fine," she replied as she pulled out her knife. "Just remember, this was your choice."

She grabbed his hand, pulling it back over the chair as she pried it open, and sliced off his fingers in one fell swoop.

The intensity of his screams filled the room as Adi casually dropped his severed digits onto the ground and resumed her position in front of him, watching as he clutched his hand, the gushing blood too much to stop. She waited for another minute before she grabbed his other hand and bent it over the back of the chair, knife ready.

"How did you survive?" she commanded.

"We went to the ranch to fight." This time the words poured out of him. "But he was waiting for us. It was over in less than an hour. We made a deal. If we told him where the village was, he'd let us live."

Adi released his hand, slowly walking back to the wall. "Your life for everyone else's." When she looked back at him, she expected an answer, to find some sort of guilt, but when he remained silent, the anger radiating from his face, she nodded.

"Time for guess number two."

He shook his head. "No."

"Come on," she said calmly. "We had a deal."

"Fuck you and your fucking deal."

The words were said with such contempt that it made Adi smile. It wouldn't really matter if he knew his death was because of Leti; he was so full of hate that there was nothing else to him. He wouldn't care that he had killed her sister. He had killed so many that a feeling like remorse, guilt, or regret was no longer possible for him. As she looked at the soulless body in front of her, she knew that the worst death she could give him would be one where he had no idea why.

Adi raised her gun to his head, sudden panic filling his eyes.

"No," he said desperately, validating her realization. "Tell me why. Please, tell me why."

She smiled sadly at him, hoping that somehow his unanswered questions would torment him forever. "You know why."

As the bullet broke through the centre of his skull, jerking his head forcefully back, Adi dropped the gun, a calm feeling overwhelming her. She had no idea what was going to happen, but for the first time in her life, she could finally let go. The pain, the fear, the guilt of the past had been dealt with, and knowing that she had fulfilled her promise and avenged her family, she could finally move on and live.

Chapter Fifteen

She hobbled away from the warehouse, hoping she had given herself enough time to escape. The moment she entered the trees, she breathed a sigh of relief, but suddenly, the air around her shook, the explosion erupting into the early morning sky. Grey and red smoke thickly billowed out, pushing Adi to run faster as the ammunition inside the building began to burst and fire in all directions. Knowing how much attention it would draw, she continued northwest, going as fast as her injuries would let her.

The pain radiating from her calf stopped her a couple hours later, and she struggled up into a tree, wedging herself into a cluster of branches, quickly falling asleep. The next time she woke, it was late afternoon the following day.

Gingerly climbing down from the tree, Adi stretched out her muscles, every one of them stiff as she walked towards the water. Her gunshot wounds were feeling better, the red sap doing its work as she slept. Digging the bullet out of her shoulder was something Adi would never forget, the pain excruciating, but as she washed the night off her face, she knew she needed to keep moving.

The sound of a stick creaking caused her to pause, if only for a second, as she continued to lift the water up to her face, listening intently. She was being watched, she could feel it, and so she stood, pretending to look at the jungle in front of her as she pulled the knife down into her hand. Turning her head ever so slightly, she saw the figure behind her, not moving as they watched from only a few feet away. Looking ahead once more, she took a deep breath and spun, the knife flying from her hand like an arrow shooting towards its target.

If he hadn't moved his shoulder at the last second, Adi's knife would have pierced him right in the chest, the blade just barely nicking the side of his shirt as it passed.

"Easy," Thiago said as he straightened back up, hands raised.

Adi was at a loss for words, too many questions filling her head. He was the last person she expected to find her, but when he said nothing else, she asked, "What do you want?"

He didn't answer right away, instead searching her face as if he was looking for the answers he needed. But when he didn't get any, he replied, "You know what you're doing, right? You have a plan, one that will get you out of this mess." He studied her face once more. "Tell me you do and I'll go."

Adi looked away. The truth was she didn't have a plan; this entire situation was new for her. While she wanted nothing more than to go back to the village and the others, she wasn't sure she should. She had done things Helena wouldn't approve of, and if she told them the truth, she wouldn't be welcomed back. "Why do you care?" she answered eventually. "You don't even like me."

Thiago smiled and looked at the ground. "It doesn't matter if I like you or not," he replied, looking back up. "Helena does. That's all that matters."

Adi studied him as she crossed her arms. "So, you're doing this for Helena. How exactly does that work?"

"Simple," he replied. He picked up the knife Adi had thrown at him and twirled it in his hands. "Helena sent us on an easy run. How pleased do you think she'll be if we return without you?"

Adi smirked. "So this isn't about Helena. You're doing this to save your own ass."

Thiago sucked in his breath sharply. "Careful what you say now, or you just might turn into a hypocrite. Or are you going to tell me that what you did back at that warehouse was for the collective good?"

His patronizing tone irritated her to the core, but she forced it down, matching his sarcasm. "What? Are you sad your friends are gone? I hate to break it to you, but they weren't the kind of people Helena would want you making deals with."

"Oh, so now you care about what my abuela wants?" Thiago replied, feigning gratitude. "Well then. Please feel free to murder some more people."

Adi snapped. "That wasn't murder," she said, instantly hostile.

"No?" he replied, meeting her anger. "Then what was it?"

She said nothing as she glared at him, refusing to be baited into telling him. What she did was justified and she didn't care if he thought so or not. She walked past him, climbed up into the tree and grabbed her bag.

"What?" Thiago mocked as she dropped back down and started walking away. "No answer? Well, this is a first! The great Adelita doesn't have anything to say."

"You have no idea what I've been through!" she yelled as she spun, unable to calm the rage inside. "Unlike you, not everyone got to have a safe and easy life. While you've been living out here with your entire family, the rest of us have been fighting, doing whatever it takes to survive." She paused, glaring at him. "You don't know shit about what people have done to us. What *they've* done to us," she said as she pointed back towards the town. "You think what I did was wrong? Fine! I don't care! But I don't regret it for a second. For once in my life, I just needed someone to pay."

Thiago said nothing, his expression unreadable. She took another breath and waited, unsure of what was going to happen, but when he didn't say anything at all, she got the hint. Lifting her bag onto her shoulders, she turned and walked away.

"You know," Thiago said, his voice slowing her to a stop, "you're a lot of things." She turned slightly, enough to see his face. "I just never knew that you were such a coward."

Out of everything he could have said, calling her a coward was not something she expected. She stood there, a mixture of confusion and anger rising up in her face.

"I mean, forget about leaving all your friends, even your brother behind," he continued. "I just never thought you'd be so scared of something you'd rather run away then face it. I guess you're not who I thought you were."

Adi glared at his smug face. She knew what he was doing: he was trying to trick her into going back and she wasn't about to fall for it. But when her feet stayed planted in place, she knew he was getting to her.

"So what's the plan?" she asked. "We go back and pretend nothing happened?"

"If you want," Thiago answered with a shrug. "It's up to you."

Adi was quiet, trying to decide what to do. She wanted to be with her family, but as Martinez's bullet-ridden body flashed before her eyes, she knew Helena would never forgive her. She was about to say so when the sound of a dog's bark diverted her attention. It took her a second to realize what it meant, but when she looked at Thiago and saw his face, she felt sick. They had found her.

Launching into a run, she followed Thiago as he led them west through the jungle away from the town. He was fast, his body effortlessly moving through the trees as she struggled to keep up, her wounds and the weight of her pack slowing her down. But when she saw the river ahead, she sped up and threw herself into the water.

The current carried them down and away from the bank, eliminating any trail for their pursuers to track. While the dogs might be able to chase them from the shoreline, it would slow them down considerably and Adi was happy to let the water do the work for her. But when she saw Thiago swimming towards the shore after only a couple bends in the river, she didn't feel so relieved.

"Stay in the water!" she said as she swam after him, but he only shook his head.

She struggled to push through the current, the strength of the water holding her hostage, but when she finally broke through and reached the riverbank, she didn't waste any time. "We haven't gone far enough. They'll find us."

Thiago silently wrung the water from his clothes. When he glanced up and saw her worried face, he nodded towards a large rock that sat along the shore. "Look for yourself."

The moment she scaled the rock, she saw the problem. Two, maybe three bends farther, the current doubled in speed, sending the water crashing over cluster after cluster of rapids. If they had stayed in the river, they wouldn't have made it out.

"Come on," he said. "They won't be far behind."

From the river they continued west, the landscape morphing from rolling hills to enormous mountains. It was the most difficult terrain she had ever seen, let alone climbed, and as they reached the top of the first hill, Thiago turned south, Adi stopping when she saw what lay before them. It was a spectacular view, rivers winding below the jagged cliffs and tall peaks of the mountain range, the warmth of the sun fading as it set in the distance. But knowing that this was their way home, she quieted the inner dread and caught up with Thiago.

"Where are Catalina and the others?" she asked when they finally stopped for the night, her muscles throbbing as she lowered herself onto the ground. They had been climbing for hours, the straps from her heavy bag digging into her shoulders and aggravating her wound.

"They've already gone back," Thiago answered. He casually sat against a tree, cutting away at a stick as he chewed on a dried plantain. "Should be home tomorrow."

"And us?" she asked. She kept still, trying to breathe out the discomfort. "When will we get there?"

"Two, three days at most. Depends on how much those slow you down."

She turned and saw that he was looking at her injuries, a concerned expression on his face. "I'll be fine," she replied, unwilling to show any form of weakness. "You've never been shot before, have you?"

He didn't answer for a moment. "No, I haven't."

She quietly rolled her eyes as she looked back up at the sky. It seemed that nothing bad ever happened to him, while death and mayhem stalked her every move. The two of them were nothing but different.

"Is that what happened to your hand?" His voice interrupted her thoughts.

She lifted it, examining the light scar that almost filled her entire palm. The last two fingers had never recovered, sitting on the end like useless blobs. Mariana said that she should be thankful her hand still worked, but as she looked at it in the moonlight, she doubted she would ever feel that way. She dropped it to her side. "No, it's not."

The following day was no better than the first. They didn't stop climbing, going up the mountains and then back down again. Adi desperately wanted a break but knowing Thiago was already questioning her condition, she remained quiet and focused all her energy on just making it to the next tree. But by the time they descended the first ridge on the third day, she didn't think she could take another step.

She didn't ask why they had stopped; all she cared about was that she could rest. She sat down on the ground, leaning against her pack as she slowly chewed on some raw pacu, and suddenly understood why they weren't moving.

She could hear the river without seeing it, a thunderous roar reaching her ears as she reluctantly pushed herself off the ground and walked towards it. When she finally saw it, she could do nothing but watch in awe as the white water raced by at an almost unbelievable pace. She had never seen anything so powerful, almost every inch of it filled with rapids and steep drop offs. When she saw how far away the other side of the river was, she knew this was going to be trouble.

"We have to cross this, don't we?" she asked as Thiago walked up, having to yell over the noise of the water.

He grinned, answering her question, and she followed him back into the trees, the noise slowly dimming as they went.

"I found a way across," he said as he stopped, finally able to speak at a normal volume. "It won't be easy, but it's do-able. Here." He reached out towards her. "Give me your bag."

"I'm fine."

Thiago's hand hit her shoulder so quickly, she found herself on the ground staring up at the trees before she could blink. Surprised, she couldn't even get an angry word out before he pulled her back up by her good arm.

"You're not fine," he said firmly, "you're injured. And if you're going to make it across this river, you'll need everything you have left."

She wanted to argue, but knew he was right. Listening to the ominous hum of the water, she took off her pack.

They walked back towards the river, Thiago taking them farther south. The current was beginning to flatten, slowing down the raging water. But when he stopped at the edge and Adi saw the line of rocks protruding through the current, her muscles convulsed in protest.

While the first few boulders were close enough to step across, the rest of them were farther apart, which meant that they would have to jump. To make matters worse, immediately following the rock line, the water suddenly dropped straight down six or seven feet, slamming onto more rocks below. She looked at Thiago, silently questioning his definition of do-able.

"Ready?" he asked.

A loud resounding "No" echoed through her mind, but instead she nodded.

With the bag strapped to his back, Thiago stepped onto the first rock, carefully making his way across. He was about a third of the way through when the rocks spaced out, so he ran forward and jumped, landing on the next rock before doing it again, hopping his way across the river. When she saw him reach the other side, she swallowed the lump in her throat and carefully stepped out into the river.

She went through the first section fairly easily, the occasional gust of wind taking her by surprise and causing her to wobble. It didn't help that her calf was cramping, but as she took her first jump and landed painlessly, she breathed a sigh of relief and prepared for the next one. She was just about to jump when she heard the river suddenly get louder. Whipping her head around, she watched in disbelief as a large tree plummeted through the rapids straight towards her.

She practically ran across the rocks, desperate to get out of the tree's path, but as she reached the middle of the river, she landed awkwardly and lost her balance, falling down hard. The second her knees touched the stone, the end of the tree slammed into her side, punching her off the rock.

She could feel herself falling, frantically reaching out as her fingers latched onto the edge of the boulder. She hung over the rapids, gasping for air as the water cascaded around her, drowning out everything else. Her grip was steadily slipping and her shoulder screamed in pain. She needed to get back up. Now.

Plunging her feet into the water, she felt around for something solid. As soon as her toes touched the rock wall that sat below the surface, she walked her feet up, putting herself into a squatting position. While she wanted to get out of there, she took a moment to steady herself. She would only get one chance to do this, and if she didn't do it right—if she messed up even a little—she would fall to her death on the rocks below. Taking one last breath, she pushed off, launching her body up and out of the water.

Flung through the air, she caught herself against the boulder, her forearms slamming into the rock as her fingertips held on for dear life. Gripping with all her might, her arms shook as she pulled her body on top.

She did nothing but lay there, every muscle clenching as she cradled the stone, refusing to let go. Overwhelmed with relief, the loud rumble of the rapids began to sound peaceful, and as her breathing slowed and her eyelids closed, a hand touched her shoulder.

Adi's eyes flew open as her body jerked, Thiago hovering above her. He looked at her for a moment before he reached down and pulled her up.

It took every remaining ounce of energy to throw herself across the rocks. Her muscles were seizing, the pain overwhelming as her jumps became sloppier with each one. When she finally pushed off the last rock onto the riverbank, she fell into the dirt, gasping for air.

"Are you alright?"

It was a simple question and said with such sincerity that Adi choked out a laugh, rolling to her side as she tried to get up. But she stopped short, the discomfort too much and she lifted up the right side of her shirt. While there was no blood, the tree had left a huge welt and she touched it gingerly, feeling the broken ribs beneath her skin.

"How bad is it?" Thiago asked, crouching beside her.

"It's okay," she replied. "I need my bag."

Handing it to her, she dug out some coca leaves, tucking a wad into her mouth.

"How much farther?" she asked, reaching out her arm.

He pulled her to her feet. "Not far. We can make it tonight if we push hard." He paused, the uncertainty all over his face.

Knowing what he was thinking, Adi shook her head. "No. If we stop, I won't get up. We gotta keep going."

He strapped on her bag. "Two mountains left."

She took a deep breath. She couldn't wait to get back to the village, lie down, and see her friends, but as she followed Thiago up the hill, she knew that she might be wandering through the jungle a lot sooner than she wished.

ψ

Adi could count on one hand the number of times she had ever been afraid of hurting someone she loved. Most of them happened when she was young, but as she walked into the village and saw Helena's anxious face, she realized two things: she was no longer a child and she could not knowingly hurt her, no matter the consequence. Even as Rodrigo scooped her up and carried her to Señorita Perez, she couldn't look away from her. Helena would never look at her the same again.

"Everybody out," Helena said softly as Adi sat on the bed, her wounds bandaged tightly.

They didn't want to go, the concern etched across their faces, but eventually they went and Adi watched as Helena sat down, patiently waiting for her to start.

It didn't take long, the silence pressing heavily against her, and she stared out the window for a minute before she looked back at Helena. "I killed three men." The details didn't matter. Helena wouldn't care why or how she did it, all that would matter is what she had done.

Helena said nothing, her face impossible to read.

"The moment I saw them, I knew I would do it."

Adi waited for a response, but none came, the seconds passing silently. After a while, Helena stood and placed a hand on her shoulder.

"Sleep."

Adi watched her leave the room, unsure of what to think. It wasn't the response she expected, but there was something in Helena's eyes that told her she wasn't done with her. Resigning to her fate, she laid down and fell asleep.

She slept for an entire day, Señorita Perez only waking her to check her injuries. No one was allowed to see her, but she barely noticed, content to lay on something soft, huddled beneath a warm blanket. When she finally woke up long enough to eat, Helena entered the room just as she was finishing.

"Señorita Perez tells me you're healing quickly." Helena hesitated. "We leave in the morning. Be ready at first light."

Normally, Adi would wonder where they were going and what was happening, but as she laid back down on the bed and pulled the blanket tight, she was calm. Whatever happened, she was ready.

Early the next morning, Adi prepared, Señorita Perez helping her put on an extra shirt and re-slinging shoulder. As she handed her a bag of supplies, she gave her a small smile and told her to go, Adi knowing where Helena would be.

The air was still in the morning light as she walked through the village towards the gate. She thought about finding Benito, but decided against it. If she saw him, she wouldn't want to leave. She stepped out of the village and onto the trail, slowing at the sight of the person ahead of her.

"You look better," Thiago said.

He was different, the hostility normally directed towards her no longer there, and she relaxed, a little relieved that she wouldn't be by herself. Hearing footsteps behind her, she didn't get a chance to reply as Helena said nothing as she passed them, Adi and Thiago simply following her down the trail and into the trees.

They hiked for hours, Adi struggling to keep up with Helena's quick pace. No one spoke and in the silence she kept her mind still, focusing all her energy on climbing up the hill. Concentrating on taking the next step, she didn't notice that the jungle was beginning to thin, but when she walked onto what looked like an old, unused road, her mind snapped to attention.

They veered off onto an overgrown path, following as it turned into an upward climb. Adi struggled to ascend the steep slope, her leg throbbing and her shoulder sore. When they reached their destination an hour later, she sat down on a mossy rock and caught her breath. It took her a few moments to see it, but when she did, she realized that they had entered an old, abandoned village.

She watched Helena and Thiago walk among the rubble, translucent rays of the setting sun streaming through the tree tops. She pushed herself up, a patch of moss sliding off, revealing a small stone structure. The jungle had reclaimed everything as bushes, vines, and lichens camouflaged most of the destroyed buildings, young trees even twisting their way along the side of the stone stacks that still stood.

Helena had stopped at the entrance of what looked like a small house and as she knelt in front of the remaining stones, her lips moving silently, Adi waited, an unsettled feeling forming at the pit of her stomach. While she was curious to find out what this place was, she couldn't shake the nagging desire to leave. Helena sat down on a stump and took out some food from her pack. They weren't going anywhere anytime soon.

"During the late sixties, early seventies," Helena said as she peeled off the skin of an orange, "this country was filled with rebel movements."

Adi watched her drop the peels into her bag piece by piece, latching onto every word.

"These groups fought against the military dictators who ruled with violence, slaughtering thousands at their pleasure. Thiago, you would have learned this in school, Adelita, I'm sure you've heard of it."

Adi nodded and she continued.

"There was one particular movement that grabbed people's attention. Its leaders were passionate, charismatic, and they connected with everyone who heard them. They were loved not only because they offered people protection, but because they gave them the chance to get their land back."

Helena smiled and took a bite of the orange. "Now, while other movements had appealing male leaders, this group was different because it was led by three women. And while being a rebel woman was nothing new—there were thousands who took up the call to fight and have been doing so for generations—these three were different. They had what we referred to as the deadly combination: intelligence and instinct."

She finished her orange and looked at Adi. "But they weren't just smart. They were destined to lead."

Adi found herself unable to look away, locked in her gaze.

Finally, Helena smiled and looked around at the ruins. "This was their home, where they stayed and built their movement. And this is where they died." She cleared her throat and looked back at Adi. "These three women were sisters. Very few people knew their names. They simply called them Las Hermanas."

As soon as she heard the words, Adi felt as though she was being transported back in time, every memory of her mother's bedtime stories hitting her at once.

"You know this name, don't you?" she heard Helena ask and she snapped out of it, looking into her knowing face.

"It's just a story," she replied, her words sounding less confident than she needed them to be. She suddenly felt nervous and took a step back, not liking the way Helena was watching her.

Helena smiled sadly. "Oh, it's more than just a story, Adelita. It's history. Your history." She paused and Adi felt naked under her stare. "The three women who formed and led one of the greatest movements in our country's history are your ancestors, Adelita Alvarez."

The moment her last name left Helena's lips, Adi felt dizzy, as though something was restricting her ability to breathe. She fought against it, demanding that she stay in control, but it wasn't working. She was such a fool, thinking they were safe when she had walked them right into another trap. She should have known it was too good to be true, she should have never trusted her. Suddenly realizing that she didn't have a single weapon on her, she willed herself to be calm. "How do you know that?" she asked, barely getting out the words. "How do you know my last name?"

Helena didn't move as she watched her, continuing on as if she hadn't spoken. "Their names were Margarita, Rafaela, and Adelita Valdez. Adelita was your abuela, your mama's mama, who you were named after."

"No," Adi said, feeling a little bit more in control. Helena might know her last name, but she didn't know as much as she thought.

Besides, Alvarez was a common name; it was just a lucky guess. "You're wrong. My abuela's name was Ana."

Helena smiled. "Ana wasn't your real abuela. Your mama, Esperanza, was born to Adelita Valdez and Leonardo Florez on March 19, 1973. I know because I was there."

The mention of her grandfather's name worried her a bit, but she pushed the thought away. She needed to focus less on what Helena was saying and more on how she was going to get back to the village. She needed to get the others. They weren't safe.

"Your abuelo was married to Ana when he met Adelita," Helena continued, oblivious to the panicked thoughts in Adi's head, "and they already had a child—Joselin, I think was her name. But Adelita and Leonardo fell in love and your mama was the product of that. I'll never forget the night Esperanza was born. It was raining so hard we thought the roof would collapse."

The more she talked, the less confident Adi was that Helena was wrong, and she once again felt the control slipping away. While anyone could know her aunt's name, there was no way Helena could know that her mother had been born during a storm. She felt the fight leave her as she leaned against a tree, the memory of her father's smiling face before her, so real she could almost touch it.

"This is your fault, you know," her father would tease when it poured for days. "God's crying again. He just didn't want to let you go."

Her mother would smile, her cheeks warming beneath his gaze as she stood in front of the stove, Mateo's hand lovingly resting on the back of her neck.

A single tear rolling down her cheek broke her from her memory and she looked up at Helena standing in front of her.

"Your abuela was one of my closest friends," she said softly as she wiped the tear off Adi's chin. "When she placed your mama into Leonardo's arms, I promised to watch over her and keep her safe.

I was there when she married your papa," Helena continued, "and I was there when Leticia was born. I was in the room when they named you." Helena began walking away, talking as she went. "I lost track of your family a few years after you were born during one of your many moves. I searched endlessly, but you had vanished. I never thought I'd see you again." She turned and faced Adi once more. "But when I saw you sitting in that room tied to that chair, I knew. I knew it was you. And I knew in that moment what I had to do." Helena moved to her with speed Adi didn't know she had, and she forcefully took her hands in her own. "You, Adelita Alvarez, were meant to find me here, in this place, so I could show you who you really are."

Chapter Sixteen

Everything was different once she walked off that mountain, but it wasn't her that changed. Helena treated her as if she was supposed to know what finding out about her past meant, but Adi didn't understand what the big deal was. The past was the past and she wasn't her grandmother. Was it somehow supposed to change her?

At first when Helena began to tell her about her family and the Las Hermanas movement, she would simply listen, thinking that the stories would eventually have a point, but when they didn't, she got frustrated.

"Why does it matter what happened?" she asked angrily. "It's over!"

But Helena would simply smile and say that one day it would make sense, continuing on where she left off.

Adi exhaled deeply as she stared out at the rolling, green mountains in front of her, replaying the last argument she had with Helena as she stood alone in the silence, watching the sun slowly sink in the distance. It was useless to fight, Helena determined to teach her something she didn't understand, so she resigned herself to it, listening to her talk about the past while she dreamt about all the things her friends were doing.

Her body shook as a shiver ran down her spine. It was beginning to get cold, the sun's warmth gone and she knew she should head back, wanting to be inside by the time the white-legged mosquitos came out to bite. She took one last look at the sky and turned around just in time to see Kaue approaching. Seeing the concerned expression on his face, she knew something was wrong.

She ran the entire way back, stifling the desire to panic as she hastily brushed a couple large tobacco leaves out of her path. While she tried to tell herself it could be a mistake, that maybe they were wrong, she couldn't help but think the worst. Entering the village, she spotted Nayara and ran straight towards her.

"Gio," Nayara said, barely getting the words out. "She's gone."

It didn't make sense. There was no way she would just leave.

"I should have known," Nayara was saying, but Adi barely heard her. She was already halfway to her room where she grabbed her bag and ran out into the trees.

They searched endlessly, Adi's anxiety building as night slowly fell. She knew it was pointless; Giovana was an excellent tracker and she would only leave a trail if she wanted to. But they looked anyway, hoping for any sign that she had been there. Adi was examining a small indent in the mud when a sharp whistle cut through the silence.

She ran towards it, hoping with all her might that it was Giovana. But when she finally got there, leg muscles burning, she saw Marcelo crouched low beside the river.

"What is it?" she asked.

"I'm not sure it's anything." He pointed to the small pile of frog skin on the rock.

"It's her."

Marcelo leaned back on his heels and shook his head. "You don't know that."

"Gio hates the skin." She knew it was a stretch, but she was determined to believe it.

"I know," he replied as he stood. "But that doesn't mean it's her."

Adi tried to figure out what Giovana was doing. If she had just eaten, she might be moving slow. "How fresh is that?"

Marcelo shrugged. "I don't know. It hasn't shriveled so maybe in the last hour."

She nodded. "And if you were her, which way would you go?"

He sighed and looked around, stepping into the water as he examined the surroundings. "There," he said, pointing to a narrow place upriver. "That's where I would cross."

She took off, running up to the spot and carefully wading through the water. She could hear Marcelo calling after her, but she didn't care. If this was the way Giovana went, she was going to follow.

The water was deeper than she expected and she inhaled sharply as it rose up past her thighs, a cold feeling passing over her warm body. She was halfway through the river when she spotted the caiman, its beady eyes peering at her along the surface of the water, but she didn't stop, locking eyes with it as she crossed, daring it to come at her. When she felt her feet hit the riverbank and saw that the caiman was still in its spot, she smirked and burst into a sprint, her legs pounding against the dirt.

She ran hard, finding a rhythm and easily moving through the trees, darting around fallen logs and dense brush as she went. Her muscles were tired but it felt good and she pushed harder, beginning to lose sight in the dark.

She heard the shot at the same time she felt it whiz past her cheek. She skidded to a halt. Scanning the trees around her, she searched for the shooter, but seeing no one, she took another step forward. The second shot landed less than an inch from her toe and she stopped, raising her hands in the air.

"Gio, please. Talk to me." She barely got the words out of her mouth before Giovana emerged from the bushes, gun aimed directly at her head.

"I'm not going back. Not without her. You can't make me."

Adi quietly lowered her hands. She didn't know what Giovana was talking about, but if she decided to pull the trigger, having her hands raised wouldn't stop it.

"Where are you going?" She had so many questions, but figured this was the best one to start with.

Giovana practically huffed at her. "Oh, so now you care?"

Stunned, she didn't know what to say.

"All you do is sit in that room with *her*. You don't give a shit about us anymore."

Her words were said with such anger that she involuntarily took a step back. But when she stood there, failing to figure out why Giovana was so mad, she decided it didn't matter.

"I'm not going back," Giovana repeated.

"Okay."

Giovana looked at her suspiciously for a moment before she turned and started walking away. But when Adi followed, she stopped. "What are you doing?"

"Where you go, I go. That's how this works."

When her hard face softened just a little, Adi knew she had her.

ψ

It took much longer than Adi wanted to convince Lupita to return to the village. She didn't understand why she had to stay while Catalina, Marcelo, and Rodrigo got to go, but eventually she went, much to Adi's relief. It wasn't just that she needed someone to tell Helena what they were doing; Adi needed to know that the others would be safe while they were gone and Lupita would do that. She wasn't just brave, she was the smartest person Adi knew and if something happened, Lupita would make the right decision.

Giovana had been headed in the right direction, the terrain feeling somewhat familiar as they followed a lightly-worn path down the mountain. Being blindfolded on the way here meant that none of them knew exactly where they were going, but when they arrived at a large river, Adi remembered the boat ride and knew they weren't far off.

"What now?" Marcelo asked above the noise of the water.

She closed her eyes and tried to picture the map in Helena's room, the one with all the x's. She remembered the marks, and if she could just remember the river, she would be able to get them around it. A sharp whistle cut through her thoughts.

They said nothing as they walked over to Thiago, his foot resting on a metal hull peeking out from underneath a camouflaged cover.

"Well?"

Climbing into the boat, they pushed away from the shore and into the current. The sudden revving of the engine gave Adi a jolt and the boat sprang to life, cutting through the water. She couldn't help but smile as the wind stung her face, making her eyes water and her hair whip behind her. She had never gone so fast, it felt like she was flying, but by the time they docked the boat a while later, she was happy to be back on land.

"I can take you to where we found you," Thiago said after hiding the boat. "But then it's up to you."

The darkness made it difficult to run as they found their way back into familiar territory. The slow pace allowed Adi's mind to wander and she wondered what exactly they were going to find. When Giovana told her she was returning for Yumi, Adi felt a pang of guilt. They had been living in a safe place for some time and only now were they returning for the others. But as they stopped for the night, she pushed her feelings aside. She had much more important things to worry about.

It took less than a day to reach the place where Adi and the others had been taken and as soon as she recognized it, she was ready to get going. Catalina led the way, running quickly through the jungle, everyone else right behind her. They travelled from sun up to sun down, stopping only when they had to and speaking little. After a few days as they neared their former home, they slowed down, unsure of what they'd be walking into.

"We're just south of the camp," Rodrigo said on their next break. "If we go straight, we'll be there by dark."

Adi nodded. "Let's go."

They headed directly north, the tension palpable as they silently moved through the trees, watching every angle. They were nearing the river south of the camp when Rodrigo suddenly signaled for them to stop, his hand shooting straight into the air. No one moved, listening intently to the jungle around them. Motioning to his right, Rodrigo crouched down low and crept forward, the others following. He stopped and Adi looked past him just in time to see an arrow fly out in front of them, striking a small capybara directly in the neck.

It was if they were collectively holding their breath, no one daring to move as they waited for something to happen. Ten seconds later, they watched as someone ran out from the trees and lifted the animal onto their shoulders. It wasn't until she turned, looking around her cautiously, that Adi saw her face and recognized the girl in front of them. Yumi.

They all jumped up at once, but she was already gone, running faster than Adi could have imagined. There was no sign of her until Giovana suddenly called out and they followed, trying to catch up. Focused on the tracks ahead, they didn't notice Yumi slip out from behind a tree and aim an arrow right at Thiago's head.

"Yumi," Catalina said, raising her hands. "It's us."

She gave no indication that she recognized any of them and as she warily looked around, Giovana walked forward.

Nothing was said as the two of them looked at each other, the seconds ticking by. Yumi still hadn't lowered her bow; Giovana's face not ringing any bells. Suddenly, Giovana rolled up her sleeve and stuck out her arm.

Adi had seen the scar before, the crisp line seamlessly splitting her forearm in two. She didn't know what it was from, but as she watched Yumi lower the arrow and turn over her arm, she was shocked by what she saw. They had the same scar, in the same place, on the same arm. In fact, if you were to measure it, it would be a perfect match, down to the millimeter.

Relief poured out of Thiago as he exhaled, his head no longer a target. Giovana had wrapped Yumi into a hug and they waited silently until she finally let her go.

"Come." Yumi picked up the capybara and turned southeast.

It didn't take long to get there and they followed Yumi into a cave, the small entrance deceiving as it opened up into a large space, the faces of a few kids coming into view. They had barely made it inside when Adi saw him walking towards them.

"Salvador!" Rodrigo said as he moved forward, dwarfing the smaller man as he happily embraced him.

Adi felt relieved until Catalina asked, "Where is everyone else?"

Salvador said nothing as he led them back out of the cave. "It happened like you said it would," he said once they were outside, his eyes resting heavily on Adi.

She met his gaze for a moment before she looked away, watching Pablo and Yumi prepare the capybara for roasting, all too familiar with how this story would end.

"They attacked hard and fast," he continued. "It was like they knew everything about us. We didn't stand a chance." He cleared his throat. "They took several girls but a few managed to escape. It was chaos and when it was over, we were completely scattered. It took me days, weeks even, to find these guys." He sighed. "I didn't know how many died 'til I went back there."

"How many?" Marcelo asked.

"Two, three dozen," Salvador replied. He clasped his hands behind his back. "Maybe more, I'm not sure. I didn't stay long, as you can imagine."

"Valentina?" Rodrigo asked, his voice quiet.

"I don't know. I didn't find her body so she might have escaped."

Adi winced. While Salvador had attempted to sound hopeful, he failed miserably. She tried to give Rodrigo a smile, but she couldn't, instead finding herself simply staring at the pain on his face.

As Catalina began telling Salvador about Helena's, her thoughts lingered on Valentina. At first, she thought it was just guilt at not coming back for them sooner, but when she remembered what Salvador said, she interrupted their conversation.

"Wait. You said they took girls."

Salvador nodded.

"How old were they?" The confusion on his face made her elaborate. "Were they younger like Lupita or were they older like me?"

He paused for a minute, thinking it over. "They were older," he replied. "All of them were your..."

He didn't have to finish his sentence as the others got it and Adi watched as they exchanged alarmed glances.

"Fuck," Marcelo cursed.

"He's alive then," Rodrigo said, the pain on his face replaced by anger. "No doubt about it."

"We need to go," Giovana said.

Adi couldn't agree more. "Pack what you need," she said. "We're leaving."

As the others ran around getting ready, Adi took a moment to try and calm the panic in her brain. While a small part of her had known she hadn't killed him that day in the village, she thought that even if he was still alive, he'd at least give up. But to know that he was still out there looking for her filled her with dread and as she paced the ground, trying to think of where he might be, Thiago walked up and planted himself right in her path.

"You know," he began, his arms folded across his chest as she walked around him, refusing to stop moving, "when I helped you in that town, I did that for my abuela, knowing how much she cared for you. And when I helped you at the river with the boat, I did that for you, thinking that somehow you had changed after our trip up the mountain. But this—whatever this is—you're going to have to explain it to me because I'm running out of reasons to help you, even if you are the granddaughter of Las Hermanas."

The mention of that name broke Adi from her focus and she was in his face in less than two seconds. "You will not say that out loud again," she said, the warning in her tone made crystal clear as she held his gaze. She glanced around, hoping no one had heard. She hadn't told the others, not even Benito, and when Helena questioned her about it, she couldn't give her an answer. Maybe it was because she didn't want to believe it or maybe it was because she was afraid people would start expecting things from her. Whatever the reason, she wasn't ready for them to find out.

"Well then," Thiago said, a knowing look on his face. "You better start talking."

It took her a while to explain the entire story, Adi skipping over the unessential details and when she finished, he was quiet.

"So, by him taking older girls, that means he's still looking for you?" he asked eventually.

She nodded, resuming her pacing once again.

"I'm sorry, but that's bullshit."

His response surprised her and she stopped.

"There are a million other reasons why he might want them," he said, giving her a look like she should know what he was suggesting. When the confusion stayed on her face, he sighed. "Sex, slavery, drugs. Pick one."

Adi smiled. "No. He's not interested in any of that."

"And how would you know?"

She opened her mouth, but then closed it, trying to think of how to explain. "You know when you meet someone," she began, "and you get this feeling like you know the deepest parts of them, like you've known them your whole life?" She looked up at him, his focused eyes staring down at her and he nodded. "Well, that's how it is with him. I know him. I know what he likes and what he doesn't. I know what he's capable of. I've known it since the first time I saw him, the first time he touched me, the first time I felt his breath on my neck." She self-consciously touched the side of her throat, as if the bruises were still there.

"Adi," she heard Rodrigo call. "We're ready."

Lost in her thoughts of him, she had forgotten Thiago was there. A little embarrassed, she gave him a strained smile before walking off towards the cave.

Thiago went to follow, but was stopped by Rodrigo's hand placed directly on his chest.

"I don't know why you're here and I honestly don't care," Rodrigo began, his hostile tone getting Thiago's full attention. "But we need her if we're gonna get outta this alive. So stop focusing on what you want and start thinking about what she needs."

Rodrigo was already walking away when Thiago asked, "Which is what exactly?"

He stopped and turned, a smirk on his face. "The fact that you need to ask just proves my point." He paused for a second, the smile quickly fading. "He's going to kill her, you know that right? No matter what happens, he won't quit. So if you care about her at all, do her a favour and start pulling your weight."

🌿

The journey back was made in silence, the little ones not needing a reminder to be quiet. They could practically taste the anxiety swirling around them.

They were a total of seventeen and as they walked with the youngest in the middle, Adi couldn't help but feel that they were going too slow. At night, it was even worse. Being unable to find a safe space big enough to hide forced them to sleep in more vulnerable places. They considered splitting up, but as soon as it was suggested, Salvador immediately said no. They would not be separated, not with what had happened, so they carried on, moving slowly through the trees and sleeping uncomfortably under the stars. She was down by the river, washing the long, sleepless night off her face when she felt the barrel of a gun press lightly against the back of her neck.

She should have been surprised or at least a little shocked, but she wasn't. In her mind, it was bound to happen.

"Hands up."

Adi hesitated, trying to think of what to do when another gun jammed into her ribs, making her double over and re-think her choice. As she slowly raised her hands, the muffled voice asked, "How many you got with you?"

"None," she lied, perhaps a little too quickly. "I'm alone."

The gun slammed into her body and she folded again.

"No one likes a liar," the voice replied. Her hands were yanked behind her and secured tightly with rope, the thread digging into her wrists.

As she was walked into the trees, Adi got a look at her captors. They weren't what she expected. Their clothes worn and their faces masked, they were strong and had caught her off-guard. She hoped the others had escaped their attention, but as they rounded the corner, she saw them sitting in a circle surrounded by armed men, Catalina held down on her stomach while Rodrigo's face dripped with blood.

Pushed to the ground and instructed to sit, she did so strategically with her back to Giovana. If anyone could get out of their binds, it was her. Adi sat close, pressing tightly against her leg, hoping she could secretly untie the knots. As soon as she felt her fingers go to work, Adi hid her smile and looked up expectantly at the men.

Three of them were huddled together, talking in hushed tones as the rest stood in silence, casually watching over the group. As she surveyed them, it became clear that they didn't work for *him*, but what wasn't obvious was what they wanted and so she waited, one of them finally stepping forward.

"Which one of you is in charge?" When no one answered, he grabbed a small girl and pointed a gun to her head.

Hearing her whimper, Adi couldn't help it. "Don't," she said.

Letting the girl go, he crouched in front of her. "What are you doing in this part of the jungle?"

She was about to give him a smart-ass answer when she saw the seriousness of his eyes. They were dark, almost black, and as they stared at her intently, she knew they weren't fooling around. "We're on our way home."

He held her stare, as if he was trying to read her, and she dared not blink. He must have been satisfied because he continued. "And where is this home?"

As soon as she heard the question, she inwardly groaned. There was no way she, or anyone else, was going to give up that information and she took a deep breath. "Ask me any other question and I'll answer it, I swear. But I can't tell you that."

He looked at her for a moment before he placed the gun against her head, some of the children beginning to cry.

She nodded. "Do it. Pull the trigger. But you'll have to kill every single one of us and you still won't know." She sat unflinching as he contemplated her answer, the seconds dragging on slowly. When he finally removed the gun, she exhaled a little louder than usual.

"What are you doing with all these children?" he asked.

"Bringing them home," she replied, keeping her word.

"Where are they from?"

Adi shrugged. "All over."

"They have no parents?"

"No."

He paused, thinking about his next question. "And why do you have them?"

She hesitated, unsure of why he was interested, but eventually she said, "We're trying to save them."

"From what?"

She paused again, wondering how much she should tell him when she decided it didn't matter. If the man came, they were as good as dead. She should at least warn him, let him know what he would be up against. "Not what. Who. I don't know his name. All I know is what he looks like."

Even behind the mask, she could see his brow furrow. "What does he look like?"

When he asked the question, something about it was different, but she couldn't put her finger on it. He seemed interested, his body rigid as he leaned even closer to her, as if he was waiting with eager anticipation.

"He's a gringo," Adi began, the man not moving. "And he has a scar that goes from his eyebrow all the way to his mouth. Like the shape of..."

"The moon," the man finished for her. He sighed and leaned back on his heels.

Surprised, Adi was suddenly unsure of who he was. Maybe she had been mistaken, maybe they *did* work for him, but as he slowly took off his mask, she could do nothing but wait.

"Cut them loose," he instructed. The men hesitated until he motioned at them with his head. He leaned forward and cut the rope from Adi's wrists before he sat down heavily on a nearby stump and pulled out a hand-rolled cigarette. He lit it, took a long drag, and blew the smoke up into the air, taking a moment to look at the sky above him before he turned back to Adi, offering her the smoke. When she shook her head, he began. "The man you have described is known around here as El Diablo."

Adi rubbed her sore wrists, watching her friends being cut from their binds.

"He used to live in this area, just south of here," he continued. "I was the one who gave him that scar."

She stayed quiet, eager to know more.

"He grew up with my son," the man said. He took another puff and exhaled slowly, the smoke coming out of his mouth in a steady stream. "But then one day his family moved and I thought I'd never see him again, until ten years later, he showed up at our door. We welcomed him in, like any friend would, but it was not the same man that walked into my house," he said, his voice low with warning. "It was something else."

Adi nodded in understanding. "El Diablo."

He grunted in agreement. "He told me he was a botanical researcher." He said it so softly, she barely heard him. "Said he was doing research for a company that made life-saving medications."

As he spoke, his voice grew louder with anger and Adi had no doubt that everyone could hear him now. "But that's not was he was doing." His eyes landed on her face and he stared at her for a moment. "He was doing what he is doing now: murdering people and burning villages to the ground. Tell me," he said, leaning towards her once more. "How does he do it?" When he saw the confusion on her face, he elaborated. "Does he kill them all at once or does he kill them one by one, like he used to?"

"All at once," she replied.

The man nodded.

"He has a group of men that he uses. But some he takes instead of kills," she continued, remembering the girls at the camp. "Some he likes to kill himself."

The man quietly studied her, the cigarette burning in his hand. "You seem to know a lot about him," he said eventually, his eyes not leaving her face. "Much more than you should."

Adi couldn't help but smirk, the sadness of the truth setting in. "He has two scars now," she said as she met his gaze. "One on his cheek, the other across his throat."

Her words surprised him and she watched a small smile spread across his face as he took one last drag on his cigarette, crushing the ash with his fingers before putting it back inside his pocket. "You've killed him then?"

"No," she replied, watching him carefully.

The man nodded. "Good." He slapped his hands on his knees and pushed himself back up.

Confused by his reaction, she stayed seated, waiting for him to explain.

"I have a proposition for you."

She could tell by his tone that it wouldn't be good, but as soon as he started telling her his plan, she knew what her answer would be.

Chapter Seventeen

"This is a horrible idea."

Adi smiled as they made their way home, finding Rodrigo's comment oddly amusing. It *was* a horrible idea, but it was the best one they had and she was all in, determined to make it work no matter how risky.

"There's got to be another way."

She sighed. While she loved him deeply, his protectiveness was beginning to annoy her. Deep down, she knew he thought he could save her somehow, but ever since she met *him*—the man—she knew that there was no way out for her.

"We need a better chance at killing him if you're gonna be bait."

She stopped walking.

"What?" he asked, stopping beside her.

Surprised, she simply smiled. Finally, they were on the same page.

They made it to the river, piling into the boat before jetting off through the water, the red marker on the tree slowly fading in the distance. When Adi agreed to the plan, she insisted on starting right away. Her new friend Jacobo left immediately to gather the rest of his men. They had decided to meet by the marked tree the next morning, but the moment Adi spotted black smoke wafting above her, she knew the plan no longer mattered. Looking back at Thiago, the boat leapt forward, the throttle jammed as far up as possible. He had seen it.

They flew up the river, the smoke thickening the closer they got, and by the time they hit the riverbank, silent fear had settled among them. For a moment, no one moved, and Adi was about to ask Thiago something when she realized he was already gone, catching only a glimpse of him as he sprinted up the mountain.

"Everybody out," Adi said as she swallowed, forcing herself to focus. "Yumi, Pablo, Gio, stay here with the kids. Salvador, do you know how to drive a boat?"

"No, but I'll figure it out," he said as he turned some nobs, the noise of the motor snapping the others out of their haze.

"Don't come near the village 'til you hear the whistle, alright?"

Giovana nodded.

Adi turned and looked at Rodrigo, Catalina, and Marcelo. "Let's go."

They ran up the mountain, ignoring the path and going the most direct route, desperate to get there. It wasn't just the smoke that alarmed Adi, it was also the silence, the jungle completely still as they climbed. Finally reaching the top, she pushed past the stinging in her muscles and found another gear, flying through the trees, the air heavy with smoke. As soon as she saw the village, she slowed down, crouching low as she approached, not seeing Thiago anywhere. The gate was open but there was no one around and she watched for a moment before she carefully moved towards it, knives out and ready.

Nothing in her life had prepared her for what she saw upon entering the village, her mind unable to form a single thought as her arms dropped down uselessly to her sides. Dead bodies covered the ground, blood staining the dirt between them as the fire hungrily burned through what was left of the buildings. She suddenly found it hard to breathe and it was as if she couldn't move, the shock of what she saw too much to process. She didn't know how long she stood there, but when she felt Catalina's hand on the back of her shoulder, she took an unsteady step forward.

They walked through the village, checking over each body as Adi's fear grew with every face she recognized, their lifeless eyes staring back at her. Seeing Mariana, she fell, her knees hitting the dirt as she lovingly touched her face, the blood smeared across it almost dry. She wanted to stay there forever, cradling her friend, but she made herself get up. She had to continue. She was afraid of what she would see next—a vision of Benito's dead body flashing before her eyes—but as she walked past the side of a house and into the centre of the village, she never could have guessed what was waiting.

She stood there in shock, hoping with every part of her that it wasn't real, that she was somehow hallucinating. But as she walked up and shakily touched the foot dangling just above her head, the breath slowly left her and she stepped back in horror. There, hanging above her, was Helena's mutilated body.

She didn't want to see it for another second, but her eyes refused to look away and she couldn't move, locked onto the sight of her. At first, she didn't notice, but as she stared, the letters suddenly jumped out, and it felt like she had been punched in the stomach. Double A's carved into Helena's chest beamed back at her. She closed her eyes as she tried to erase the image, but she couldn't. Suddenly hearing a noise around the corner, her eyes shot open.

It was as if she had lost the ability to speak, her tongue so big it filled her mouth as she helplessly watched Thiago walk towards the wall blocking his view of his grandmother.

"Adi," he said as he approached, the devastation on his face fading into confusion when he saw her tormented expression. The moment he turned the corner, she looked away, unwilling to watch as he saw his grandmother's body for the first time.

She felt helpless as Thiago tried to take a step forward, his body failing as his knees buckled out from underneath and he hit the ground, a small gasp escaping his body. She knew she needed to leave, to keep looking for the others, but as she stood there trying to find the will to keep going, she realized she no longer wanted to. No matter what they did or where they went, he would find them, and as she watched another family being ripped to shreds, she no longer cared to try. It was over. She was done.

She didn't bother turning around as Catalina and Marcelo walked up, their stunned silence saying more than words ever could.

"Those are A's," Marcelo said slowly after a minute, his tone a mixture of shock and awe.

"Have you found him yet?" Adi asked, no longer wanting to be there. When they didn't answer, she turned around. "My brother."

"No," Catalina replied. "He's not here. None of the children are."

A small surge of hope jolted through her, but she shut it down, unwilling to let it cloud her judgement. She had been living in an illusion, a fantasy, and she would no longer allow herself to be so naïve. Just as she turned around, an urgent whistle cut through the air.

Catalina and Marcelo ran towards the signal, but Adi simply walked, knowing nothing she did would save any of them. Catalina looked at her oddly, but she ignored her and went up to where Rodrigo was crouched down, examining a hole in the wall.

"It's small," he said as he glanced up at her, but getting no response, he looked back at the hole. "But big enough for them to squeeze through. They might have made it out."

They looked at her expectantly, waiting for her to say something, but when she didn't, Marcelo said, "We'll go check it out. You should let Gio know it's safe."

Adi almost laughed as Rodrigo nodded, Catalina and Marcelo leaving the village. While the people who had done this were gone, safe wasn't the word she'd use. But as she listened to Rodrigo send one loud long whistle into the air, she told herself not to care and got to work.

It was pointless, she knew, but Adi lifted another body onto her shoulders and carried it to the corner of the village, determined to keep busy as she waited for the others to return. She should have gone and looked for Benito herself, but in that moment, she was too afraid of what she'd find. As she started digging the next grave, she felt incredibly ashamed. It was a new feeling for her and she dug faster, trying to keep the giant ball of emotions that threatened to destroy her at bay. She would not feel anything.

She dragged the body into the hole, quickly shoveling the dirt on top before stepping out, ready to go get the next one. As she dropped the shovel and turned, a hand latched onto her arm, pulling her back.

"What?" she asked, Rodrigo's worried face looking down at her.

He was quiet for a moment, his eyes searching hers as if he wanted to say something important, but simply sighed. "You need to do something about Thiago."

Adi bristled, becoming defensive. She didn't need to do anything. In fact, she was tired of it. Tired of always being the one running around fixing things. She was about to tell him as much when he continued. "He's been sitting there, holding her body for hours. He needs to let her go."

Adi took a moment, fighting to control her anger. "Why do I have to do something?"

A look of disbelief passed over Rodrigo's face, but he closed his eyes and took a breath. "Because," he replied evenly, "I tried talking to him and he shoved a gun in my face."

"And what makes you think he'll listen to me?"

This time, Rodrigo didn't react so nicely. "Are you about done?" he asked, his tone hostile. "This pity party you're throwing yourself, is it almost over? Cuz I've had e-fuckin-nough of it."

She struggled to find the words, feeling so angry she could only glare at him.

"You think you're the only one that's hurting?" he almost yelled at her, the frustration tumbling out. "That you're the only one who's struggling with this? You're not!" He was up in her face, hands angrily placed on his sides. "So you don't get to do this. You don't get to check out and give up. That's not how this works."

She kept scowling at him, wondering what made him think he could talk to her that way, even though deep down she knew he was right. Unwilling to admit that to him, let alone herself, she stormed off, feeling the weight of his stare on her back.

She had planned on leaving the village, wanting to go into the trees to cool off, but as she walked past Thiago sitting there, she couldn't help but stop. He was on the ground, exactly where she had left him, holding Helena so gently she almost cried, but she looked away, quickly shoving the tears and the feelings down.

Walking up, she crouched in front of him so he could see her face. At first, he didn't look at her, his eyes focused on his grandmother. But when Adi reached out and softly placed a hand on top of his, he almost jumped, looking up to see her there for the first time.

"I'm sorry." It wasn't enough, she knew that, but it was all she had.

He didn't reply and instead looked back down at Helena, the pain twisted on his face.

Adi stayed there for a few minutes before she stood back up, having no words of comfort. She knew Rodrigo would want her to try harder, but Thiago clearly wasn't ready to give Helena up and she wasn't going to make him.

"It's your fault you know."

The voice was so quiet and low that Adi barely heard it, but it stopped her dead and she turned to look at him.

"It's your fault," he repeated, his voice growing louder. "She's dead because of you." This time he looked at her, his bloodshot eyes filled with so much hate that it was all Adi could do not to look away. "You just had to do it, didn't you?" Tears welled in his eyes. "You just had to kill those men, not caring about what it would do to us—to her."

As much as she wanted to, Adi couldn't deny the truth in his words. It was the only thing that made sense, the only possible way he could have found them. This time, she forced herself to feel it, every ounce of hate, as his stare burned into her. The moment he looked back down at his grandmother, Adi turned away, trying to calm the storm building inside, the pressure growing with every second. But as she did, her eyes landed on Catalina entering the village, the body of a boy in her arms.

The world seemed to fall away as she watched her come closer, every muscle clenching uncontrollably. She didn't have to look to know who it was, the answer written across Catalina's face, but even as she stopped in front of her, Adi refused to look down.

"No," she said defiantly, trying to reject what was right in front of her. But the longer she stared at the pain on Catalina's face, the less she was able to deny it, and she dropped her gaze, her heart shattering into a thousand pieces.

ψ

They finished burying them at sunset, the darkening sky a welcome sight as Adi stood in front of the grave that held Benito's body. She was broken, so much so that she wanted nothing more than to crawl in with him, but as she felt Nayara's hand gently squeeze hers, she knew they'd never let her. She was standing there, staring down at the small mound of dirt when she heard, "Adi!" and looked up.

His fist hit her face faster than she could blink and her head snapped back, unsure of what shocked her more, the pain or the unexpected assault. But she didn't get to think further as the second blow hit her stomach, crumpling her as she clutched her body. She could have defended herself, even fought back, but as she looked into Thiago's enraged face, she simply waited for the next punch. It came a moment later, the strength of his clenched hand striking her cheek and sending her sprawling into the dirt. She looked up just in time to see Marcelo and Catalina rush forward and take him down, Thiago fighting against them on the ground.

"Let him go," she said painfully. She pushed herself up into a seated position, spitting out a mouthful of blood. "Just let him go."

Nayara and Giovana were already at her side but she shrugged them off, crawling towards Benito's grave as Thiago stormed away. Wanting nothing more than to be alone, Adi ignored their stares, laid down in the dirt, and closed her eyes.

She woke up to the sound of a paradise tanager, its vibrantly coloured body flitting around her head, landing on Benito's grave for a moment before flying off, its song blending with the morning light. She stared up into the sky for a few minutes, letting its blue hue soothe her before she sat up, the pain a reminder of the night before. As soon as she saw him, she let out a big sigh.

"If you're gonna kill me, just do it already. I've had as much as I can take."

Thiago said nothing as he continued to stare past her, sitting less than ten feet away. Adi could see some of the others, carefully watching them at a distance but not close enough to hear. She looked back at Thiago, his red, puffy eyes telling her about his sleepless night. He met her gaze.

"This man," he said, taking a moment to clear his throat. "This man with the scar. Do you know where he is?"

Adi studied him as he refused to look away from her. She didn't have to think hard to figure out what Thiago wanted—it was the same thing they all did. But as he sat there in his fragile, emotional state, she wasn't sure she should tell him. "Yes," she replied.

He nodded and was quiet for a while before he spoke again. "I want..." he stopped. "I need you to help me. I need you to help me kill him."

His measured words rang clearly through the air and Adi watched as Rodrigo took a couple steps closer, an uncertain look on his face. While she had made a similar deal with Jacobo just a couple days earlier, she knew that what Thiago was asking was different. He didn't want to entice the man; he wanted to hunt him down and kill him. It was simple. No waiting, no games. While both options were risky, what Thiago was suggesting was without a doubt more dangerous, downright foolish even. They would be in enemy territory, taking on a man who had endless resources and absolutely no moral limitations. If they failed to kill him, they would not get a second chance.

As she thought about it, perhaps that's what made it so appealing, knowing that after it was over, only one of them would still be breathing. She would either die or get to live in a world without him. As she looked at her brother's grave beside her, she knew what she wanted to do.

She expected some resistance when she told the others, but as she surveyed the serious faces standing around her, she got none. Even when she started to explain how slim their chances were, she was stopped midsentence when Catalina placed a hand on her cheek, letting it rest there for a moment before she gave her a small smile and walked away. As the others left, needing no instruction on

LAS HERMANAS

how to prepare, Adi remained where she stood and found herself alone with Lupita.

Never before had Adi seen such a tormented look on her face. "You don't have to do this if you don't want to," she said. "You can go with Nayara. You don't have to come."

Adi knew how much Lupita hated being touched, but seeing the tears suddenly fall down her soft cheeks was too much and she dropped to her knees, gently placing a hand on her arm. The moment she touched her, Lupita took a deep breath and quickly wiped the tears away.

"I'm sorry," she said, the words almost bursting out.

Adi didn't understand.

"Benito, I..." she stopped and steadied herself. "I couldn't save him."

Adi wanted to give her a smile and tell her that it wasn't her fault but when she opened her mouth, nothing came out, so she simply nodded.

When she took her hand off her arm, Lupita stepped forward, gave her a quick hug, and disappeared into the trees.

Adi had no strength to push herself off the ground, but as she watched everyone diligently preparing for a fight that wasn't their own, she buried the overwhelming sadness and stood back up.

She spent the rest of the day with Jacobo discussing how they were going to do it. Upon hearing the new plan, he flat-out refused to participate, but when Adi told him that they were doing it with or without him, he reluctantly agreed. It was the best chance any of them had at getting what they wanted.

Jacobo surprised her with how much he knew about the area, producing several semi-recent maps. It took over an hour to update them, Adi relying on what she had seen on Helena's map and Thiago adding in what he knew, but when they were done, she was pleased with how much information they had. It was more than she expected.

Adi grimaced as Nayara pressed the rag against her swollen face, taking a small sip of the hot drink in her hand. The night was quiet and she could see small groups of people huddled together against the destroyed buildings, others sitting silently around the fire. She stared at the tea, watching the small bits of leaves float around for a while.

"Are you scared?"

Nayara didn't answer, taking a minute to finish cleaning the cut on her cheekbone. Adi didn't doubt that it was broken, the swelling almost forcing her right eye shut. Her stomach was still sore and would be for a few more days, but she was grateful that she could at least keep her food down.

Nayara sighed as she rinsed the rag in the bowl, slowly ringing it out, her face illuminated by the moonlight. "I feel," she said finally, struggling to find the right word, "torn when I think about tomorrow." She gently scrubbed some dirt off Adi's chin. "I'm sad, but mostly I'm just tired."

Adi listened to her friend, noticing how much she had changed. She tried to permanently etch Nayara's face into her memory. While her face was beautiful, it was her soul Adi was trying to capture, and as she watched her talk, she hoped that when the time came to say goodbye, she'd be able to take a piece of her with.

She rinsed the cloth once more. "Are you?"

Adi didn't know what to say, although she thought she knew the answer. She should be scared—she was going to try and kill an invincible man—but she wasn't, and that was what frightened her. She was about to answer when a shadow fell over Nayara's face.

A few moments of awkward silence passed before Nayara stood and handed him the bowl. "I've already done her cheek," she said, her tone clearly conveying how she felt about him. "Her lip still needs cleaning."

Adi looked down and smiled as Nayara angrily walked away. Her reaction had caught him off-guard and he stood there surprised as he watched her go.

"Think she'll ever forgive me?" He sat down, a hint of a smile on his face.

"Doubt it."

Thiago quietly studied her, his brow scrunching together in a knot.

Although it was dark, Adi could read him easily and she knew why he was there.

He sighed and reached down into the bowl. "Do you think my abuela would forgive me?" he asked as he rung out the rag and gently placed it against her lip. "For what I've done to you?"

There was something different about the way he was talking to her, a kindness she didn't expect, and as the cloth began to loosen the dried blood on her mouth, she reached up and took it from his hands.

"I'm sorry." He held her gaze. "For all the shit I threw at you." He was about to continue when she stopped him.

"Okay."

When she said nothing else, he asked, "So, does that mean you forgive me?"

She could tell he was a bit afraid of the answer, as if he expected her to say no, so she looked away for a moment and took a breath.

She didn't punch him as hard as she should have, her fist landing squarely on his eye, but she made sure the blow drew blood and she sat there for a minute, enjoying the sight of him hurting as he grabbed his face.

"Now I forgive you," she said. She scrubbed the remaining blood off her mouth.

The sad regret covering him had turned to shocked anger, and Adi smiled as she rinsed the rag in the bowl.

"Everyone's packed and ready to go," she said as she leaned forward, pressing the cloth firmly against his eye.

He winced but didn't back away.

"Nayara and Talita will take the little ones up to that abandoned village, the one Helena showed us." She rinsed the cloth again. "They should be safe there for a while at least, even if we don't make it back."

She dropped the rag into the bowl for the last time. Taking a sip of her tea, she offered it to him, watching with amusement as he reacted to the unpleasant taste. But when the sadness returned to his face, she said solemnly, "You need to be ready."

The sound of her voice grabbed his attention and when he looked at her again, she continued.

"If you're not, you shouldn't come."

He paused, taking a long drink of the tea before passing it back to her. "You should get some sleep."

As Adi watched him walk away, she sighed. If only it were that easy.

Chapter Eighteen

She barely slept but that didn't come as a surprise, her mind full of her brother as she lay alone in the dark. Although today wasn't the day she would face the man, she knew she needed to get Benito out of her head before she did. Grief was dangerously unpredictable and as she watched the darkness fade into the morning light, she threw off the blanket, determined to leave Benito behind, if only for a little while.

"I'll see you soon," she said as she knelt, her hand feeling the dirt that covered him. For some reason, she expected leaving to be easier, but it wasn't, and as she forced herself back up, it felt like she was slowly being torn in half.

"Come on," Rodrigo said, seeing that she was struggling. He walked over, wrapped his arm around her shoulders and gently steered her away. "We'll be back before you know it. Besides, we got some assholes to kill."

Adi smiled and took a deep breath. It was time.

They silently travelled through the jungle, all thirty-two of them. While they were being careful and quiet, it was almost impossible to be stealthy when a group that large was moving quickly through the trees. As they stopped to take a break a few hours south of the town, Adi realized it didn't matter. Whether he knew it or not, they were coming for him.

"We can't be seen here," Jacobo said as he sat beside her, munching on some smoked caiman wrapped in a cloth. "This town is full of people who work for the rancher, officially and unofficially. They even have an ammunitions factory here."

At the mention of the warehouse, Catalina coughed and Adi had to suppress a smile.

"What?" Jacobo asked as he looked at the two of them.

"Nothing," Adi replied and so he continued.

"I have a friend who can help. She owns a small farm just north of here."

"And you trust her?"

Jacobo nodded. "I once tried to arrest her, back when I was a government official." He smiled at the memory. "But she was too smart, and a Sister, so she was impossible to find."

"What's a Sister?" Giovana asked.

Jacobo grunted, realizing he needed to explain. "It's what the members of Las Hermanas called themselves. If you were a Sister, you were practically invisible."

Adi felt Thiago looking at her, the hairs on the back of her neck prickling, but she ignored it. "You're sure she's trustworthy?"

"Yes."

He led them around the town, taking them straight west and then north. It was late-afternoon when they arrived and as Adi spotted the little house in the clearing, they stopped.

"Wait here," Jacobo said. He took off his bag and tucked his handgun under his shirt. Adjusting his cap, he casually stepped out of the trees and walked towards the house.

He was inside for much longer than Adi liked, making her wonder if something had happened. When she heard someone whisper, "He's coming," she stood.

As soon as he was back beneath the trees, he approached her. "We can stay in one of the barns, but only for tonight. We'll move when it's dark."

His eyes held hers as he stopped talking, everyone else returning to what they were doing before. "Strange things have been happening in the town," he said quietly, just for her to hear. "The ammunitions factory is gone. Someone burned it down with the bar."

She said nothing, her face unreadable.

"They're looking everywhere for the person who did it," he continued. "Rumour is, it was a woman."

Adi didn't flinch.

"$2000 American dollars for her capture."

Although she knew Jacobo was suggesting something, she refused to give him anything. What she had done cost her more than she could fathom, and if she had known the consequences of her actions, in that moment and as hard as it would have been, she would have walked away. "Good thing we avoided the town then."

He smiled. "Yes. Good thing."

They waited until dark, slinking through the trees towards the barn that sat against the tree line. It was tight fitting all of them in, but as Adi lay up in the loft, squished in between Lupita and Catalina, she felt relaxed. They would arrive tomorrow, which meant they were nearing the end, and for the first time since Benito died, she felt a small flicker of satisfaction.

She woke up to angry voices, getting louder as they entered the barn. Peering down through a crack in the floor, she watched as Jacobo's men pushed five people dressed in camo into the centre, forcing them onto their knees.

"What's going on?" Giovana groaned irritably as she woke up.

Adi shook her head, struggling to hear the voices below.

She watched Jacobo walk over to them, squatting on his haunches in front of a woman. He stayed there for a few minutes talking with her, until he suddenly looked up.

"Adelita. You have a visitor."

Adi didn't move, a feeling of uncertainty passing over her. She wasn't sure what bothered her more, the fact that Jacobo had used her full name, which he never did, or that there were strange people asking for her. As she looked at the faces around her, Catalina giving her a quick nod, she pushed herself off the floor and climbed down from the loft.

He met her at the bottom of the stairs, giving her a knowing look as he handed her a piece of paper.

It was a good drawing, the likeness uncanny. There was only one man who knew her face this intimately and she smiled. She was looking forward to their meeting. They had a lot to talk about.

"So what?" she asked. She looked up, handing the paper back. "You gonna turn me in?"

A smug smile spread across his face as he answered. "No, I'm not, but they might."

He stepped out of her path and she walked forward, feeling the eyes of the barn as she approached. While they could try to kill her, and maybe even do it, they wouldn't make it out alive. She found that thought comforting as she stopped in front of the people kneeling on the ground.

"It's you." A smile spread across the woman's face.

Not knowing what she meant, Adi remained silent. Rodrigo casually leaned against the wall behind her while Catalina walked around the captives, her hands resting comfortably on her knives as she slowly sized them up. Adi could tell that Catalina was making them nervous, and as she watched their reactions, their eyes anxiously trying to keep track of where she was, she relaxed.

"And you are?" she asked, looking back at the woman.

"Melina," she answered, eager to tell her. "I'm Sofia's daughter." When she could tell that Adi didn't know who that was, she said, "The woman who owns this barn."

Adi nodded. "What do you want?"

Melina opened her mouth to say something, but then shut it, pausing for a moment. "When I saw you sitting there on the ground this afternoon underneath the trees, I knew it was fate."

The first part did nothing to calm Adi—knowing she had been spotted without her knowledge—but the second part interested her and she chose to focus on that. "Fate?" she asked skeptically.

"Yes." Melina nodded. "You see, ever since they started putting up these posters around town, I knew that one day we would meet. We are fighting the same war, you and I."

Adi folded her arms across her chest.

"I moved back here five years ago," Melina continued, "when they revoked my law license for trying to put together a land rights case against a well-connected businessman. It took me much longer than I care to admit to realize that the government wasn't interested in hearing about farmers being pushed off their land. By the time I did, it was too late. They told me I would never practice law again so I came here, trying to do some good."

Catalina had stopped circling and Adi caught sight of Giovana, her legs swinging back and forth over the edge of the loft, Lupita practicing her knife jabs beside her.

"What I came back to was not what I expected." Melina was staring at her. "Did you know that the rancher's men do whatever they want here?" Adi could feel her anger as she spoke, and Melina paused, trying to regain control. "One of them even lived with a family for an entire month, raping their twelve-year-old daughter every night. Do you know what that does to a person?"

Adi didn't answer, knowing it was rhetorical. Nothing she said would provide comfort and she couldn't help but think of Nayara and Talita with all those kids, making their way to the mountain alone.

"When he finally left, her parents went to the police, but they told them there was nothing they could do. They wrote to the government asking for help, but again, nothing. When they finally came to me, asking if there was any legal recourse they could take, I knew I couldn't turn them away."

"What did you do?" Adi asked.

She looked back up at her. "What could we do? We killed him."

It was not the answer Adi expected.

Melina smiled at the memory. "We made it look like an accident, crashing the jeep and sending it into the river. But really we tricked him into stopping at the side of the road and put a bullet in his brain."

Melina almost chuckled at the surprise on Adi's face. "If my mama only knew the things I did..." She paused for a minute before she spoke again, remembering why she was there. "When you blew up that warehouse, everything changed. It was like people finally woke up and realized that things could be different. For the first time in a long time, they're actually willing to fight for something— for themselves. When I saw you in the trees just outside my house, I knew it was fate. We were meant to meet. We were meant to help each other."

"How exactly?" Catalina asked, stepping in front of them. Adi could tell that she was wary of Melina, unsure of what to make of her, but Adi stayed quiet, content to let the two of them work it out. "How exactly are we supposed to help each other?"

A confident smile spread across Melina's face. "What do you need?"

Catalina laughed. "We need an army."

Adi looked back at Melina, expecting her to falter, but she didn't.

"What else?" she said.

Adi smirked. This was going to be fun.

☙

By the time they worked out the particulars, Adi wasn't so excited. What Melina wanted in return was nothing short of a miracle, as if their own goal wasn't hard enough. But seeing as she had given them an army of over fifty people, a hidden camp near the ranch to prepare, and years of information on their defenses, movements, and habits, Adi didn't have a choice. She'd get her the rancher or die trying.

At first light, Melina took them to the camp only a few miles north of the ranch.

"They don't come up here," she said as they walked. "They're not interested in the north for some reason."

Adi didn't really care. All she wanted was a safe place to hide as they made their plans and when they finally arrived, she was pleasantly surprised. The building was so overgrown with plants, vines, and lichens that it was as if the jungle had decided to keep it, wrapping it into its loving embrace. Adi walked around, seeing no way in until Melina drew her attention to a rusty, metal handle barely peeking out of the green. She jerked on the knob, the door reluctantly pushing open, and Adi stepped inside.

Other than the musty smell and some dust, it was unusually clean for an old building. Makeshift beds lined the walls and several tables sat in the centre, with chairs and stools strewn about. The moss over the windows dulled the light that managed to sneak through the trees and as Adi looked past the old, faded flag that hung from the middle of the ceiling, she nodded. It would work.

As they waited for Melina's fighters to arrive, they began to prepare, learning as much as they could about what they would be facing. The ranch was owned by Daniel Guzman, whose father acquired it in the late 1960s. It was the typical story: land stolen from its rightful owners and given to political allies, breaking generations of familial ownership and livelihood. So when the land-less farmers began quietly working the idle fields, Guzman didn't just push them off his land, he violently lashed out.

"He started taking over the neighbouring farms, piece by piece," Melina explained as she pointed to the spots on the map. "If someone refused to sell, he'd just kill them and buy it from whoever owned it next." She leaned against the table. "He met some resis-tance but it didn't last. Anyone who opposed him died." Melina paused, the frustration obvious. "And then when the rumours started about him wiping out entire villages," she whistled, shaking her head. "It's damn near impossible to fight something like that."

"Especially when he has El Diablo," Jacobo said, his tone low and angry.

"Tell us about the men," Adi said before anyone could ask ques-tions. She wasn't interested in stories, only in how they could win.

Altogether, Melina estimated that there were about three hundred men, the bulk of them at the ranch. While normally they were spread out, watching over the vast amount of land Guzman had stolen, they returned after the warehouse explosion. He was determined to find the culprit.

"Most of them are mercenaries," Melina explained, "but some are locals. Former military mainly."

"So basically we're fucked," Marcelo said, his arms crossed against his chest.

Adi looked around the table, watching shades of hopelessness seep into their faces.

"How the hell are we supposed to beat that?" he asked.

"Countries have been won with less." When Salvador had told her he was coming, she wanted to talk him out of it—he was no fighter—but as she watched him walk up, she was glad he was there.

"We're not fighting for a country," Marcelo replied.

"Aren't we?" Salvador's question silenced him and he continued. "They have the numbers, that is undeniable, but that doesn't mean we can't win. As long as we're smart and use our position to our advantage, we stand a chance."

"How do we do that?" Giovana asked, leaning against the table.

"We take them by surprise," Thiago answered. "Defenses?"

Melina nodded. "The ranch is surrounded by seven guard towers," she replied, pointing them out. "They sit just inside the tree line and have some sort of detection system."

"Cameras or motion sensors?" he asked.

"Both, we think. We've never gotten close enough."

"How many men in each one?"

She shrugged. "Two to four."

Distracted by the door opening, Adi watched as several people entered, nodding to Melina as they passed.

"Okay, so we take those out first," Catalina said. "Then what?"

"Then you gotta get through the field," Melina answered.

Pablo chuckled. "There's no way. They'll mow us down like sheep."

"That's why we need to draw them in," Adi said. "Fight them in our territory. These men don't know the jungle like we do. I've seen them move. They're loud, clumsy, and don't know shit about the land they live in. That's what Salvador meant by taking advantage. We use their weaknesses against them."

"Lure them into the trees," Thiago said.

Adi nodded. "Kill as many as we can."

"How we gonna get the house?" Yumi asked. "That's the goal, right? To get the house?"

"We sneak in here," Rodrigo said, pointing to the area directly west of it. "The house sits about a hundred feet from the tree line. All other sides are surrounded by open fields. It's the only way in."

"That's their weakest point," Marcelo argued, shaking his head. "They're gonna guard the shit outta that. We'll never get in."

"We will because they'll be distracted by what's happening all around the field," Rodrigo replied. "What do you think they're gonna do when all the towers suddenly go out? Just wait? When they send men to check, we take the house."

As heads nodded around the table, more people trickled in and Adi turned to look at the fighters Melina had got. While no one jumped out at her as a born killer, they appeared to be in good shape and seemed to be equipped with decent weapons, although Adi would have accepted anyone at that point. When she turned back around, the table was silent. "Okay. Who wants to take out some guard towers?"

Chapter Nineteen

They attacked at midnight, determined to take advantage of the darkness. First, they sent out seven teams of two—Giovana, Catalina, Yumi, and Thiago among them—to eliminate the seven towers, while Jacobo and Marcelo led a group of ten to the west side of the ranch. As soon as the men ran south towards the trees where Adi, Rodrigo, and Melina were waiting, they would take the house.

A cold chill ran down her spine as she waited in the darkness. There were approximately sixty of them spread out among the trees surrounding the field, trying to appear larger than they were. As she watched the first tower catch fire and light up the night sky, she hoped it would be enough.

The sound of a few gunshots cut through the silence, adding to the already mounting tension as they sat low in the trees, waiting for their prey. The sky brightened again as another tower was set aflame, monkeys and birds protesting angrily at the disruption. Adi looked to her right, spotting Lupita sitting a few trees away, calmly watching the field in front of them. They were the closest to the open pasture, only a couple trees in, and as soon as Adi heard the trucks roar to life, she exhaled slowly. It was about to begin.

They sped towards her, headlights bouncing as they drove through the field. By the time they arrived at the bottom, all seven of the towers were lit and Adi watched them jump from their vehicles, disorganized in the chaos. When they entered the trees twenty feet north of them, Adi shook her head at Lupita. They couldn't go yet.

All was quiet and then suddenly it wasn't. A scream and several bursts of gunfire erupted into the air. She was disappointed at having to wait, her muscles twitching in restless anticipation, but as she looked back out into the field, she saw that she was about to get more than she asked for.

Gripping a knife in each hand, she waited as the men exited the trucks, the feeling of steel steadying the adrenaline pumping through her veins. They entered the trees cautiously, automatic rifles aimed in front as they walked single file, oblivious to the danger above. She wanted to pounce, eager to release some rage, but she forced herself to wait, watching as the last man stepped into the bush.

Nodding at Lupita, she dropped with her knife at a downward angle. She drove it hard into his neck, a surprised groan squeaking out as he fell dead onto the ground. Landing on top of him, she pulled her knife out of his body and dove behind a tree.

Bullets peppered the other side of the trunk as she waited. She was more than happy to be the distraction, knowing that Lupita and the others would be closing in. When she heard the screams and panicked voices as they were killed in rapid succession, she stepped out.

There wasn't much left of the men, their bloodied bodies stripped of anything useful. Adi picked up an AK-47 and was slinging it across her back when Lupita handed her a sack. She wasn't surprised when she saw the grenades, remembering how many were in the warehouse, but just as she tucked them into her pack, a barrage of gunshots ripped through the night sky.

They crept towards the field, watching as dozens of men unloaded at a single spot up ahead. There would be too many men for whoever was there to deal with. She needed to do something fast.

"Get ready," she said to the others and ran out into the field.

The first grenade she threw missed the now-empty trucks by a mile, sending dirt and grass high into the air as it burst; but the second one hit, the sound deafening as the explosion rocked the vehicle, bright flames and black smoke billowing up. Adi didn't stick around to watch, sprinting back under the trees as fast as she could. She knew the noise would bring the men back to the field and that's where she would meet them.

Running north, she stopped behind a cluster of small trees, searching for her target. She saw the first one, his light skin practically glowing in the dark as he came towards her. She didn't move, patiently waiting for the group to pass before she crept up behind the last man and slit his throat.

The gurgle of blood alerted the man ahead but as he turned, Adi lunged forward and ripped his neck open, the curved, serrated side of her knife creating a gaping hole. Before his body hit the ground, she was already safely under cover, calmly leaning behind a tree as the bullets flew. She stayed there, expecting the shooting to eventually stop, but when it didn't, she lost her patience and climbed the tree.

She sat about a foot above them, her opponents oblivious to her position as they kept their guns aimed at the ground. Not waiting for them to figure it out, she balanced herself against the trunk and grabbed the gun off her back.

The first shot caught everyone by surprise, Adi almost falling out of the tree as the gun kicked hard, missing by a mile. She was too busy pulling herself back up to see that they were looking right in her direction, but seeing no one, they turned away. She didn't miss the second time or any time after that, shooting round after round in quick succession, bodies littering the green floor. As her feet dropped down into the dirt, she heard a whistle.

Adi stepped away from the trunk, making herself visible in the moonlight as she whistled back. As soon as she saw Catalina running towards her, she couldn't help but smile.

"You okay?" she asked.

Catalina nodded.

"Come on."

By the time they got back to the field, they could see that their strategy wasn't working. A dozen trucks were heading south and as they sprinted towards them, large angry bursts of gunfire seemed to spit out from everywhere.

The chaos only increased as they ran into the thick of it, the darkness making it difficult to see whether they were fighting enemy or friend. As Pablo's dead body slumped to the ground in front of her, Adi whipped out her knives, desperate to gain control.

She sprinted towards the man on her right, striking him with a lethal blow to the back of the neck, his heavy head pulling the rest of him down. The second one she slashed across the leg, his angry grunt loud enough to block the deadly snap of his neck as she twisted it hard. The third man was already coming at her, so she ran to meet him, dropping at the last second and slicing straight up into his thigh. She could taste the blood as he crumpled on top of her, his weight pinning her down. When she finally pushed him off, she saw that she was in trouble.

The bullet grazed her leg as she dove out of the way, sending her flying into the dirt. She could see his shadow carefully searching the ground, but just as he came into view, she hurled the small knife tucked against her ankle.

She had never heard screams like it, the anguish rushing from his mouth like a waterfall. Not stopping for a second, she grabbed her gun and pumped a bullet into his chest. He fell back and she scrambled to her feet, looking at her knife sticking out of his eye as his body went still. It took a couple tries to get it out, the eyeball wanting to come too, but when she finally wrenched it free, the fighting had almost stopped.

Death had come quick and dirty in the confusion and it didn't take long for it to be over. Snipers in the trees were picking off what was left of the men. They had forced them back with such velocity that they fled, dropping their weapons as they dissipated. Adi and Lupita chased after them, managing to kill a few more as they retreated, but as soon as the men ran out into the field, they stopped and turned around.

The night was silent once more as Adi looked at the bodies piled up among the trees, dark lumps covering the jungle floor. It was hard to tell who they were but as she searched, she found more than a few of their own, and as soon as she spotted her face peering out from under someone's arm, she started digging.

She carried Yumi out, gently placing her bullet-ridden body on a clump of thick ferns. Looking around at the surviving faces, she asked, "Where's Gio?"

A low rumble in the distance caught her attention and she turned, the sound growing louder. It was coming from the field and as she headed towards it, unsure of what was happening, she realized what it was.

"Get down!" The warning came at the same time the cargo truck crashed into the trees, sending them diving for cover.

She expected to be attacked, or at least hit with something, but when they heard nothing but the engine slowly ticking off, they crept out. A few of them ran forward, guns pointed at the truck as they checked it over. Shaking their heads as they looked in the cab, they moved to the back, stopping in front of the large canvas tarp that covered it. Glancing at Rodrigo, he nodded and they flung the cover open.

It was hard to see what was in there, so Adi stepped forward, the shadow of a man coming into view. The closer she got the more she saw and by the time she reached the bumper, she realized who it was. There, hanging in the back of the truck, was her father.

⚐

She couldn't move, staring at the frail, mutilated man above her as the air slowly left her lungs, sending her down in a heap. She was suddenly exhausted and could feel every single stab of pain as her muscles cried out, unable to look away from the blood dripping down his skin, her name carved deep into his chest.

"Adi." Rodrigo gripped her by the shoulders. "Adi, look at me."

She could do no such thing.

"Look at me!" He didn't give her a choice, roughly grabbing her face as he knelt directly in front of her. "You can't do this." His voice broke as he held her face in the palm of his hand. "Not now. Not when we're so close."

She had no words, staring blankly past him as he spoke, not hearing a sound.

"Hey!"

The hard shake snapped her out of it, and she finally looked at him.

"We need to go," he said firmly. "Now."

Adi didn't resist as he helped her up, her legs shaking as she turned and walked away from the truck. Every step felt like a betrayal, like she was abandoning her father, but when the explosion ripped through the air and slammed her into the ground, it no longer mattered.

Sight and sound faded in and out as she fought to regain consciousness. She tried to get up, but her arms buckled and she rolled to her side, desperately looking around.

Very little was left of the vehicle, black smoke billowing up into the air. She watched Rodrigo help someone stand and remembered that Catalina had been right behind her.

She stumbled towards the bodies with a renewed sense of panic, hoping that some, *any* of them were still alive. Finding Salvador, she knelt down and touched what remained of his face, the smell of burning flesh stinging her nostrils. She looked around and didn't bother getting up. They were all dead.

"Come on," Rodrigo coughed as he ran up. When she didn't move, he crouched beside her. "Look."

Adi followed his arm and saw what he was referring to. There, coming down the field towards them were more men.

She forced herself up, following Rodrigo as they ran through the trees, hearing the sound of gunfire behind them. The jungle was beginning to thicken and after a few minutes, they stopped, struggling to find a viable path through the trees.

Adi bent over, leaning against her legs as she caught her breath.

"We need to regroup. Find the others," Rodrigo said, recovering much quicker than her. "Then we can decide what to do."

Adi crouched down on her haunches trying to think. While they had killed a lot of men, they were losing badly and if something didn't change, they'd never make it. She stood up.

"Go."

At first Rodrigo didn't understand what she meant, but as she held his gaze, she watched the realization sink in.

For a while, he simply shook his head, his hands running through his hair as he looked away. It was clear he didn't like it, but as he turned towards her again, she knew he wouldn't try to stop her.

"Let me come with you."

She smiled and shook her head once. "You'd just slow me down."

He almost laughed at her attempt at humour, but it died on his lips and he walked forward, pulling her into him. She closed her eyes as she felt his strong arms wrap about her, holding her tight. After a moment, he let go but didn't look away.

"Kill the fucker."

Adi didn't wait to watch him leave, heading in the opposite direction. She was tired and sore, but she wasn't beat—not yet. She made her way through the jungle alone, knowing that this twisted game of cat and mouse that started four long years ago was going to end today, one way or another.

She sat inside the tree, protected by its leafy canopy as she watched the ranch, the morning light eating away the darkness. At first it was quiet, the rancher safe and secure in his extravagant house, but then all of a sudden it wasn't and Adi watched with curiosity as a flurry of activity took over. Men spilled out of the house, quickly pulling up several trucks before going back inside, others standing guard. For just a minute, everything was still again, but as she watched the men come back out, she realized what was happening. The rancher was running.

She couldn't believe it. The asshole was actually leaving. But as she watched them load more and more things into the vehicles, the smirk dropped off her face. If they didn't want to lose him, Marcelo and the others needed to attack now. When nothing happened, Adi scampered down the tree.

She sprinted towards the road, staying under cover. She could hear the truck engines turning over so she ran faster, determined to get there first. Arriving at the edge of the field, she dropped to her stomach and crawled up the small slope next to the road just as the trucks began to rumble down the long driveway. The wait seemed to go on forever, the noise heightening with her anticipation, and as soon as she saw the vehicles in range, she pulled the pin and threw it.

The grenade landed in front of the first truck, Adi panicking when there was no explosion as the vehicle approached. She launched two more, the grenades landing on the road one after another. Suddenly the first one burst, a loud explosion shattering the stillness.

Adi kept her head down as the others detonated, sending metal shrapnel in all directions. Peaking over the top of the slope, she watched as the trucks burned, flames bulging around them as men poured out, desperate to get away.

They didn't stand a chance, Adi picking them off one by one as she shot, the black smoke masking her position. The remaining trucks were already reversing back down the road as quickly as they came, not bothering to save their friends. She knew what would happen next. He would come for her. She slunk back into the trees and eagerly awaited his arrival. She was ready.

It took longer than expected but as she sat silently in her perch, several metres away from where she had blown up the trucks, she watched the camouflaged bodies sneak through the trees, closing in on their target. There were dozens of them, many more than she had accounted for, and she was beginning to doubt the sanity of her plan. But it didn't matter. He only had to be close.

Gunfire ripped through the air as they lit up the edge of the field, hitting dirt, tree, and animal indiscriminately. They were shooting anything and everything within a twenty foot radius, and Adi watched for a moment before she took out the last three grenades and pulled the pins.

She threw them as far as she could in opposite directions, the bombs arcing above the treetops before falling back down onto the ground below. The men stopped shooting as the grenades went off, unsure of where the assault was coming from. At first, they canvased the area around them, but when they cautiously moved back, all heading in the same direction, Adi smiled. She knew where the bastard was.

Sliding silently down the tree, she crept in his direction. The plan was to avoid the others altogether, but when she saw one coming straight towards her, she had no choice.

Slinking in behind a tree, she slit his throat as he passed, his body dropping heavily to the ground. The closer she got to him, the more men she encountered, and she had managed to kill four more before one of them saw her.

Adi darted away as the bullets whizzed past. She hoped he would follow and wasn't disappointed when she watched him run up, not seeing her behind the rock. The first shot pinged off his helmet and he spotted her just as she fired again, this time the bullet lodging in his neck.

Blood spurted through his fingers as he clutched at it, falling helplessly onto the ground. She could hear more coming towards her, the gunfire drawing their attention as feet thudded through the dirt. She was searching all around her when she spotted it, the perfect cover, and quickly dove underneath the thick vines, watching as the jungle filled with men.

At first, she didn't recognize him, but as soon as she saw the thick, pink scar across his throat, she realized who it was. He was much skinnier, his face sunken and pale. He looked like he'd aged ten years since the last time they'd met, but as she stared up at him, she could still see his dark, ugly soul.

"Adelita Alvarez!" another man called out, the sound carrying through the trees. "Surrender or die!"

Adi couldn't stop the smile spreading across her face. There was no way he would pass up an opportunity to taunt her. She must have taken away his voice, and now, she was going to take his life.

She crawled soundlessly through the vines until she reached a tree big enough, quickly scaling it before settling down on a thick branch about halfway up. While they stared up into the trees above them, she was twenty feet away and lining up her shot.

The abrupt movement of a scarab beetle dropping from a higher branch startled her at the same time she pulled the trigger, the flinch sending the bullet off target. Instead of blasting through his skull, the lead struck his shoulder and Adi ducked down as the men returned fire. She desperately wanted to poke her head out and see where he was, but as the shots flew around her, she reluctantly slid down the tree and waited.

He had been right there, in her sights, and she had missed. The frustration was too much to take and she was just about to risk running out when she heard the sound of a single shot.

Adi paused, listening intently as the men continued to pummel the trees with bullets. But when she heard the sound a second time, she glanced past the tree and watched as a man crumpled to the ground.

The men stopped shooting just as a third shot ripped through the air, causing them to turn and face the opposite direction. Seeing her chance, she ran out, not bothering to look behind her as the gunfire began again.

The sound of death danced all around, but she didn't stop, knowing she had to find him. She ran all the way back to the tree line, pausing only to kill those standing in her way, but she was too late. He was gone.

The only thing she felt was anger, her jaw clenching in frustration as she pumped a bullet into the back of a wounded man's head as he crawled. She couldn't believe he had gotten away. She slowly exhaled, the rage boiling inside, when she heard a noise and spun around.

"I missed," she said, her voice cracking as she watched Catalina and Rodrigo approach, struggling to keep control of the jumble of emotions running through her.

Her two friends exchanged a look, but just as Catalina opened her mouth, gunshots burst into the air.

They sprinted towards it, the noise growing louder with each second. Adi could see a few men off in the distance, hastily retreating through the trees. As she got close, she saw what they were running from. Giovana sat crouched in the tree, killing off man after man while Lupita snuck along the ground, attacking with such precision and speed that they had no time to react.

Obviously not needing her help, Adi went after the runaways, Catalina and Rodrigo right behind. There were only a few dozen men left and she followed as they ran out into the field. She was looking across the pasture, surveying the opposition, when her eyes locked onto the body of a man stumbling towards the ranch house.

"Go!" Rodrigo didn't need to tell her twice.

She saw nothing but him, running at a pace she didn't think was possible, the adrenaline rushing through her veins. She should have been exhausted, but as she closed the gap and descended upon him, she never felt more alive.

She launched her body into his, using her momentum and speed to push his frail frame forward, slamming him into the ground. She bounced off his body when they hit the dirt, but the moment he rolled over, she was on him, pummeling with her fists.

Blinded by anger, her punches fell into a rhythm and she didn't see his palm jut up, his hand striking her throat. Stunned by the amount of pain and lack of air, she grabbed her neck, desperately trying to breathe. He threw her off with ease, Adi feeling the swift kick of his boot bash her in the ribs as she attempted to stand, forcing her back down. She tried to roll away, but he was too quick and he jumped on top of her, pinning her down with strength she didn't know he still had. The moment she felt his long fingers wrap around her neck, she was transported back to when she was eleven, the memory of the first time flashing before her eyes.

"You are an interesting individual," she could hear him say all over again. "It's a shame you didn't last longer."

"No," she said, the word not making a sound as she fought against him, trying to stay conscious. She would not do this, not now, not ever and as her eyes flew open, she heard Rodrigo's voice: "Kill the fucker."

She punched him in the shoulder, remembering where she had shot him, and the grip of his left hand faltered just enough for her to quickly inhale and focus on what she had to do next. Bringing her leg in towards her body, she tucked it underneath his chest and suddenly pushed up, forcing him away from her. He struggled to hold on with his fingertips, but she was too strong and she kicked him off, jamming her heel directly into his wound.

His voice rasped out in pain as he fell back, Adi gasping for air as she scrambled into an upright position. As she stood, she saw the knife swing towards her and leaned back, but not fast enough as she felt the blade catch her cheek. She didn't hesitate, countering as she hit him hard and fast, warm blood trickling down her face, her fists connecting with his jaw. As soon as she saw him stumble backwards, she ripped the knife off her back and began slicing at him, her strength increasing as she attacked.

At first, he was able to fend her off, even getting a few cuts in, but she eventually overwhelmed him, the months of training with Mariana taking over. She fell into a familiar rhythm, manipulating his movements as she forced him to react exactly how she wanted— hitting left to make him go right—and when her knife ripped open his calf, she knew she had him.

He buckled, sinking to the ground unwillingly as he dropped his knife. She paused her attack, looking at him kneeling below as shock and displeasure stared back at her. If his vocal cords hadn't been severed, he probably would have said something to hurt her and wear her down. While a year ago, she might have been curious to hear what he had to say, now she no longer cared. She was finished with him. Distracted by her thoughts, she almost missed him reach behind his back.

She stepped to the side, feeling the bullet tear past her through the air. Not waiting for him to take another shot, she swung her knife down and watched as his hand fell to the ground. His raspy screams sounded ghost-like as he doubled over, clutching his severed limb in pain. His mouth was open but there was no sound and as he looked up at her one last time, she knew it was over. Gripping her knife in both hands, she chopped down as hard as she could and watched the life drain out of him.

Chapter Twenty

Adi stood there for several minutes, staring at the lifeless body in front of her. Years of running and hiding had come down to this moment, and he was dead. She expected to feel something, anything, but as she looked out into the field, the green grass covered in flesh, she felt nothing. It was only when Giovana walked up, and said those three words, did she finally feel.

She tried to run, but couldn't, stumbling down the gentle slope to where the others were standing, the silence of the dead so loud she could barely hear. The sight of him dropped her and she shook as she reached out and touched his face, his empty eyes refusing to look at her. She lost control—the rage, the pain, the anguish tumbling out all at once—as she held him in her arms. It wasn't supposed to be like this, he wasn't supposed to die, but none of that made any difference. Rodrigo was gone.

The sun had risen, its bright light shimmering over the field as she slowly walked towards the house. It felt like she was floating, unconnected to her body's movements, but when Marcelo touched her arm, she looked up and watched the pain flicker across his face.

"He wants you." He tried to smile, but it fell halfway up. "He won't talk to anyone but you."

She followed Marcelo through the house, the walls leering at her as she entered. She might have noticed the brightly painted stone mosaics and the richly woven rugs had it been any other day, but it was not, and she numbly walked down the hallway suddenly feeling cold. Marcelo stopped in front of a door, nodding before he opened it and walked through.

It was a large room, complete with a bed, two couches, and several chairs, but as soon as Adi entered, she saw him, his face bloodied as he sat tied to his seat. Melina said nothing as she passed, the rancher smirking as Marcelo led her to a chair directly in front of him. Adi sat down, taking a moment to look at him before slowly removing the layers of weapons strapped around her body. While there were other people in the room, they stayed silent, the only sound Adi's guns dropping onto the floor beside her.

"Enjoy this while you can," the rancher said as she pulled a dead man's automatic rifle over her head, finally feeling only the knife on her back. "It won't last. Tomas will return and finish the job, like he always does." When she didn't reply, he leaned forward. "Want some free advice? Run."

She looked at the others in the room, their tired, angry faces watching the rancher with contempt. It wouldn't matter what he said—the reasons why, the empty promises he would make—none of that would give them back what they had already lost. Finally turning towards him, she said, "No."

"No?" He practically spat out the word.

She nodded and stood, turning towards Melina. "He's all yours."

She could hear his screams as she walked out of the room, his confidence wavering as he spewed vulgar threats. She knew it wouldn't take long until he started begging, but as she walked out through the front door and into the light, she forgot all about him. Her Sisters were all she needed.

Acknowledgements

Thank you to Kayla Feenstra, April Jenkins and Stephanie St Hilaire for reading one of my first drafts. The fact that none of you have excommunicated me for making you read an absolute pile of garbage speaks to your grace and decency as human beings. I promise to never put you through such a terrible and painful ordeal again.

And to Matt, who unfailingly believes in me and is my biggest supporter. I wouldn't want to do this without you.

Printed in Canada